GRAVE MATTERS AT ST BLANE'S

An Alison Cameron Mystery

MYRA DUFFY

www.myraduffy.co.uk
http://myraduffy-awriterslot.blogspot.com

Cover design by Mandy Sinclair
www.mandysinclair.com

Also by Myra Duffy

The Isle of Bute Mystery series

The House at Ettrick Bay

Last Ferry to Bute

Last Dance at the Rothesay Pavilion

Endgame at Port Bannatyne

****

The prequel to the Isle of Bute Mystery series

When Old Ghosts Meet

THE ISLE OF BUTE

The Isle of Bute lies in the Firth of Clyde, off the west coast of Scotland, a short journey from the city of Glasgow.

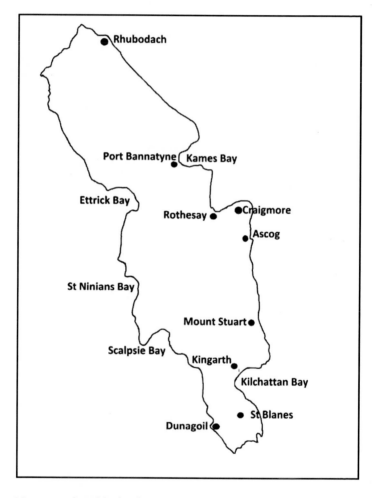

Map reproduced by kind permission of Brandanii Archaeology and Heritage www.discoverbutearchaeology.co.uk

For Paul, who shares a birthday with St Blane

PROLOGUE

'Why did you insist on dragging me up here?' The portly man stopped halfway up the hill and bent over, wheezing loudly as he sat down on the nearest large boulder.

The younger man stood a little further up the slope, gazing at the view from this grassy knoll at Kingarth towards Dunagoil, the vitrified fort on the west side of the Isle of Bute. He wheeled round and shrugged, eyeing the older man with some disdain. 'I thought you'd want to see for yourself, Mr Crombie, since you're the one investing money. Not much further to go.'

Alexander Crombie frowned. 'What do I pay you for, Dexter, if it's not to deal with the day-to-day business?'

'This is an unusual circumstance, Mr Crombie.' Dexter glanced upwards at the darkening sky. 'We'd better get on. The light will be fading soon.'

Alexander Crombie got to his feet, staggering a little from the effort of regaining his balance and slowly began to follow Dexter, now bounding up the hill. Why had he thought it was a good idea to buy this field? It was such a long shot and what's more, he'd had to come up with a plan to obtain the necessary permission to develop it.

He couldn't remember who'd first suggested building an historical theme park: 'Historical tourism' was all the rage, but here on this windswept hill he was beginning to suspect this wouldn't be the solution to his problem.

'People can't get enough of the past,' he'd been told, but he fretted about how much it would cost. And what if it was all for nothing? Eventually he'd been persuaded, had bought the field after a fair bit of wrangling. With the plans for the theme park drawn up and planning permission granted, the survey had at last gone ahead.

Now this. He dreaded to think what Dexter had found: it was sure to be some unexpected hitch, ancient field drains or some such that would mean spending a lot of money to sort out. He'd already spent plenty with nothing to show for it.

'Over here.' Dexter was beckoning him towards the top of the site, hidden by a screen of large trees and overgrown bushes. Crombie cursed as he caught his jacket on a thorny bush and moved forward, tentatively watching for any hazardous rabbit holes. He stopped to peer in as Dexter pushed back a thick hedge and slowly pulled off the grimy tarpaulin covering a shallow pit.

'The worker who found it didn't realise what it was …and I didn't enlighten him, told him to leave everything as it was. As well it wasn't that manager, Benjie, or one of the archaeologists.' He winked. 'Something to keep to ourselves, eh?'

Alexander Crombie ignored him. Dexter was a necessary evil, a man he could trust, but then Crombie knew Dexter's little secret. He leaned over as a burst of late sunlight shafted through the clouds, illuminating the pit. As he tried to catch his breath he recognised the outline of what seemed to be an ancient box, shaped like a little house, only partly visible above the soil and heavily encrusted with mud. He knew enough to recognise what it was: a reliquary, designed to hold the relics of a saint, and there was no doubt it was old, very old indeed.

Alexander felt a sudden surge of excitement. Perhaps this venture wouldn't be such a waste of time and money after all. On the other hand, they'd have to think of a way of dealing with Benjie.

It wasn't what I expected to see as I drove off the ferry from Wemyss Bay, eager to begin my latest commission on the Isle of Bute. Over in Guildford Square, opposite the ferry terminal, a large group of people seemed to be involved in a show for tourists but as I drove slowly past to find a parking space, I'd a good view of the banners waving in the breeze.

'NO THEME PARK ON BUTE' said one and 'KEEP BUTE THEME PARK FREE' said another. From time to time the motley crowd behind the banners set up a chant, but it was difficult to make out what they were saying. The heavily built man at the front appeared to be trying hard to organise them, with little success.

Before heading to my hotel, I had to find out what this was about. The theme park was my reason for being on the island and when I'd signed up to write the tourist guide there'd been no suggestion there'd be any objections. On the contrary, the project had been sold to me as something which would be of great economic advantage, encourage visitors.

With my car squeezed into the last remaining parking space at the far end of the square, I locked up and walked over to have a closer look at the protesters. By now they'd attracted a fair number of onlookers, some clearly day trippers, others island residents. What they all had in common was a look of total bewilderment as the leader of the protesters gave full voice to his demands.

'We want to keep our island as it is. We don't need any tat here. We have enough to attract those who want to enjoy our unspoiled beaches, our forest walks, our …'

'Our lack of things to do,' shouted a voice from the crowd, momentarily throwing the leader off his stride.

He glared at this interloper. 'What do you know? Do you want Bute overrun by hordes of city folks, throwing their litter everywhere, bringing their foul ways …?'

'Better than not coming at all,' shouted someone else.

As this debate was likely to continue for some time, I sidled off, wondering how important this protest was. It might be no more than a few residents concerned about the effect building a theme park would have on the environment but, whatever the reason, it could prove to be a problem.

As I was about to unlock my car, I was startled to hear a voice say, 'Why, hello, Alison, fancy meeting you' and turned to face a tall, white-haired man.

'Good gracious, Harry, what on earth are you doing here?'

Harry was a colleague, rather than a friend, from some years before when I'd been a teacher at Strathelder High school. He hadn't been the most sociable member of staff and it was a surprise to everyone when he married and came to live on Bute after he retired. I'd met him again when my friend Susie had inherited a house at Ettrick Bay, but after the tragic death of his wife, Greta, he'd left the island for good. Or so I'd been told.

'Are you living on Bute again?' I said, trying to conceal my astonishment.

He shook his head. 'Only temporarily. I've been asked to help with a new enterprise out at Kingarth.

They're building a theme park there, based on the ruins of the monastery at St Blane's, and I've a contract to do the research.'

Before I could reply there was a loud shout from the crowd and we looked round in time to witness a scuffle break out. After watching for a moment or two I said, 'What a coincidence. I'm working on that too, though I'm writing the visitor guide. They told me there would be a history expert on hand, but I didn't realise it would be you.'

'Yes, strangely enough, the 7th Century was one of my specialisms, one I've continued to be interested in. I once thought about doing archaeology instead of history so this is right up my street.'

'So we'll be working together?' I hoped we'd be able to collaborate without running into difficulties, remembering how taciturn Harry could be.

'Looks like it, Alison. See you later.' With that he turned on his heel and walked quickly across the road to the Albert Pier, leaving me staring after him. He'd been perfectly polite, but as reserved as I remembered.

Between my encounter with Harry and the demonstration by those opposed to the theme park, this commission was shaping up to be interesting.

2

As I drove away, the crowds in Guildford Square were beginning to disperse, some wandering towards Montague Street, others heading for the seafront. After a showery start as we'd sailed across on the ferry from Wemyss Bay, the sun had come out from behind the clouds, leaving a clear day. Boats bobbed at anchor in Rothesay Marina, their new paintwork glinting in the afternoon sunlight, the smell of brine and diesel oil in the air. On the pontoons, several people scrambled back and forth as a queue of boats waited in line to exit the harbour as soon as the bridge leading to the Ferry terminal was raised. There was no time to waste on this west coast of Scotland: best to take advantage of every opportunity to sail on the waters of the Firth of Clyde.

Once out of the car park, I drove slowly down to the main road and headed for my hotel. The traffic lights went to green as I passed the bus shelter at Guildford Square and I jerked the car forward, glancing in the driving mirror to catch a last glimpse of the leader of the protesters. He was now engaged in a heated discussion with two of the few remaining onlookers.

In the muddle of our encounter I'd forgotten to ask Harry where he was staying, but I'd see him soon enough. As for me, I'd booked into a hotel near the Bute Sailing Club on the outskirts of Rothesay. It wasn't somewhere I'd stayed before, but I'd reckoned that with this short contract it wasn't sensible to rent. In truth, I'd had enough of that on my previous visits to Bute and this time I wanted to finish quickly with no interruptions, no sudden remembering I'd run out of milk or coffee or other essentials. No, it would be good to be able to concentrate on preparing the visitor guide and have all the practicalities taken care of.

Any further concerns about the demonstration I'd seen in Guildford Square would have to wait: the clock on the dashboard showed I'd have to speed up. A meeting of everyone involved in the project had been called for lunchtime in the Kingarth Hotel, once an old coaching inn and now a popular restaurant on the road to Kilchattan Bay. The last time I'd been there was when writing my history of the Rothesay Pavilion, while renting the old fisherman's cottage at Kilchattan. I remembered with pleasure the tasty food I'd enjoyed in the restaurant on more than one occasion.

Benjie, the project manager, had said in his last e-mail, 'I thought it would be a good idea for the team to meet over lunch, let us get to know one another,' a suggestion that met with my wholehearted approval.

I'd brought less luggage than usual with me, but was well aware it could be cold on the West coast at this time of year, even when the sun did break through. If I was to be outdoors exploring the site at St Blane's I'd need warm clothing. With that in mind I'd packed several sweaters and thick trousers as well as a change of jacket and some boots, hoping these would see me through my time on the island.

There was so little traffic it took me only a few minutes to reach the Bute Sailing Club and find the Crannog Hotel. I don't know quite what I'd expected from the pictures on the website, but it certainly wasn't a large double fronted house with the white paint of the exterior flaking off and the small front garden covered with drifts of last autumn's leaves, a few of which had made their way into the entrance porch. The reception area had a vinyl floor, cunningly disguised to look like

8

marble and the website photo had obviously been taken at a tilted angle as it was a good deal smaller and more cramped than it appeared online. The smell of overcooked food drifted from the room to the left and through the glass door I glimpsed several small tables set out for a meal.

Whatever its shortcomings, this hotel would have to do and as I waited at the Reception desk behind a very smartly dressed woman I heard the receptionist say, as she consulted the large book open in front of her, 'I'm sorry, but Room Nine on the first floor is the last one available this early in the season.'

The woman said in clipped tones, 'I booked through your website several weeks ago and specifically asked for a room on the ground floor.'

'Ah,' said the receptionist, nodding her head, 'but did you confirm it in writing.'

'No, of course I didn't,' the woman snapped. 'I told you that I booked it through the website.'

The receptionist shrugged, tapping the book as though an answer would emerge. 'That's the problem, then. The website doesn't always work.'

'Oh, for goodness sake,' shouted the woman as she grabbed the key from the startled receptionist's hand. 'I can't waste any more time on this.' With that she headed for the stairs, dragging a heavy suitcase behind her, as she muttered, 'And I suppose the lift doesn't work either.'

The receptionist, her large black and white badge identifying her as Freida, sighed as she gazed after this impatient guest. 'Of course the lift works. Some people are always in a hurry.'

Fortunately I'd better luck. 'Mrs Cameron? Room Six on the ground floor is ready for you,' she said handing over my key. 'What people don't understand is that we only open some of the rooms at this time of year.'

I pushed through the swing doors leading to the rather gloomy bedroom corridor. The Crannog was a small hotel with few rooms, but for a moment I was perplexed as I identified room five and then seven, but the number between them was nine.

On closer inspection, as my eyes became used to the shadows, it was clear what had happened. The top screw had come loose, allowing the number to swing down. I'd have to mention this on my way out.

After rummaging in my case to find and a fleece and my parka jacket, I left for the Kingarth Hotel, intending to speak to Freida, but Reception was deserted.

As I reached main door the smartly dressed woman who'd been checking in ahead of me came hurrying out, pushing past me without a word. Ignoring this rude behaviour, I collected my car from the road in front of the hotel. This would be the first time I'd met the whole team and I didn't want to get off to a bad start by being the last person to arrive.

3

So why did I do it? Return to Bute when I'd vowed to stay away, given that every time I returned to the island difficulties followed. Not that I actively sought trouble. It seemed to find me.

There was much about the place I loved: the quiet beaches edging the waters of the Firth of Clyde or curving round at Ettrick Bay; the long stretches of sand at St Ninian's Bay where the wild geese gathered in the autumn; the sheltered coves where boats from all corners of the world overwintered, nestling snugly against the rough winds; the little town of Rothesay with its quaint streets and even quainter shops; the walk from Port Bannatyne round the locally named Loop that took you high above the village and boasted spectacular views over the waters of the bay.

Truth was, I couldn't seem to avoid complications whenever I was working on Bute. A natural curiosity, coupled with a series of unfortunate incidents was my problem.

The letter of invitation had arrived one morning in February and thinking it was yet more junk mail I'd gone through to the kitchen, intending to give the contents a cursory glance before consigning it to the recycling bin.

Simon put down his coffee cup and looked up from the newspaper where he was frowning in concentration over a crossword puzzle as he heard my, 'That's a strange thing to do.'

He raised his eyebrows in that way he has, waiting for an explanation.

'Who came up with this idea?' I muttered.

'So what is it this time?' he said lifting the envelope postmarked Rothesay I'd laid on the table beside him.

'It's almost too incredible to be true,' I said, waving the letter at him. 'You can read it for yourself. You know the St Blane's site at the south end of the island, the one with the ruins of the 7th century church and the monastery reputed to have been home to St Blane?'

'Mmm. I recall a little about it. Who was St Blane again?' His mind was still on the crossword.

'He was a 7th century monk, educated in Ireland before coming back to found the monastery on Bute. His name survives in lots of Scottish place names - Dunblane, Strathblane, Blanefield are a few of them. Someone's decided to build a theme park based on his life out at Kingarth.'

'They're going to build a theme park about a 7th century monk?' Now I had his full attention. 'Who on earth would want to do that?'

'Oh, they don't call it a theme park. It's described as an "educational and historical facility", but it has the appearance of something that might have been dreamed up by Hollywood. I heard vague rumours about it last time I was over, but most people dismissed it as a fanciful idea that would never get permission.' I shrugged. 'Apparently the bid has been accepted and they've started clearing the field. I think the archaeologists are there at the moment, surveying the site before building work begins.'

He ran his fingers through his greying hair, rumpling it roughly. 'So what would they want you to do? Act the part of one of the characters, St Blane's mother perhaps? Show tourists around dressed in 7th century garb? Though you don't quite look the saintly type.' He laughed loudly at his joke.

'Now you're being silly. They're looking for someone to produce a short guide for visitors.'

'You're well qualified for that. But that's not a good enough reason for agreeing. You don't have to accept everything that comes your way.'

He was right. Having left teaching to set up as a freelance writer, I'd been lucky with the number of commissions so far. But times had changed. Money was tight and one-off projects few. I couldn't afford to turn down work and this was a very enticing offer, well paid for the few weeks involved. Besides it would solve a problem for me. We'd had our ups and downs over the years and the money from this would let me organise a surprise holiday for our anniversary. On several occasions we'd gone as far as sending for the brochure for *Canada Coast to Coast*, a journey from Vancouver to Halifax, taking in the Rockies, the Great Lakes and Nova Scotia. Our son, Alastair, had told us so much about the country and this journey was something we both wanted to do, but couldn't readily afford.

And that was it. In the end, in spite of some misgivings, I decided to accept. Or perhaps the idea of the holiday spurred me on. All I had to do for this contract was spend a couple of weeks on the island, explore the site as it was being constructed and work with the researcher before heading back to Glasgow to write the visitor guide in the comfort of my own home.

'I can see you're wavering.' Simon looked a little uneasy, possibly remembering my previous visits to the island.

'It looks interesting and the money's good,' I said briskly, 'and I'm probably worrying about nothing.'

Simon merely grunted. His unscheduled early retirement from his post as a head of department in a

Further Education college hadn't left us on the breadline but, although he worked hard, his educational consultancy had its highs and lows. At the moment, in the present economic climate, these were mostly lows.

I read the letter again. 'Benjie Anderson is in charge of the project. I don't know him, but I've heard about him. '

His eyes widened. 'Really? How come?'

'I read about him somewhere. He specialises in managing historical projects. He was responsible for the Roman villa project in Kent and the Stone Age village in Northumberland. He comes with good credentials.'

'As long as you take care and keep to your contract, don't get involved in anything you shouldn't.'

The silence stretched out for a moment and, ignoring this last remark, I headed for my study to write my acceptance. 'Of course I won't. It's not as if they're using the St Blane's site – that's a scheduled monument – but an empty field nearby where they'll recreate the 7th century ambience.'

As I left the room he said, 'Are you sure you want to go back to the island on your own? This consultancy of mine doesn't finish until the end of March. I'm waiting on the statistics for the Appendix and from the looks of it, those won't be finished any time soon. '

'It'll be fine,' I said. 'It would be great if you could join me at some point, but I will be working. Why don't you think about having a few days on the island if you do finish on time, before I come home? We could enjoy doing that West Island Way walk we've always promised to do, but never quite got round to.'

He didn't reply and I laughed. 'Don't look so worried. Everything will be absolutely fine.'

I should have listened to his concerns. I was wrong …and not for the first time.

4

As I drove back through Rothesay and out on the road past Craigmore towards Kilchattan Bay, all I could think about was the meeting with Harry. What on earth had prompted him to come back to the island? He might be feeling lonely, be at a loose end and the money for the commission would be a useful supplement to his pension. Or was there more to it than that?

After the death of his wife, he'd left Bute as soon as possible, vowing never to return, but it would appear he'd changed his mind. What's more, I strongly suspected, given his taciturn nature, he'd keep his reasons to himself, but as luck would have it we arrived at the Kingarth hotel at the same time and walked in together.

Up close, I had to admit he appeared to be much better than when I'd last seen him on Bute. His hair was whiter than ever, if that was possible, and there were a few more creases round his eyes, but all in all he looked pretty well. 'Are you staying in one of the Rothesay hotels?'

He shook his head. 'No.'

I tried a different approach. 'I'm staying in the Crannog, the hotel between Rothesay and Ardbeg,' I said. 'It didn't seem worthwhile to lease a place for such a short trip.'

'Mmm.'

'I think it was originally called something else – it's been taken over recently, given a new name,' I gabbled on to fill the gap and was about to change the subject, when he suddenly said, 'You're probably surprised I came back to Bute after all that happened?'

'I did wonder,' I said warily.

'This project is one that intrigues me and time does hang heavy at the moment. Does that give you enough information?' He gave the ghost of a smile. 'Still the same old Alison, wondering what everyone's up to.' By which he probably meant "nosey as ever" but was too polite to say.

I needn't have worried about arriving on time. As I pushed open the door to the Kingarth, with Harry close behind me, the restaurant area was empty apart from two people sitting in the far corner at a table marked Reserved. Even in a busy restaurant it would have been easy to spot them by their very workmanlike clothes, worn and rather grubby, a sure sign they'd been working out at the theme park site. They could only be archaeologists.

'Hi, there,' I said sliding along the bench at the trestle table opposite where they were sitting deep in conversation. They turned to look at us as I said, 'I'm assuming this is the St Blane's group?'

The younger of the two men grinned, displaying a set of teeth that gleamed against his ebony skin and extended his hand after giving it a cursory wipe on his jeans. 'I'm Ryan McNab and,' gesturing to the silver haired man beside him, 'this is Sven Horensson.' Ryan couldn't have been any older than his early thirties and the most striking thing about his appearance was the long, tightly matted dreadlocks he sported, trailing halfway down his back, tied at the bottom with what looked like a knitted cord of many colours and topped with a woolly hat with a large bobble. He had a wispy beard, a striking contrast to his mass of hair.

The older man looked up from perusing the menu, unsmiling, almost sullen and gave a brief grunt before

17

returning once more to the bill of fare. It was possible he didn't speak much English and though that would be most unusual for a Scandinavian, it was the only reason I could think of for his bad-mannered behaviour. Given his grizzled appearance, he looked more suited to be a Professor of Archaeology in a university rather than someone still occupied with the day-to-day business of excavations.

Harry leaned across the table saying, 'I'm Harry Sneddon,' and I'd only just said, 'And I'm Alison Cameron,' when the back door to the restaurant suddenly swung wide open, letting in a blast of cold air and to my surprise the young woman I'd encountered at the hotel strode into the room.

I lifted the menu, pretending to study it as I took the opportunity to examine her closely. She was tall and thin; her coal black hair was pulled back from her face, swept up on top of her head and she wore a severe black business suit and high heeled shoes more suited to town than country. As she came towards us, it was clear her carefully applied make-up of thick black mascara and a slash of bright red lipstick was designed to give her an air of authority.

'Take it easy, Zofia, chill out,' said Ryan, getting to his feet and grinning broadly. 'What's the hurry? The others ain't arrived yet.'

Zofia edged along the bench beside me, pulling down her skirt. 'This isn't good enough,' she said, frowning and whipping the tiniest mobile phone I'd ever seen out of her jacket pocket. 'Everyone was told *exactly* when to be here. I hope they've a good explanation.'

Whatever the reason for their lateness, it couldn't have been the traffic. One of the best things about the island is that it's virtually traffic free, except in the summer when a huge number of visitors swell the usual population of some six thousand.

Zofia made no attempt to introduce herself and started to talk into her phone, or rather shout, so that several people in the bar at the far end of the room craned round to see who was making so much noise.

'Hello, hello,' she shouted, 'is that you, Dexter? We've arrived at the Kingarth. I thought you'd be here.'

We couldn't hear Dexter's reply, but Zofia started to frown, making it clear she was far from happy. 'Okay, okay, but I think you should join us. We *need* your input.'

She snapped the phone shut, gazing round at our expectant faces. 'For the benefit of the new arrivals Dexter is in overall charge of this project: he works directly for Alexander Crombie and it's almost impossible to do anything without his say-so. *Unfortunately* he seems to have priorities other than contributing to our first full team meeting.'

Ryan leaned over and laid his hand over hers. 'Zofia, cool it, cool it. You know what these people are like. They want the work to be done, no hassle. So let's get on with it. Sven and I have come off the site to do the necessary and it'll all be fine.'

Zofia jerked her hand away and tossed her head back, letting a couple of strands of hair escape their confinement and she impatiently smoothed them back into place. 'You don't understand what it's like it is to be in charge of a team, Ryan.'

'Oh, no, you don't say,' muttered Ryan, suddenly looking solemn, 'I'm only in charge of a team of twelve.'

For a moment I thought I'd misheard. 'Sorry,' I said, 'I thought Benjie Anderson was in charge of this project. I've been dealing with him since I agreed to take on the work.'

Sven and Zofia exchanged glances. 'There has been a problem, Alison,' said Sven shuffling his feet and avoiding looking at me.

'What kind of problem?' The letter accompanying my contract had been most specific about Benjie being in charge, stressing his credentials, listing them in bold type at the top.

Before anyone could reply, a young man came in through the main door and waved to us. He was closely followed by a woman wrapped up in a high viz jacket over a pair of overalls. She and this new arrival seemed to know each other well, judging by the way he shepherded her towards us and as they reached the table, they smiled at each other in a conspiratorial way, confirming my suspicions.

They squeezed in beside us and the young man introduced her as, 'Luann Hempster, the project engineer,' before introducing himself as Nathan Fortune, the project photographer, though I should have guessed that from the large professional camera slung carelessly round his neck. His chiselled features and lean body hinted that at one time he might have been on the other side of the camera and his outfit of jeans, blue shirt and matching pullover, though casual, looked well cut and expensive.

Luann, on the other hand, looked far too little to fit my idea of an engineer, her mass of curly blonde hair and oversized spectacles with black rims hiding much of her face.

'What's all this about a photographer,' Harry leaned over and whispered to me. 'I thought I'd be taking the photos for the visitor guide?'

I shrugged to show I knew no more than he did and luckily, before I could say anything, the waitress came over to take our order.

Zofia waved her away. 'Come back in ten minutes,' she said, rather rudely I thought. It had been a long time since breakfast in Glasgow and the appetising smells drifting out of the kitchen reminded me I was hungry.

And there was no answer to my question about Benjie. 'Did you realise we'd lost the project leader?' I muttered to Harry.

But Luann had overheard. 'You didn't know?'

She looked towards Zofia who was engaged in discussing some problem or other with Ryan, judging by the grimace on both their faces. 'Benjie isn't around at the moment.'

Harry and I said together, 'What do you mean? Where is he?'

Luann made a face, replying hesitantly, 'I don't know the full story, but from what I've heard he upped and left several days ago. No one knows where he's gone, or if they do they aren't telling.' She hunched forward, pushing her hair back messily behind her ears and said in a loud voice to Zofia, 'Alison and Harry didn't know about Benjie. Perhaps you'd better bring them up to speed.'

Zofia tapped her fingers impatiently on the edge of the table. 'I've not been told much more than the rest of you,' she said. 'He didn't turn up for the last scheduled meeting and Alexander Crombie wasn't best pleased. No one's been able to contact him and his mobile seems to be switched off. I'm the project consultant, but *I've* been asked to fill in meantime.' She seemed edgy, unsure.

'Seems a bit odd if he left suddenly like that, without a word of explanation,' I said to Harry.

Turning to us Luann said, 'Yes, but the word is that he wasn't happy. He and Dexter, Alexander Crombie's right hand man, had fallen out over the way the site was developing. The next thing we knew he'd gone AWOL.'

'So he's a missing person? There's a police investigation?' My heart sank. I'd hardly been a day on the island and here was a problem already.

'No, no, not at all. It's more likely he'd had enough. I think he and Dexter had different views about how the site would develop. Word is they had a terrible row and Benjie stormed off.'

There was a slight chill in the atmosphere, almost too subtle to notice and then Zofia said brusquely, 'It's not really any of our business. The problem's been solved – I'll be leading the team until a substitute can be appointed. It's up to Alexander Crombie what he decides to do about Benjie's defection. Now can we get on?' Her phone rang and she snatched at it, almost as a reflex action, then after checking the screen she pressed the button to silence it.

Nathan moved up the bench nearer Harry, leaned over and whispered, 'Zofia was asked to step up at very short notice. We thought the project might have to be abandoned after Benjie's disappearance, but Crombie knows Zofia well and was luckily able to get her to agree, though I heard she'd another consultancy for a theme park in Greece lined up.'

Good heavens, was the whole world to be covered in theme parks?

'Now,' Zofia said, lifting her case from the floor where she'd dumped it, 'we need to get on and the first thing is to focus on the team outcomes. This is a preliminary meeting, but it's *important* that we define our objectives, benchmark our aims, build in controls, agree how to take fail-safe action…'

'Whoa, whoa,' said Ryan, cutting in, 'let's eat and chill out. We know what we've to do, Zofia. Benjie briefed us well. All this mumbo-jumbo of management speak won't get the job done any better …or any quicker. We'll report back to you if there are any problems, that's for sure.' A wicked grin crossed his face. 'Management by exception, ain't it called?'

Zofia didn't reply immediately. She was now searching in her case, flicking through papers as though to hide her anger at this attempt to undermine her authority.

'That's all very well,' she replied, sniffing. 'There's a lot of money invested in this project. It's not one of your amateur excavations, you know, where people have to make do on a shoestring.'

'Pity they're not paying us well, then,' muttered Nathan with a sideways look at me, but Zofia ignored him, instead turning her attention to Luann. 'It wasn't the best of ideas to meet here, Luann. I know you're trying your best in difficult circumstances but it's too informal. I wanted to have a *proper* plan of action set out, analyse our goals, schedule meetings, have roles and responsibilities clearly understood and allocated.'

My immediate thought was that Zofia's habit of emphasising random words could soon become extremely annoying.

At this point the waitress came over again, hovering uncertainly in light of the reception she'd received earlier.

'We should order,' said Luann, pretending not to notice Zofia's bad humour and purposefully lifting the menu. She turned and gave the waitress a dazzling smile, a smile that lit up her face, transforming her from someone rather ordinary. 'I'll have the salmon salad, no fries…and,' with a defiant look at Zofia, 'a glass of house white.'

As though inspired by this bold decision, a choice that didn't please Zofia judging by her pursed lips, Ryan and Nathan clamoured to order a pint of beer with their steak pie and chips, while Sven indicated he would stick to water.

My order was far more modest. At this time of day a sandwich and cup of tea were more than enough, though I was sorely tempted, but it was unnecessary of Zofia to say, 'Black coffee is all I want.' The tension in the air was palpable, everyone on edge, uncomfortably silent as we waited for our order.

None of this looked promising for our working as a team, no doubt why Harry said after a few minutes, sounding conciliatory, 'We could arrange another meeting somewhere we could work more easily, if that would suit you better, Zofia. But don't you think it's been a good idea to meet like this for the first time as a sort of bonding session? Especially after the news we've received about this change of personnel. Alison and I knew nothing about Benjie's sudden departure.'

Whatever Zofia had in mind for this first meeting it evidently wasn't a bonding session, not by the way she glared at these remarks from someone new to the team.

Fortunately at that moment the waitress appeared with the first orders, including Zofia's coffee. She gulped it down with a little moue of displeasure as the hot liquid caught her unawares and before we had time to start on the meal stood up, saying, 'I don't have time to waste waiting about here. I'll book the Lesser Hall at the Rothesay Pavilion for nine o'clock tomorrow morning. I expect everyone to be there *promptly*, ready for a proper meeting.'

'Will that include Dexter?' said Luann, but Zofia continued as though she hadn't heard her.

'We've lost enough time as it is with all this. If you haven't had the opportunity to see the site at St Blane's I suggest you go over there and make yourself familiar with the terrain.'

Nathan sniggered, then changed it into a cough, hiding behind his hand as he lifted his glass of beer to take a long gulp, after taking off his camera and placing it carefully at the far end of the table.

She stomped out in a flurry of papers, briefcase and laptop, shrugging on her jacket and leaving us looking after her, perplexed by this outburst.

Ryan was the first to speak. 'Whoa hey, what was that all about?'

'Seems to me she's being a bit high-handed.' Harry added his tuppence worth, and now I was consumed by curiosity.

'Does anyone know anything about her? I don't recognise her name.' Though I'd every intention of checking her out on the internet as soon as I'd access to my computer.

Ryan and Sven exchanged glances as though uncertain about how much they should say. Harry broke in. 'I've heard about her I'm sure. She's been a consultant on several projects like this one, mainly in overseas countries.'

But it was Luann who stepped in to answer his question. 'I doubt if she's had any jobs where she's been more than a consultant, has managed anything like this. Sure she has a reputation, or we've been told she has, but this theme park at Kingarth is a big deal. There's lots – careers and money – riding on it. Benjie was so easy to work with, so enthusiastic about everything. Let's hope he has a change of heart and returns soon.'

Something had been nagging away at me ever since I'd received the letter offering me the contract and someone in this group might have the answer. 'Why choose this place to develop a historical theme park? There are plenty of sites on the mainland where it would be much easier to do this kind of thing. And where there would be the possibility of attracting bigger crowds? I mean,' I blustered on, not wanting to offend any of them, 'it's a lovely island but to make a theme park pay you'd have to be sure lots of people would visit regularly.'

Luann grimaced. 'You mean a bit like that place in the North East of England? The Beamish Museum Park? You'd think so, wouldn't you? But it seems Alexander Crombie who's funding the project was born here and left for South Africa as young man in order to make his fortune. Now he wants to give something back to the local community and thinks this is the way to do it. If it comes off, there will be lots of employment opportunities on the island and if it doesn't, at least the building firms here will have had some work during its construction.'

'I suppose someone will benefit.' It still seemed like a huge gamble.

'That's if the protest group doesn't scupper the whole idea.' Nathan frowned as he spoke.

'There are always people who object to anything new,' I said, thinking about my encounter with the protesters on my arrival.

'This is rather more than a few people on the island who don't like change. They think the theme park will cheapen, devalue the site at St Blane's. They've been gathering support for a few weeks now and from what I hear they're a determined bunch.'

Ryan was nodding in agreement, his dreadlocks moving about as though with a mind of their own. 'Sure could be a problem, folks.'

'Nonsense,' Luann retorted. 'Most people realise the place will be a boon to the island economy. A few people frightened of progress won't upset the plans.'

That made sense, of a kind, but from what Nathan said about the protesters, I couldn't help but think the whole project might turn out to be some kind of white elephant. Alexander Crombie must have very deep pockets to take such a risk and I was looking forward to meet him at some point. Still, it was no concern of mine. I'd a contract and once it was done, though I'd be interested in what happened eventually to the theme park, I wouldn't be involved.

'I think I'll do as Zofia suggested and head over to St Blane's,' I said. 'It's some time since I was there and it would be good to refresh my memory before the meeting tomorrow.'

Harry slid along the bench and stood up. 'I'll come with you, Alison. To be honest I haven't ever been to St Blane's even though I was here for some time before…' He stopped, but I could guess he'd been about to say, '…before Greta died.'

To cover this awkward pause I intervened quickly with, 'Of course. Good idea. We can think about how we want to tackle this together, match the research with the need to keep the visitor guide easy to read.'

As we were about to leave, a small dark-haired man came bursting in and after hesitating for a moment in the doorway, gazing around, hurried over to join us saying, 'Sorry I couldn't get here earlier. I'd a few phone calls to make.' He stopped. 'Where's Zofia?'

'You've just missed her.' Ryan grinned. 'No worries. We've all to turn up tomorrow at the Pavilion.'

In reply to my whispered, 'Who's that?' Luann said quietly, 'That's Dexter, making out as usual how important he is. Phone calls my foot. He wants to show he's too high and mighty to keep to our schedule.'

'And he's in overall charge?'

Luann shrugged. 'I expect you could say that. He's certainly Crombie's right hand man.'

Dexter gazed round. 'Why is Zofia not here? I tried to call her, tell her I'd be late.'

Ah, so that was the phone call Zofia had ignored.

'She has gone.' Sven looked up. So far he'd said very little, contenting himself with observing what was going on around him.

'…decided we'd be better to meet tomorrow at the Pavilion. It's too informal for her here,' added Luann. 'Zofia isn't big on socialising.'

'Damn,' Dexter growled, twanging a dark blue elastic band he wore round his wrist. 'I made a special effort to come out here.'

'Now you're here you may as well have something to eat,' said Nathan, making room for him on the bench.

Dexter declined with an abrupt shake of his head saying, 'There's too much to do,' but Nathan persisted, 'You might as well join us and sample the excellent menu.' He smiled and I immediately warmed to him. He seemed relaxed, easy going, which was great given we'd have to work closely with him to produce the visitor guide.

Before Dexter could complain about wasting time, Luann said, 'We'll finish our coffee and then join you over at the site later, if that's what you prefer.'

He fiddled with the elastic band on his wrist again and without another word hurried out.

'Let's go, Alison,' said Harry steering me by the elbow, evidently as keen as I was to get away from the friction in this group.

We left the others sitting drinking coffee and chatting in an unhurried way, almost as if in defiance of Dexter. Let them all squabble as much as they wanted to. I was here to fulfil a contract and once I'd collected all the necessary material, I'd be off back to the mainland. I'd no intention of getting involved with the problems of this particular group.

5

We agreed to travel separately by car to Kingarth, an arrangement which suited me perfectly. I wasn't too sure how well Harry had recovered from the death of his wife, nor about his motives for returning to the island, and it would be better to avoid discussing personal matters.

I followed Harry as he drove out of the car park at the hotel, though given the spaces were tight, I only narrowly avoided a disastrous brush with a large black Landrover. Accident avoided, I kept closely behind Harry as he turned left at the Kingarth cemetery and accelerated along the road leading to St Blane's.

From Kingarth to St Blane's is no more than a couple of miles, but the road narrows to a single track with passing places as it approaches the site and the last part winds steeply upwards. At the farm at the top of the hill a large tractor was parked beside the milking shed and we had to wait for a few minutes as the farmer deftly manoeuvred it to the edge of the ditch to let us pass. A few hundred yards from St Blane's we passed the last building on the left hand side, newly renovated and whitewashed, probably another farm bought as a holiday home as so many are on Bute, before reaching the rubber matted verge where the roadway ran out at the foot of the field.

Once out of the car, I looked up, remembering this part of the island was hilly and we'd have a bit of a scramble up to the ruins of the chapel at St Blane's. The field destined to become the theme park looked no easier a climb.

In the meadow on the other side of the road several inquisitive lambs came trotting over to the five-barred gate, their little stumps of tails wagging. They showed no fear and their size, even this early in March, was an indication of how sweet the grass was in this corner of Bute.

A temporary entrance of sorts had been put up in the chain fencing surrounding the site of the theme park and we headed there, eager to see it for ourselves.

The ground sloped gently upwards, ending in a sharp escarpment dotted with trees and a number of excavating machines were already at work on the lower slopes, stripping off large sections of earth. Halfway up the hill large pallets of bricks were stacked to the side of several concrete blocks and as we watched a yellow digger came trundling up. There were several mounds of earth, the outline of a structure or two, (though it was hard to identify their exact purpose at this early stage), the usual assortment of portaloos and a Portakabin for the workmen, outside which sat a motley collection of buckets and tables with trowels, brushes and sieves. In the distance, near the top of the hill at the escarpment, several figures scurried backwards and forwards, their shouts drifting down in the still air.

'Where shall we start?' said Harry, gazing round. 'It looks busy here, not to mention dangerous, and we haven't been given any safety equipment.'

'Let's head over to St Blane's,' I said. 'After all, that's what we'll really have to understand if we want to produce a good visitor guide. It's so long since I've been there it'll be good to refresh my memory. I'd forgotten how difficult the access road is to Kingarth. It must be a nightmare for all this heavy machinery.'

'Agreed. This is my first visit, so I'll have to rely on you.'

We picked our way carefully back down to the road, walked a little way along and then opened the gate at the foot of the slope leading to St Blane's, edging our way through the turnstile before starting to climb the hill. There was a path of sorts which helped, but it was still a fair step to the ruined chapel. The sheep, grazing in the lush pasture, looked up at this disturbance before returning to munching contentedly.

'Keep to the wall,' I said, 'that way you've some hope of avoiding the sheep droppings.'

'At least it's dry,' said Harry, pulling his jacket closely round him. 'I wouldn't fancy doing this in the wind and the rain.'

'I know what you mean,' I said, glad of the chance to pause to catch my breath. From halfway up, there was a clear view of the menacing square outline of the vitrified fort of Dunagoil far in the distance, bordering the water's edge. Even on a bright day like this it looked dark, threatening and I shivered a little, before looking to the distant horizon.

'What a view,' I exclaimed, shading my eyes against the sun. 'Simon and I once climbed out to Dunagoil over there.'

'I thought it wasn't accessible?'

'Not from the coast side it's not, unless you have a boat, but you can get over from this side. It's quite a walk and you need good stout walking boots.'

As we reached the top, we once more stopped, charmed by what lay in front of us. The site was more extensive than I'd remembered, the remains of the chapel rising up from the rest of the ruins amid the trees and cliffs.

'There's not much left, is there?' said Harry gazing round at the signs indicating the foundations the Pilgrims' dormitories, the stone basin where pilgrims would have washed their feet, the tumble of stones, once the monks' round cells, the mysteriously named *Devil's Cauldron*.

We wandered back to the ruined chapel and stepped inside. Harry traced his hand along the line of mortar. 'Ah, here's the mark to show where the Third Marquess of Bute made the restoration.'

We lingered for a few moments, savouring such a quiet spot on this part of the island. Only the sound of birdsong and the occasional bleat from one of the sheep, carrying in the still air, disturbed the silence.

Although he wasn't admitting it, it was clear Harry was as puzzled as I was. There was little to see at St Blane's, so how would the theme park make use of this? Perhaps that was the intention – Alexander Crombie could give free rein to his imagination. Once again I thought he must be very rich indeed to have taken on a project such as this.

Harry said, as though echoing my thoughts, 'They'll have to do a lot of work to make a theme park based on this a paying proposition. It's a lovely spot, but there's not much to it.' He peered at a large sign where only a few stones were evident. 'That's the remains of the manse where the Parish priest and, after the Reformation, the minister lived.'

'They couldn't have had a large congregation,' I said, looking round at the empty landscape. 'It's hard to believe it continued to be used for so long.'

'Well, you'd be surprised. I've done some research on the site and in the Middle Ages, when almost every saint had an annual fair or market associated with his name, this was a pretty lively place.'

'So people travelled here in some numbers?' I found that hard to believe.

'Indeed. The St Blane's Fair was on 12th August and for centuries cattle came to the fair, not merely from the island but also from the mainland, swimming across the narrows at the Kyles of Bute or ferried from Ayrshire by Kerrycroy. It would have been quite a sight. '

'It must have been a very wealthy place.'

'Extremely, though the guess is that most of the precious items from the monastery were lost in the Viking raids on the island.'

'But wasn't some treasure found here? I seem to remember reading about the St Blane's Hoard found over a hundred years ago by some workmen digging in a field some way from here.'

He paused, frowning as he recalled the details. 'They found some twenty or so coins, a couple of gold rings, three gold bands if I remember correctly, and a small bar of silver. But nothing else was ever discovered from what I know, though there were a number of excavations over the years.'

'Surely that's strange? There must be more objects somewhere on the site, waiting to be found.'

'Don't get overly excited, Alison. Sure there are likely to be some bits and pieces found from time to time. The Hoard might not even have been buried. It might have ended up there by chance.'

'But some people think there is still treasure to be found?'

He raised his eyebrows. 'So, has anything been discovered? No, of course not. The field where the Hoard was hidden…and the site at St Blane's… have

34

been well searched over the years, but nothing of value has turned up. Most likely the monks managed to make off with anything valuable when it became clear the Vikings were on their way.'

The sun had disappeared behind clouds some time before and now little spits and spots of rain began to fall. I shivered as the temperature began to plummet.

'Time to go, I think,' said Harry. 'Those clouds look pretty ominous and we're not really equipped to be out here in the rain.'

'Good idea,' I said, suddenly remembering I'd left my coat in the car. Surely by now I should have known how quickly the weather can change on this Atlantic coast: bright sunshine one moment, rain the next.

We hurried back down the hill as the rain began in earnest, plump drops falling faster and faster and by the time we'd reached the road it was coming down so heavily I was almost soaked through in the short distance to the car.

'I guess our visit to the site will have to wait,' Harry yelled above the noise of the rain.

In the field where they were building the theme park, there was no sign of any of the workmen. Doubtless they had sought shelter from this storm in the blue Portakabin halfway up the slope.

'Good idea,' I said, tugging open the car door. 'I'll see you tomorrow at the Pavilion.'

We scurried into our respective vehicles and I drove off, turning up the heater to maximum in an attempt to dry out, glad to be able to follow Harry along the narrow road back down to Rothesay. By now the clouds were low and threatening: it was getting dark and the combination of the gloom and the rain didn't make for easy driving.

By the time I'd tooted goodbye to him at Craigmore and reached the town I stopped off at the little Co-op for a bar of chocolate. Dinner at the hotel wouldn't be for some time and I was badly in need of comfort food to keep me going.

Supplies bought, including a couple of extra bars for emergencies, I headed for the hotel, looking forward to a long hot bath before dinner. If nothing else, this project was turning out to be interesting and I wondered how Zofia would deal with us all in the morning.

6

The Rothesay Pavilion sits near the shore at the edge of the town, its splendid façade promising a stylish interior. I'd a particular fondness for the place, having written a history of the building recently and I was pleased to be back.

We'd been instructed to arrive on time: I was there a good twenty minutes early, partly because I hadn't yet accustomed myself again to the speed with which one can travel round the island; partly because I didn't want to incur Zofia's wrath so early in our dealings. She struck me, even from our limited acquaintance, as someone with a fiery temper, prone to sulking if she didn't get her own way. As the mother of three children (now fortunately grown up) I'd had enough of childish tantrums. Maura and her husband Alan have been living in Kent for several years, Alastair is a lecturer at the University of Maple Ridge in British Columbia and our youngest, Deborah is currently living in Manchester, working on an Arts project, though what will happen when the funding comes to an end, goodness knows. I expect she'll come back home as she usually does between jobs or courses.

Although Zofia was also staying in the Crannog Hotel, I hadn't seen her again but no doubt would bump into her sooner or later. I wouldn't say I was exactly avoiding her, but this lack of social contact suited me fine.

With a few minutes to spare before the start of the meeting, I sat outside on the low wall at the car park in front of the building, waiting for the others, enjoying the freshness of the morning. The storm which had raged for most of the night had passed and the sky was clear and blue, though it was a little chilly with the wind blowing off the water, the billowing sails of a yacht far out on the bay showing how breezy it was. Even so, it was good to sit quietly with the sun on my face, smelling the sea air, aware it would soon be Spring.

As I gazed around, I caught sight of something odd on the lampposts outside the building and went over for a closer look. Someone had been fly-posting and the message was clear. HANDS OFF OUR HERITAGE, one of them proclaimed and the other NO THEME PARK AT ST BLANE'S. I walked further along the road, counting the number of lampposts with similar posters. There was nothing to indicate who might be responsible, but it could only be the work of the protesters. That was worrying: they were organised enough to have produced these posters as well as rallying a number of people to their cause.

Luann came strolling down the road to join me, brushing away some imaginary dirt on the wall before levering herself up to sit beside me. 'Madam not arrived yet?' she said consulting a large watch which made her thin wrist look even thinner. She'd made an attempt to control her wild hair by tying it up in a topknot, but little tendrils kept escaping, and from time to time she'd impatiently thrust them back into the glittery bobble she'd used. She rummaged in her pocket and found a couple of Kirby grips and pushed them in to her hair.

'Apparently not, though I haven't been inside yet. Thought I'd take advantage of the fresh air in case the weather changes again.'

'Yes, that was some storm yesterday evening,' said Luann. 'That's the problem about a project like this –

for the first part at least you're totally weather dependent. I popped over to the site before coming here and thank goodness they've managed to get started again this morning. I thought the ground might be too boggy, but most of the rain has drained down the hill. One of the advantages of being on a slope.'

'What's all that about?' I said, pointing to the posters.

She laughed. 'Haven't you noticed them before? They're all round the island. That's the protest group, objecting strongly to the theme park. They claim it will ruin the heritage site.'

'Yes, I saw one of their rallies as I came off the ferry yesterday. Why are they so concerned? The theme park won't be anywhere near St Blane's.'

'Exactly. It's the usual group of people who don't want change. The theme park will bring a lot of advantages to Bute: more visitors, more employment. It's all nonsense.'

At that moment Nathan came sauntering along the promenade, pausing occasionally to look out over the bay and focus his camera.

'We've been lucky to get Nathan on this project. The word is Crombie had to pay a fair amount of money to tempt him.' There was a note of pride in Luann's voice as she looked over at him.

Feeling rather ashamed of my ignorance on the matter, I said, 'Oh, so is he well known?'

Luann laughed. 'He's only the best archaeological photographer in Britain. It must have taken a fair bit of persuasion, or possibly money, to get him here from London.'

One by one the others arrived and we trooped together into the small hall on the ground floor of the

Pavilion, where we tried with limited success to make ourselves as comfortable as possible on the hard plastic chairs. As the minutes ticked away with no sign of Zofia, one or two of the group became restless and any conversation petered out into an oppressive silence.

'That's great, folks,' said Ryan, pointedly consulting his watch for the umpteenth time. 'She tells us to make sure we're here on time, but can't manage it herself.' Today Ryan had tied his dreadlocks back with what appeared to be a coloured ribbon and he'd shaved, highlighting his fine features.

Harry came and sat beside me, the frown on his face showing how displeased he was.

'What's wrong?' I said.

'It's the arrangements for taking the photos for the visitor guide,' he grumbled. 'I bought a new camera specially. A waste of money.'

'You can take as many photos as you want. I'm sure they'll be useful,' I said more sharply than intended. Was Harry going to make this complaint at every opportunity?

Sven was sitting at the back of the hall, scrolling through his phone, deep in concentration. He was a man of few words, was Sven, and I didn't think his problems were to do with language difficulties. Any time he did speak, his English was faultless. Perhaps he preferred not to waste words. As he rolled up his sleeve, it was clear he'd had a tattoo done at some stage but it was so faint he'd obviously made an attempt to have it removed. I squinted over to see what it was, but he hurriedly rolled his sleeve down again and continued fiddling with his phone.

Suddenly the door was flung open and Zofia came striding in, laden down with a laptop, a bundle of papers and dragging what looked like a portable screen.

Without a word of apology for her lateness she dumped everything on the desk at the front of the hall, while the screen clattered to the floor. 'Glad to see you're all here,' she said. Her phone, piled up on the table with all the other stuff, started to vibrate and for a moment she looked as if she was about to answer it before deciding to ignore it and put it in the pocket of her coat, slung carelessly over the back of her chair.

Luann opened her mouth to make a remark, but a nudge from Ryan silenced her.

He was right. There was no point in causing yet more problems.

Zofia finally managed to set up the screen and sort out the laptop. Interestingly, no one offered to help her and I was sure they didn't have my excuse of being pretty hopeless with the technology. I wondered if it was anything to do with Benjie, if he'd been popular and now he was no longer on the scene there was a degree of hostility towards Zofia for having taken his place. Not your problem, Alison, I told myself. You're here to do a job and forget about everything else.

'I thought,' she said, glaring at us and switching on the laptop, 'it would be good to show you the mock-up I've had sent through and give you an idea what the theme park will look like when it's finished.'

'Is this something new? I would've thought you'd have seen this before?' hissed Harry to Luann.

'We've seen the plans and the drawings, of course we have, but nothing like this. I think it's a computer generated set of images and should be interesting,' Luann whispered back.

'If you could please pay *attention*,' said Zofia, stabbing at the keyboard, trying to find the right link on the computer.

Feeling a little like naughty schoolchildren we looked towards the front as the title *A Great Day out for all the Family* appeared on the screen.

'This is only a working title,' said Zofia, forestalling any criticism. 'We'll have something a lot *snappier* when we're finished and the marketing people have done their work.'

'That's if the protesters don't manage to get the project cancelled,' said Nathan in a loud voice from the back of the room. 'I hear they've been going round the island, drumming up support for the petition they intend to present to Historic Scotland in an attempt to have the plans for the theme park cancelled.'

Zofia appeared flustered for a moment, but only a moment. She shook her head, 'You're exaggerating as usual, Nathan. There are plenty of people on the island who're looking forward to having opportunities to encourage tourists. Has anyone approached you? No, I thought not,' as Nathan shrugged his shoulders. 'It's rumour and gossip, nothing more. The people on this island know the *benefits* this will bring.'

Remembering the protest at Guildford Square and the posters on the lampposts I knew this wasn't strictly true, but wasn't about to speak.

She turned back to her laptop. 'Now, let's get started. We've wasted enough time as it is.'

Suitably rebuked, Nathan disguised his discomfiture by fiddling with his camera, avoiding meeting her gaze and, pleased she'd won this round of the argument, Zofia pressed the icon on her laptop to start the slideshow.

I sat back in anticipation, thinking this would be especially useful for Harry and me, as without some overall idea of what the theme park would actually look like, we'd find it hard to do it justice. Perhaps Zofia had more sense than we'd given her credit for.

7

The film started, overlaid by a rather sombre musical soundtrack, but as the tour of the St Blane's Theme Park began there was sound of a sharp intake of breath, followed by silence.

Where the original St Blane's was quite small, with little apart from the shell of the church and the information signs beside the ruins of other buildings, the proposed theme park was gigantic, covering the entire area of the field nearby right up to the edge of the wooded escarpment.

The camera panned round to give us a view of the reconstructed chapel, an ornate building of white stone with no resemblance to the original and more suited to a Greek island than to the harsher climes of Bute. 'It's designed to be suitable for weddings,' said Zofia defensively, as we gasped at the elaborate stonework and the clock tower with the large bell. 'It can hold a maximum of eighty guests, though seventy would be more comfortable.'

This was only the start of the surprises. The refectory, allegedly constructed using information from a number of excavations across the country, was a long low building, revealed on closer inspection to be a large restaurant: the inside not at all the kind of place where the monks would have eaten their frugal meals, with its bright modern décor and shiny laminate tables and chairs.

Spread over the site at the bottom left, near the entrance, were a variety of attractions which looked more suitable for a funfair: they'd all been labelled up in line with the original sites at St Blane's but that was as far as the resemblance went. The camera panned over the *Giant's Wheel*, the *Devil's Ride*, the *Sith Experience*, the *Ertha Wishing Well*.

'What's a Sith?' I whispered to Harry

'A kind of fairy, I think,' a reply which left me not much wiser.

Halfway up the hill there was a very strangely shaped pond surrounded by a wooden platform with the sign, Catch Your Own Dinner, showing it was intended to be a fish farm.

'Hey ho, that's a wicked idea,' said Ryan, slapping his thigh. 'If you don't catch anything, you don't eat, I expect.'

Zofia failed to recognise the note of sarcasm. 'Now you're being silly,' she said. 'Of course there are other options and many people will want to take their catch home with them.'

The camera swung up to the top of the site where a number of round buildings apparently made of stone and roofed with turf sat clustered together. 'What are those?' asked Harry, leaning forward to peer at the screen.

'They look like the old monks' cells,' I whispered, 'but what use would they be?'

Zofia looked pleased at this sign of interest. 'Let me show you.' She clicked on one of them and the interior came into view. This might have been a building modelled on a monk's cell, might have had the appearance on the outside of something very basic, but the inside was, in a word, palatial. The rough exterior concealed a low level sitting area complete with gigantic television, a kitchen equipped with all the latest gadgets including an American-style fridge freezer, a large built-in cooker, a microwave and a coffee machine. On the ground level there were two bedrooms, each with an ensuite bathroom.

'Are they all like this?' asked Harry, once we'd recovered from the shock of seeing such luxury in the so-called monks' cells.

'Oh,' said Zofia airily, 'this is one of the smaller ones. Some of them have more bedrooms.'

No matter what you thought about the concept, you had to admire the ingenuity of the architect who'd designed them. On the outside they looked so unprepossessing, but inside, well, wow! Though quite what they had to do with the reality of life in the 7th century was difficult to see. On the other hand, no doubt it would have been impossible to attract visitors if they were expected to live as the monks once did.

The camera continued to pan round the site, stopping outside the proposed Apothecary shop. 'The monks were big on herbal medicines,' she said, 'and we plan to have a large selection of herbal *remedies* for sale. There will be staff qualified in various techniques, like,' she made a vague movement with her hands, 'Indian head massage, aromatherapy and hot stones massage.'

Trying hard to control my desire to laugh, I glanced over at Harry, hoping to catch his attention, but he deliberately ignored me and sat tight-lipped as further details of this theme park were revealed. This mangle of history and fantasy wasn't likely to meet with his approval and I'd be interested to hear his opinion when I'd the opportunity to speak to him alone.

As though he read my mind he said in a gruff voice, 'Exactly what period of history is this meant to represent?'

'Oh,' replied Zofia, dismissing his question, 'It's not meant to represent a particular period; it's not for *real*,

Harry.' She giggled as though this was a very strange idea. 'It's meant to be an *experience*. So while the site will have the appearance it might have had when St Blane was there, the opening event will be more like the medieval fairs that took place.'

The look on Harry's face showed what he thought of this explanation and for a fleeting moment I felt some sympathy for the protest group.

'And who exactly do you think will come to this theme park?' Nathan sounded incredulous, unable to contain himself any longer, voicing everyone's thoughts.

'You'd be surprised, 'said Zofia, whirling round. 'It's all been well thought out after proper investigation and a great deal of research. There's been plenty of consultation. People love this kind of thing. It makes them feel they have an affinity with the past, but with all the comforts of the modern age. Isn't that so, Luann?'

Luann, who had remained quiet all through this extraordinary presentation, merely nodded, sending her cascade of curls bouncing.

'I thought it would be a much simpler affair,' I ventured. 'A reconstruction of the original St Blane's with a little more in the way of home comforts. I thought that was why I'd been recruited to write a visitor guide.'

Zofia looked astonished at this statement. 'Whatever gave you that idea? You and Harry have been recruited to produce the guide, but people now want more than a replica of a few ruins. They want *excitement*, something for the kids to do and above all they want their home comforts.' She sniggered. 'I suppose you'd have been happier if the monks' cells had stuck more closely to the originals. Possibly bare earth with a bit of rush matting and an animal skin or two for protection and warmth?'

'Not exactly.' I didn't want to start an argument with her, but this concept was surely as far removed from the original idea of St Blane's as night was from day.

Zofia shrugged, unable to hide her disappointment at our reaction. 'I'm sorry if *you* don't like it,' she sniffed, 'but all the decisions have been made and it's our job to make sure everything goes smoothly.'

She snapped shut the laptop and perched on the end of the desk, swinging her legs. 'We must make certain everyone understands the schedule. The theme park is to be opened on 12th August, the birthday of St Blane and it will take a lot of dedication to make that happen.'

'A miracle it would have to be,' muttered Sven, the first time he'd spoken throughout the presentation, but if Zofia heard him, she gave no sign, continuing to talk with increasing enthusiasm.

'It will be a really big affair with lots of craft stalls, someone demonstrating weaving, someone else showing how the old coracles were made, a group of singers and lots of *food* stalls based on what they would have eaten in the 7th century.'

This all sounded like a proper mish-mash and I was glad when Nathan said in a languid voice which had a steely edge to it, 'And I'll be doing the photographs for this brochure, Zofia?'

'Yes, of course. Mr Crombie wants you to take photos of the site as it progresses, photos to go in the souvenir brochure and some of the opening event.'

'That'll keep you busy,' said Luann, making a face.

Yes, I thought, especially if you're also providing the photos for the visitor guide.

Zofia seemed to have lost her train of thought at this interruption. 'Now, where was I? Oh, yes, the 7th century food.'

'Oh, really,' said Sven. 'And what might that be, Zofia? Beef burgers and cola?'

'Of course not,' she replied. 'Let's not be silly.'

'They ate very little meat,' said Harry quietly.

'Vegetables, that's what they ate,' said Ryan, 'peas, cabbage, parsnips, carrots…'

'…apples, blackberries, raspberries…' added Harry.

'And they drank beer and mead and…' Ryan chimed in again.

By now there was much laughter as this litany was taken up by others in the room.

'…and milk and cheese and celery…'

'…and lots of bread and butter and…fish and…'

Zofia stamped her foot. 'Be quiet all of you. This is a serious business.' The laughter died away apart from the odd giggle, quickly suppressed in the face of Zofia's anger.

'And what about the monks this theme park is supposed to represent?' Harry spoke. He looked cross, no doubt seeing all his research into one of his favourite periods in history going to waste.

Zofia shook her head as though this comment was of little consequence. She was becoming increasingly tetchy at being interrupted, not to mention the poor reception this grandiose scheme was receiving. 'Of course that will be recognised. It's planned to have a group of people dressed as monks singing Gregorian chant in the chapel. Several of the stalls will have monks as stallholders, others will be dressed as St Blane and his mother Ertha and of course there is the main event.' She stopped, waiting for a response and

49

wasn't disappointed as all eyes were fixed on her, wondering what could possibly trump what she'd shown us so far. 'There's going to be a Viking invasion as the day draws to a close. They will sweep in from across the bay and storm the place, dressed in *authentic* costumes.'

The faint sound of a phone ringing somewhere in the building, footsteps hurrying up to the main hall, the squawk of seagulls outside the windows were the only sounds as we sat in silence, trying to make sense of this latest announcement and fully aware of the shock she'd created, Zofia stood up and lifted the pile of papers on her desk.

'Here are the timescales for each of the items. Please highlight your own contribution and check it carefully as now is the time to ask any questions. We have to press on and I don't want any unnecessary delays.'

'She means the protesters,' Luann whispered to me as the papers were handed round.

There was so much detail to take in and at this moment I wasn't particularly in the mood for it, so I shuffled the documents together and put them in my bag. I'd read them later, back in the hotel.

Sven looked up and waved the sheaf of papers at her, his voice sharp with anger. 'I do not understand, Zofia, why we have to have the information for everyone, rather than have only our individual instructions. It is a lot more work to read all this.'

Zofia glowered, unable to hide her annoyance at this contradiction of her grand plan. 'We are a team, Sven, a team. We have to be aware not only of the contribution each of us will make, but also be able to analyse what everyone else will be doing. That way we can empathise, support one other, build a proper framework for team dynamics, networking and rating each section of the plan. It's the only way we can assess work patterns and work out our priorities.'

This management speak sounded as if it was her way of trying to control us. Or to be fair to her, perhaps having only recently taken over from Benjie, presumably without any briefing, she was struggling to get a grip on the whole project.

'Bet you're sorry you asked, man,' tittered Ryan as Sven subsided into muttering to himself, but whether that was because he didn't want to antagonise Zofia further or whether it was because he'd no idea what she was on about, was hard to tell.

8

'Everyone happy?' Zofia stood up, clearly expecting a positive reply, though no one spoke. 'I have a meeting out at the site now. I dare say I'll see you there at some point. We'll meet here in three days at the same time. It's important to maintain the *impetus*, to identify any difficulties, problem solve before things get out of hand. It's the only way we'll manage to keep to our brief.'

Luann raised her eyebrows and I had to admit from what Harry and I had seen, even on our short visit to the site, there was a lot of work to be done. The archaeologists would have to complete their survey soon if the building work was to be finished in time for the planned opening date.

But that was the least of our problems at the moment. As we came out of the Pavilion together, chatting among ourselves, everyone carefully avoiding walking beside Zofia, we were met by a sea of angry faces.

'Good grief, what's going on here?' said Nathan, who was first out through the double doors leading on to the street.

A sea of banners greeted us, most of them obviously amateur efforts with slogans displaying a united hostility to the theme park at St Blane's.

NO THEME PARK HERE said one. KEEP BUTE RUBBISH FREE said another, obviously recycled from a different event. The largest of all looked as if someone had taken a bed sheet to write on it in large blue letters the words

SAY NO TO THE THEME PARK.

We stood looking to Zofia for guidance, taken aback by this display. At a guess there were almost fifty protesters, wedged closely together so that there was no way through without being bumped and jostled.

'Don't worry,' said Harry, 'I'm certain they won't hurt us. All bark and no bite.'

I wasn't so sure. Right at the front was the tall, ruddy faced man I'd seen at the demonstration in Guildford Square, looking more determined than ever.

'Keep Bute theme park free,' he shouted and the chant was taken up by several of the others, one by one, but not exactly in harmony so that it became a cacophony of noise.

'No desecration of our sacred site,' called another waving his banner right in front of our faces.

Zofia appeared to be rooted to the spot, as did the rest of the team, taken by surprise. It was as though we were unable to move, waiting to see what would happen next.

In the end it was Sven who broke the impasse and saved the day. He strode to the front, pulling himself up to his full height. 'You must let us through,' he said facing down the leader of the protesters.

'Oh, do you think so?' There was a note of anger in the leader's voice, his colour rising as he glared at Sven. 'We've every right to be here.'

'Yes, you must, because if you do not,' Sven raised his voice to make sure he could be heard at the back of the crowd, 'if you do not, I shall call the police and you will all be arrested for harassing us.'

A small, frail looking lady who must have been at least eighty, tugged at the leader's sleeve. 'Perhaps we should go, Everett. We've made our point and we don't want to be arrested, do we?' she whispered.

Everett rounded on her angrily, shaking off her hand and she shrank visibly beneath his wrath, moving back a step or two. 'Don't be so stupid, Muriel. This is an entirely peaceful protest. We're entitled to be here by law.'

But by now there were other murmurs of dissent in the crowd and several of those at the very back began to edge away, crossing the road to move along the promenade towards the Discovery Centre, quickening their pace and furling their banners.

It was a moment or two before Everett noticed their defection and when he did he rounded on those who were slinking off. 'Come back, come back,' he yelled to their departing backs, but his words had no effect.

He clambered up on to the little wall surrounding the front car park, balancing precariously on tiptoe as he shouted, 'Do you want your island invaded by hordes of grubby people who will have no respect for our culture. These people are making a mockery of our legacy.'

A cheer went up from the few remaining loyal supporters, banners waved wildly as he spoke.

Fortunately this meant that this little group had moved over towards Everett, away from the main door to the building and we were able to creep off, leaving the last of the stalwarts to their protest.

'You wouldn't really have called the police, would you?' I asked Sven as we walked quickly to our cars parked at the back of the Pavilion.

He shrugged. 'I might have. These people are no more than a nuisance. They do not want progress, claim to be preserving their heritage, but how many of them know anything about the St Blane's site? It would not surprise me if most of them had not ever visited it. They are only out to cause trouble.'

This was a long speech for Sven and delivered with a passion I wouldn't have thought him capable of. Perhaps there was more to him than first appeared.

9

Harry and I had agreed to meet for coffee the next morning at the Ettrick Bay tearoom, one of my favourite places on the island, not least because of the range of home-made cakes on offer, a temptation I should probably have avoided.

Too late, as I drove from Rothesay through Ardbeg and Port Bannatyne and took the left turn past the lodge at Kames Castle to head for Ettrick Bay, pulling down the sun visor and squinting against the bright morning light, the thought occurred to me that this might not be the best place in the circumstances. It was at the Ettrick Bay tearoom that Simon and I had met Harry and his wife Greta the year we'd come over to help my friend Susie with her inheritance of the large Victorian house on the hill at the far side of the bay, a venture which had caused so much grief to everyone, but mostly to Harry. Surely it would have been better to arrange our meeting somewhere else?

Don't be silly, I told myself, almost anywhere on the island will have associations with Greta for Harry. He would surely have said if this arrangement didn't suit him. Comforted by this thought, I drove quickly past the farm and the old blacksmith's cottage to turn left into the car park for the long low building overlooking the curve of the sands at Ettrick Bay.

Harry had arrived before me and was standing outside the tearoom, gazing out over the bay, watching the waves ripple in to the shore. The beach was empty at this time of day; the only sign of any recent activity the tracks of a tractor in the sand where the farmer had taken the short cut across to his farm. The herd of cows in the nearby fields came lumbering down in a line to stare at us over the stone wall, our presence a welcome diversion from the uneventful morning.

Harry turned as I locked up the car and walked over to join him.

'Strange, isn't it, to think that this place was once so busy, the beach crowded with people? And now look at it. Not a soul in sight.' He waved in the general direction of the sands where only a few oyster catchers strutted at the edge of the water, shrieking noisily.

'Not really,' I replied. 'It's still only March. Early in the season for tourists. And anyone with any sense is comfortably seated inside the tearoom, admiring the view from the window rather than out here on the beach in the chill wind.'

He smiled. 'You're right of course, Alison. Let's join them.'

We found a table for two in the little inshot in the far corner and ordered coffee and cake, though Harry had to be persuaded to add the cake to his order, saying, 'I don't usually eat much at this time of day.'

Fortunately he changed his mind when I directed his attention to the large chocolate cake nestling in the chilled cabinet beside the serving counter and we settled down to a preliminary discussion of how our guide might best be of help to visitors to the theme park at Kingarth.

Harry pre-empted my first question with, 'What do you think of this group, Alison? A rum lot aren't they? We've met many strange people in our years in education, but this team is something else. Do you remember Mr Blackstock? How he came to be a head teacher beats me. Fortunately he didn't last long. Then there was that French teacher. What was her name? The one who ran off with that young technician in the Science department and…'

While agreeing with his analysis, I'd no inclination to be distracted from our purpose by idle chitchat and gossip, nor spend time reminiscing about our time at Strathelder High school.

'Fortunately we won't have a lot to do with them,' I replied, interrupting him. 'We can get on with the visitor guide and agree how we'll present the information. Once we've finished our brief, it's over to others to decide how they want to use the rest of the material.'

He looked crestfallen at this reluctance to engage in speculation about the group, sighed and pulled out a set of papers from the case he was carrying. 'You're probably right. Let's see where it's best to start.'

Most impressively, Harry had managed to do much of the preliminary research, including finding a number of anecdotes about St Blane.

'One of the most interesting is the story that Blane was bringing a load of holy earth from Rome up to the shore when the cord tying the container broke. There was a woman down by the shore, gathering shellfish and Blane asked if he could borrow her girdle to bring the load up. She refused and he cursed her that whenever she tried to gather shellfish, the tide would run high, which I assume means she'd have no luck.'

'That's not likely, surely,' I said. 'I thought his nickname was Blane the Mild?'

Harry chuckled. 'It's probably only a story. Still, it makes the whole thing more interesting and that's the kind of information we might want to include.'

We chatted on for some time, our papers spread out over the table as we tried to agree what we might include and what leave out. As a researcher, Harry wanted to incorporate every last detail: as a writer I knew the guide had to be simple and slick.

'I've some concerns,' I said hesitantly, sitting back and frowning at the ache in my shoulders as a spasm of pain caught me, the result of so much sitting around and little exercise. 'This is going to be more difficult than I first anticipated.'

'How come?' Harry looked puzzled.

As I moved my head from side to side to relieve the crick in my neck, out of the corner of my eye I caught sight of someone I'd rather not meet. In the seat by the door, Everett was sipping from a large mug, staring directly at us. My first thought was that he'd followed us out here, was stalking us. Not that it would help his cause much, if he was trying to upset us. There were more important people than we were working on the Kingarth site.

I turned back to Harry, but I couldn't help but glance over at Everett occasionally. 'Sorry, what were you saying?'

He said patiently, 'Why do you think this is going to be difficult?'

'Oh, yes. Quite simply the theme park is designed for people who want to come to the island to have a bit of fun, have an experience of what they thought of as the time of St Blane, not the reality. I don't see many of them being very interested in the historical information.'

Harry's shoulders sagged and too late I realised I shouldn't have been quite so blunt and hastened to recover lost ground. 'What I mean is that you've done a great job on the research but we'll have to be careful in the way we put everything together.' I stressed the 'we' hoping that would make it sound at least part of the difficulty might be to do with me.

Seated as he was in front of one of the large picture windows that took up most of the wall, with the light behind him, it was difficult to read his expression but from his next comment it was obvious this had failed to reassure him. He shook his head. 'No, you're absolutely right, Alison. What they'll want is something full of stories, whether the stories are true or not. This isn't going to be the educational facility we were led to believe. It's going to be more like a Hollywood theme park.'

I glanced over at Everett. He was still sitting in exactly the same position, staring straight at us in a way that was most unnerving.

'What's wrong, Alison?' Harry followed the direction of my gaze.

I leaned forward and hissed, 'It's that man who was leading the protesters. He's sitting over there watching us.'

'What man?' said Harry and I turned to find Everett was no longer in the tearoom.

Of course the idea he'd been deliberately watching us had been my imagination. The tearoom was a popular venue. I was beginning to be obsessed by these protesters and returning to the subject under discussion said, 'Well, we're not giving up now. If they don't like our version of the guide they can find someone else to write a different one – after they've paid us, of course.'

Harry visibly brightened. 'Yes, that's the spirit. It's their problem, not ours.'

And suitably cheered at having made this decision, we celebrated with more coffee, though Harry declined to join me in another slice of cake.

10

Having examined the schedule from Zofia by the simple method of tearing out the pages directly concerning me and throwing the rest in the bin, I couldn't see that the task of writing a short guide for visitors would take me nearly as long as my contract suggested.

Most of my work, after sorting out the research with Harry, could be completed back in the comfort of my home in Glasgow, something that lifted my mood, though I was still waiting to hear if Simon would be able to join me on the island any time soon.

I'd called him immediately after the first meeting at the Kingarth as much to elicit sympathy as to update him on recent events, but Simon had some news of his own and didn't seem to be in the mood to listen to my concerns.

'Yes, yes, that's all very well, Alison, but I did warn you when you signed up for this project that it sounded a pretty dodgy proposition. I mean, who would really want to go to Bute to visit a theme park? Anyway,' brushing aside any possibility of further discussion, 'there's other news. Maura's been trying to contact you.'

With a feeling of guilt I remembered I'd switched my phone off the previous night and had ignored the "three missed calls" when I'd switched it back on.

A tight knot formed in my stomach. 'What's wrong? Is there a problem?' Maura, as the eldest of my three children is the most sensible, so why would she be trying to contact me so urgently?

Another thought. 'There's nothing wrong between her and Alan is there? Is she ill? Is she having problems at work or...'

'Don't worry, don't worry,' said Simon, 'it's only to say she's coming up to Scotland in a couple of days and wanted to catch up with us.'

'And what did you tell her?' I could feel my stomach returning to a calmer state.

'Well, I explained you were on Bute, so she said she'd try to come over to the island to meet up with you, even briefly.'

This caused the knot in my stomach to tighten again, especially as Simon had no further information about their plans and evidently hadn't thought to ask. As I said goodbye I began to think of all the possible reasons she might be coming north at such short notice. She works with a small, busy advertising agency in London and I couldn't imagine how she'd managed to organise leave so quickly. I had to phone her, find out more, but my call went to voice-mail, so I'd have to fret a little longer.

In the meantime there was work to do: Zofia had decided to change the meeting venue once again, summoning us by a phone call to meet her the next day at the site.

This seemed a strange choice, unless there was some new management theory decreeing it was useful to conduct meetings in the open air. In truth, nothing would have surprised me. I hoped it would be a fine morning, remembering our last visit to the site and made sure I was wrapped up in plenty of layers with a pair of wellingtons and a waterproof jacket stowed in the boot of the car in case of a sudden downpour.

We were in luck and as we gathered at exactly nine o'clock outside the Portakabin halfway up the hill, it was on a bright if frosty morning, the grass shimmering, the indents of our footprints showing clearly our trail up the hill.

Wishing I'd remembered to bring gloves, I put my hands in my pockets, hunching my shoulders against the stiff breeze blowing in from across the water as we joined Ryan and Sven and trudged up to where Zofia awaited us. Ryan introduced us to the young man walking alongside him. 'Meet Vernon, nicknamed Vernon the Dig,' he said, 'the man who has to keep the volunteers in order. Not so easy, eh, Vernon?'

Vernon nodded in acknowledgement. 'We've a good number of volunteer diggers,' he said, 'trouble is they're not trained archaeologists and need a lot of guidance.' Vernon was small and sturdy, his face weather-beaten and solemn, not someone you'd want to cross, but exactly the kind of person to keep a group of volunteers in order.

Ahead we could see Zofia waving wildly. 'She's some woman,' grinned Ryan.

Unfortunately it was windy at this high point in the field and as Zofia gathered us round her, we had to lean in to catch what she was saying.

'My plan is that we walk round the site together and I'll point out the features from yesterday's presentation. You'll remember that there are a lot of different elements to this project. It's important to have a comprehensive view of the site, to understand the plan.'

'I'd be much better keeping an eye on the diggers,' complained Vernon. 'All I need to know is what I'm supposed to be doing, not what everyone else has to do. We're on a tight enough schedule as it is.' So Vernon had also been having some problems with the amount of paperwork Zofia insisted on foisting on us.

Zofia was having none of it. She glowered at him. 'This is exactly the attitude which causes a project to come to grief, Vernon. This lack of understanding of the whole... ' she waved her hands around to encompass the site '...and only thinking about your own bit. Alexander Crombie sees this as something which will attract people from far and wide. We need to have a vision which will transmit itself to everyone, ensure it's something that will repay the money spent on it.'

'She's off again,' muttered Luann coming up to stand beside me. 'Why doesn't she shut up and let us get on with it. This is only delaying the inevitable.' She looked again at her watch and said, 'Damn' under her breath. Today she'd tied her unruly mop of hair back, drawing attention to her broad forehead and snub nose.

'Problem?' I said.

She bit her lip. 'I'm supposed to be meeting the main contractor in half an hour. Doesn't give me much time to see this and get back into town. I might have to duck out.'

If Vernon heard this, he gave no sign, but contented himself with staring at the ground and muttering.

'Anyone else have any problems with the way this project is being organised?' Zofia glared round defiantly, daring any of us to speak, but no one said a word. 'This way, then,' she said striding ahead up the hill as quickly as her unsuitable footwear would allow and we trooped along meekly in her wake.

That Sven was so much older became apparent as we climbed to the top of the hill and he paused a couple of times to catch his breath, wheezing loudly.

'Are you okay?' I went over to ask him, as Zofia was paying no attention to his difficulty.

'I am fine, or I will be in a moment. I smoke too much, that is my problem.'

'I would have thought the fresh air and exercise as an archaeologist would have countered at least some of the effects of smoking,' I said as much to give him time to recover and then stopped as I realised it sounded very much like a lecture.

'You know about such things?'

'No, no, I've no medical knowledge,' I said hastily, alarmed he might ask me for advice, but suddenly there was a loud shout from the top of the hill and Zofia began waving her arms to attract our attention. 'Come on, come on,' she said. 'We don't want to take all day to do this.'

Fortunately both Sven and I were too far away to make a response and together we made our way up to join the group as, out of politeness, I slowed my pace to match his.

'We can't waste any more time.' If there was one thing Zofia liked, it was being in control.

'I hope you and Harry are taking time to become familiar with this site, Alison. It has to mirror St Blane's as closely as possible and we want every visitor to have the full experience.'

'They'll probably be paying enough for it,' said Nathan, but if Zofia heard this she ignored it.

Zofia wittered on for a further half hour, occasionally moving to another part of the site, pointing out features where work had begun, asking us to imagine what hadn't yet been started. Unfortunately there were more features that hadn't been started than had.

'Do you think you'll make the deadline?' I whispered to Luann.

She shook her head. 'Very doubtful. I can't imagine how everything will be completed on time. Why, the archaeologists aren't anywhere near finished with their survey and if they turn up anything of importance, well...' Her shrug of the shoulders said more than words could.

It was becoming increasingly cold here out on site and Harry said, stamping his feet, 'Zofia, do you not think we've seen enough for the moment? We can surely take our own time to look round later.'

Zofia scowled. 'You have to understand, Harry, that one part very much depends on another. It's fine going off at a tangent but everyone has to keep *on-message* if the project is to go well.'

There was a murmur of discontent as she finished speaking. It was one thing to be briefed, quite another to be treated like children. There were tensions simmering under the surface, about to explode in a couple of cases.

Zofia walked over to the partly excavated site where the *Wheel of Destiny* was to be sited. This was no more than an overblown version of a Tombola wheel, but from what we'd seen on the computer generated images it was designed to be tricked out with all kinds of 7th century additions, such as having runes instead of numbers. I doubted very much if the monks, being of a religious persuasion, would have had any truck with this kind of nonsense.

As she turned to the group, no doubt to give us yet another lecture about our duties or some kind of pep talk, Zofia stumbled, almost toppling into the gaping hole of the nearest trench.

'Easy, easy there,' said Ryan, catching her by the elbow. 'You gotta wear more sensible shoes on site. These are useless on boggy ground like this.'

'I thought she was experienced in this kind of project?' I whispered to Harry. 'Surely she'd know she needed stout footwear?'

Ryan kept hold of her arm as she steadied herself, but instead of appreciating his concern, she shook him off angrily, 'If people would be more careful about sealing off the area round the trenches there would be no problem.' Tetchy as ever, Zofia was plainly the kind of person who couldn't bear criticism.

Ryan sighed. 'Whatever, Zofia. But don't blame anyone else if you end up in big trouble. This is a building site, remember.'

'I'm not likely to be that stupid,' she said smoothing down her jacket and patting her hair. 'Not likely to do something silly.'

'Trouble, Zofia?'

Busy as we were watching this incident with Zofia, none of us had heard Dexter come up behind us.

She whirled round. 'No, there's no problem, except for some people not pulling their weight.'

If she was trying to unsettle him, she failed and he smiled, saying mockingly, 'Most of us know what we are supposed to do, Zofia and get on with it.' He pinged the elastic band on his wrist so violently it broke and fell to the ground. 'Damn,' he said, before reaching into his pocket for a replacement.

'Amen to that,' said Ryan, rolling his eyes.

'I have to go. There's something I want to check out,' said Vernon, turning and heading off.

'That will be all for today,' Zofia said through gritted teeth, possibly realising others would follow his example. 'I'll see you at the Pavilion tomorrow at nine sharp. In the meantime, remember to keep to your individual targets and fill in the appropriate sheets as you go. I'll collect them at our next meeting.' Without any word of farewell she headed down the hill, picking her way carefully over the uneven ground and, dismissed so abruptly, what could we do but follow her until Dexter stopped us with a wave of his hand.

'Mr Crombie will be visiting soon to see what progress has been made.'

A ripple of laughter went round, quickly quelled as he glared at us, twanging the elastic band on his wrist again. 'It's no laughing matter. A lot of money's been spent on this project. The survey and the dig have to be finished before any other work can begin.' This latter remark was addressed to Ryan and Sven, but no one was in the mood for criticism.

'I don't know about anyone else,' said Harry, 'but I'm heading for the Kingarth for something hot. I'm freezing standing around in this cold. Care to join me?'

'Man, she can whistle for her target sheets,' said Ryan. 'As if we ain't enough to do without this nonsense.'

'I'm heading over to St Blane's,' said Luann snapping shut her phone. 'There are a couple of things I want to check out and as I've had to reorganise the meeting with the contractors, I may as well use the time productively. They're not pleased at yet another delay.'

Sven opted to keep at work with the other diggers, leaving Dexter alone. He turned on his heel, muttering as he hurried down to catch up with her, 'This won't do. I have to speak to Zofia.'

But as we were about to go our separate ways, one of the diggers came racing down the hill. 'You have…have to come…to come at once,' she said breathlessly, her face red with excitement.

Everyone turned to look at her and Harry said, 'What on earth has happened?'

'Vernon says you have to get everyone together, come up to the escarpment, like right now.'

Given the recent heavy rain the ground at the site was still boggy in sheltered parts of the field, making the going difficult as we started to squelch our way up to the huddle of figures at the top of the escarpment. Once or twice my foot caught and I almost slipped.

There was a buzz about the place we hadn't seen before, people shouting to one other, their voices drifting in the breeze, though it was impossible to make out what they were saying. I hurried to reach them, doing my best to catch up with Harry, rather put out he hadn't had the courtesy to wait for me.

I needn't have worried. As he came to the crest of the hill he stopped, bending over to catch his breath as I came up beside him at the thickly wooded topmost part of the field, well away from where the theme park was to be built.

'Where's Luann?' I said, looking round as though she might suddenly materialise from behind a bush.

'No...no...idea,' gasped Harry, 'but I can hear voices from the undergrowth over the top of the hill in the wooded area.'

'What are they doing there? I thought the site ended further down because it was too expensive to clear all that woodland?'

Intrigued as to what we might find, together we made out way into the wood and not for the first time I thought it wouldn't be a bad idea to have some kind of transport on site, perhaps a cable car system. Most of it would be far too hilly for anyone except for the young and the fit. It struck me as strange that this particular field had been chosen, that there was no need to have the theme park so close to St Blane's.

At the edge of the wood the other members of the team had gathered, chattering excitedly, Luann standing with Ryan and Sven and several of the volunteer diggers, looking down into a shallow trench. Summoned by Ryan, Zofia came hurrying up to join us as quickly as her inadequate footwear would allow, but stood a little further back, as though this show of excitement was beneath her.

'Hi,' I called. 'What's going on?'

Luann was moving restlessly from foot to foot, hugging herself and shivering, though it was unlikely to be because she was cold, well wrapped up as she was in a thick jacket.

Sven and Ryan moved nearer and the thought crossed my mind to ask what they were doing here. This wasn't where the archaeologists should have been at work. No matter, it wasn't my concern, so I contented myself with saying, 'Ah, so you've found something of interest?'

Luann whirled round and nodded, her eyes shining.

'We sure have, or at least Vernon here has. He's trying to excavate it now, but he's having to be very careful.' She pushed her glasses back up on her nose, then decided to take them off, before finally putting them on top of her head.

Harry peered over and said what I'd been thinking. 'Why are they digging here? It's nowhere near the proposed site, it's far...' He broke off, realising how snippy he sounded, not that anyone appeared to be taking notice until Luann turned to say, 'I know, I know, but Vernon decided on a hunch to try using his metal detector.'

71

Visions of a hoard of gold coins appeared before me. That would be a find indeed and a very good reason to get excited. Never mind the theme park: this would be the real prize for the archaeologists.

Vernon made a waving motion with his hand but it was clear he was intent on continuing to uncover whatever was in the trench, preferring to get on with his work without the rest of the team hovering around and interfering.

'I'd an idea this part of the site might yield something,' he said, his voice breaking with excitement. 'It's well away from where most people would think to look.' He shrugged, trying to appear modest. 'I was fooling around really, trying out this new metal detector.'

'Yeah, this is the tricky part,' said Ryan. 'He has to be careful not to break whatever it is he's found.' He sounded nervous, anxious, so unlike his usual sunny self.

There was a palpable air of anticipation as Vernon worked away slowly and steadily with his trowel and occasionally a stiff brush, bit by bit uncovering the find, until suddenly he gave a shout of triumph and held aloft what appeared to be a small circular object, though it was difficult to tell, it was so encrusted with dirt. I felt a surge of disappointment. This wasn't what I'd expected, though the archaeologists seemed mightily pleased.

Sven sprang forward into the pit and almost wrested it from Vernon's hand. 'Hey, watch out, man,' said Ryan, 'whatever it is, it's fragile.'

'Be careful, Sven,' added Luann, motioning him back with her hand.

Sven paid no attention but whipped a small brush from his pocket and little by little began to ease the dirt from the object. There was a flash of what looked to me like dull silver, then a gasp of disbelief followed by a loud cheer from the archaeologists.

'Can it possibly be...?' said Ryan, peering closely at the object.

Sven narrowed his eyes. 'It looks very like a religious object, a silver plate.'

'What do you think it is?' I hissed behind my hand to Harry.

'No idea, but it's clearly something of value,' Harry said brusquely before turning to Ryan, 'But why would it be buried here? The monastery is over there on the other side of the field.' Harry waved vaguely in the direction of Saint Blane's.

'It's a silver paten, the monks would have used it in the communion service,' said Vernon, turning round to join in this conversation. 'It's an incredible find, we couldn't have hoped...'

Ryan interrupted him. 'Hey, hey, wait...there's something else here...under the paten.' He crouched down and using his brush, got rid of another layer of dirt before showing us a fragment of slate, holding it carefully by the edges. He blew away the remaining soil.

Vernon gasped. 'It's another of those slates, or a fragment. One was found at St Blane's a number of years ago and there are examples from all over Scotland in the National Museum in Edinburgh.' He wiped beads of sweat from his brow, muttering, 'I can't believe this is happening.'

Zofia pushed her way forward, intent on showing who was in charge. 'Here's Nathan at last,' she said.

She waved to him. 'Over here, over here.' He came ambling across to join us.

'What's all the excitement?' he said.

'We've made a discovery,' she said, 'and we need to have some photographs.'

'I found it,' said Vernon, whirling round, making the ownership absolutely clear as he determinedly seized the slate from Sven.

Ryan was brushing the remains of dirt from the paten. 'Easy, easy, guys. We don't want any damage.' He handed it carefully to Vernon.

Nathan pulled his camera out of the bag slung across his shoulder. 'Great. Well, let's get a few shots. We shouldn't need the tripod for this, though I'll set it up if need be.' He fiddled with the lens for a moment before saying, 'Go back into the trench, Vernon and pick up your trowel. That's right, now if you could crouch down a bit. A little further over. That's it.'

With the ease that came from long experience, he positioned Vernon for the photo saying, 'That's fine for the first one. Now let's get that silver object into focus. Put it back where you found it and raise your trowel above it.'

While this was going on, Harry, who'd been busy snapping away since we'd arrived, now stomped off, indicating his displacement by Nathan was again a source of grievance.

Vernon laid the slate carefully at the side of the trench and passed the paten to Zofia. 'We'll do this first. Hold it for a minute while I position myself.' He clearly seemed to be enjoying his moment of glory. He turned and stretched out his hands. 'Ready now.'

Very reluctantly Zofia handed over the precious object, making a movement to shake more dirt from it as she did so.

Sven sprang forward. 'For goodness sake, be careful. Do not shake it about like that. You might damage it.' Then he added, 'You be careful as well, Nathan. We do not want it spoiled.'

Nathan grinned. 'Don't worry. I've lots of experience in this kind of thing.'

Sven looked unconvinced and hovered over him, moving restlessly to keep them in view.

'That's fine, Vernon, you're doing great. Move it a little to the right.' Nathan ignored this spat and focussed on the task in hand.

'It was found further over,' muttered Vernon.

'I know, I know, but this is about getting the best shot, the best angle...'

Ryan interrupted, 'It's all fine, no worries. We've recorded it properly. This is just for the publicity and...' He gestured to a woman, one of the young archaeologists, who was sitting nearby, balancing a sketch pad on her knees and she grinned to acknowledge his comment. 'I'm finishing the sketches right now.'

'And now the fragment of slate. I'll have to get a close up for this one; try to capture any of the markings on it.' He frowned, adjusting the lens, fiddling with the settings until perfectly satisfied. 'That's great. If you step back another fraction...'

He clicked the camera a couple of times, but before he could continue there was a shout from Vernon as he sprang out of the trench as though hit by a bullet.

'What have you found?' Luann jumped, startled by Vernon's sudden action.

We moved forward again, eager to see this latest find. Perhaps there would be a hoard of gold coins after all.

Vernon was choking, breathless, as he scrambled to his feet. 'There's something else there,' he finally managed to gasp. 'I stood on it.'

There was a ripple of excitement as everyone surged forward, craning to see.

'More finds?' The eager look on Sven's face showed his anticipation of further riches.

Vernon shuddered, waving his arms about wildly as he peered in to the trench. 'Stay back, stay back. No, it's not an artefact. It's something else, or rather someone.'

Ryan jumped down into the trench, laughing at this reaction. 'Come on, man, you've seen enough skeletons in your time. It'll be one of the monks. That would explain how it came to be here. You gotta have found another graveyard associated with the St Blane's site.'

But Vernon had climbed out of the trench and was fast disappearing off towards the bushes on the far side where we could hear the sounds of retching.

'I will give you some help,' said Sven, jumping down beside Ryan, trowel at the ready. 'You have to be careful uncovering this if it is a skeleton.'

'It's not like Vernon to be squeamish,' said Luann, heading off to catch up with him.

'This will hold everything up even more,' muttered Zofia. 'We'll have to call the police, not that there should be any problem about an ancient skeleton, though it will cause even more of a delay.'

'Bloody hell, man, what the…' Ryan's sudden shout drew our attention back to the trench.

I peered over Luann's shoulder. It was a few seconds before I could focus on what was lying in the bottom, now that some of the earth had been cleared away. Expecting at the very least a jumble of bones, all I could see was what looked like some bits of blue rag. To my horror I realised I was looking at the remnants of a sleeve, pieces of cloth attached to what looked very much like an arm and a fleshy arm at that. This was no skeleton.

'Don't disturb it,' said Luann, leaning forward and grabbing his jacket, but Sven shook her off and kept scraping away, revealing more of a body grotesquely contorted, the face unrecognisable.

'Stop it, stop it,' said Harry, coming up beside Sven and tugging at his jacket to pull him away. 'Don't you know, you above anyone, that you shouldn't be doing that. Leave it! Right now!'

'Who is it?' Nathan sounded frightened.

None of us had an answer to this: instead we all stood round looking at the partially uncovered corpse below us. Thanks to Ryan's piecemeal efforts, more of the face could be seen clearly, a thin faced man with a straggly beard, matted with the soil in which he'd been found.

Whoever it might be, there was one thing certain. This was no monk's skeleton, no guardian of any treasure. It was a body and a recent body at that. The police would most certainly want to know about this.

12

Silence, broken only by the sound of sheep baaing in the distance, the sharp cry of a curlew overhead and then everyone moved at once. Zofia ran forward to pull Sven out of the trench, yelling, 'Leave it, leave it. Don't you realise you're tampering with a crime scene!'

Ryan, as if suddenly understanding what lay at our feet, scrambled out to stand, shaking and trembling, beside us but Sven continued brushing away the soil till Harry stopped him by leaning over and almost dragging him out of the trench.

'Oh man, oh man,' Ryan kept repeating over and over. 'How was I to know what it was?'

'I'll phone the police,' said Harry, ever practical, 'that's if I can get a mobile signal out here.'

He moved off, walking further and further down the hill and I could see him waving his mobile this way and that until eventually he disappeared from sight only to appear a few minutes later, looking decidedly relieved.

'Success,' he said, trudging up to join us again. 'I managed to get through and they're on their way.'

This was of little comfort as we stood waiting, uncertain what to do next. It was Luann who finally said in a firm voice, taking charge, as Zofia stood still as a statue, her face a mask, 'There's no point in everyone hanging around here. We'd be best to head for the Portakabin and have a cup of strong sweet tea. Someone can wait for the police to arrive.'

Zofia didn't seem to register this, but stood staring at the partially exposed corpse as though mesmerised. Usually her reaction to anyone who tried to usurp her position would have been swift and determined, but she made no movement, finally rousing herself to do as Luann asked and trail behind us down the hill to the Portakabin, leaving Sven to stand guard over the body. Vernon by now had recovered a little and walked unsteadily back to join us.

'Won't they want to interview us all? About the body, I mean.' The colour was beginning to creep back into his face, but he was still shivering and clearly in shock.

'Yes,' said Luann, 'but there's no point in all of us standing round here.' She jerked her head in the direction of the trench. 'Sven will remain on guard until the police arrive. Best we keep together and get some hot, sweet tea brewed.'

'That's a good idea, Luann,' I said. 'Vernon could certainly do with something. The police can as easily interview us in the Portakabin as here.' Although I did recollect being told the story about sweet tea being good for shock was a myth, this was no time to be quibbling over the niceties.

We headed for the Portakabin, but as we started down the hill Harry changed his mind, insisted on staying with Sven. 'Just in case,' he said. 'You don't want to be left out here on your own with a corpse,' but the blank look on Sven's face made it difficult to tell if he appreciated this suggestion, though what could he do but offer a grudging, 'Thank you, Harry,' as he turned away and I noticed Harry had whipped out his camera once more.

At the Portakabin several of the diggers and the other workers were having a break, some reading the newspaper, others taking the opportunity for a hand of cards. Everyone turned to look at as we tumbled in and with no time to hide our distress, we'd no option but to give them a potted version of events before deterring them from hurrying out to have a look.

'Surely someone must know who he is,' said one of the diggers, a young man showing a keen interest in this unforeseen discovery. He pulled out his tobacco tin and cigarette papers before he noticed the scowl of disapproval from the man opposite. He held up his hand. 'Okay, okay,' he said, getting to his feet. 'I'm going outside to smoke it...and no, don't worry, I'm going nowhere near that trench.'

All we knew about the body was that it was apparently a male and even I could tell it hadn't been there very long, had all the appearance of a hurried burial. The spot at the top of the hill, within the woodland, was well away from the range of the survey area and if Vernon hadn't been so enthusiastic, trying out his new metal detector, it might never have been discovered.

Vernon grabbed a seat in the corner and I took over some tea which he cuddled with both hands, still shaking, as though afraid he might spill it but he made no move to actually drink it, in the end slopping a little over the edge before putting it down suddenly, adding wet rings to the shabby table top.

'Who can it be?' he said. 'It doesn't seem real somehow. I've seen lots of skeletons in my work, but never an actual corpse.'

'It's possible whoever buried him thought it a good place to hide a body. With such thick woodland and scrub I heard it was decided it wouldn't be worthwhile clearing it for the theme park. Far too expensive.'

Luann put two tea bags into each of the remaining cups. 'Better if it's as strong as possible.'

Ryan didn't say a word, but started slowly to sip this second cup as soon as she gave it to him, blowing on the hot liquid to cool it.

The silence in the Portakabin stretched out till we heard the sound of the police car approaching and Luann and I went outside with strict instructions to the others to make sure Vernon stayed where he was.

'I'll have to go and find out what's happening,' said Luann, as Ryan hung back.

'I'll come with you,' said Nathan.

We headed back up the hill towards the shallow grave, everything else forgotten as a million questions raced through my brain. One thing was for sure, whoever it was couldn't have buried himself: someone was trying to cover up an accident or else he'd deliberately been killed.

As I reached the trench the police were already at work, deftly sealing off the area round the trench with tape and moving everyone back out of the way, much to the disappointment of some of the other diggers who had now come up the hill to join us.

Luann arrived first and Nathan had his arms round her shoulders as though comforting her. She'd lost all her previous calmness and now was racked with sobs, her body shaking. What on earth was wrong now, was my immediate thought and as I approached I heard Harry say, 'There's no way you could have known about this,' but Luann's reply, in between her sobs, was too quiet for me to hear.

Ryan came up behind me and made straight for Luann while I waited, willing him to frame the questions I didn't want to ask, didn't want to have my suspicions confirmed.

The police continued to secure the area round the body: the scene of crime officers had been called and would arrive soon.

There was an animated discussion between Harry and Ryan and then I saw Luann turn away, point to the trench and bury her head again in Nathan's chest. Then she seemed to collect herself and pushed him away, as one of the policemen came over. The expression on Harry's face as he joined me was grim.

'What's going on? Is there some news?'

'Of a kind. Luann and Ryan think they know who it is. Luann recognised the logo on the blue jacket as they took the body out. It's very distinctive apparently because of that. The only one on...'

I cut in, hoping to stop Harry giving me a full description of the clothes. 'Yes, but who is it?' I asked, although by now I'd a good idea.

Harry raised his eyebrows as though surprised at this question. 'You haven't guessed? Why it's Benjie Anderson, of course.'

So I'd been right. It all made complete sense, explaining why Benjie had apparently disappeared so suddenly. He hadn't abandoned the project after all. Whatever had happened, it wasn't because he'd decided to leave voluntarily.

It was no good: I had to see for myself, get as close as the situation would allow and without replying to Harry scurried further up the hill.

The police were already busy unravelling the final bit of tape to seal off the crime scene, but I snuck further up, overlooking the trench, to find a spot where I could see clearly. This was tricky and involved pushing my way through the thick bushes on the far side of the trench,but I finally managed it.

The police continued to wave everyone back, though they had a difficult task. By now almost all the workers and the diggers who had been in the Portakabin had joined the original group, anxious not to miss any of this excitement and it was some time before order was restored and the police satisfied there would be no contamination of the area. Given the muddy nature of the site, a number of people slipped and slid on the wet grass and there was an intake of breath as one of the diggers went down with a thump.

While everyone was engrossed in watching the police, I looked round, suddenly remembering how the body had been found. What had happened to the silver paten…and the broken slate with the markings on it?

I tried to think back, recollect the exact train of events. Vernon had found it, started to clean it, aided then by Sven and Ryan, but he'd laid it down when he'd come across the body. Or had he handed it over to one of the others? No, I was sure I remembered he'd put it to one side. Carefully of course, but he had laid it down at the edge of the trench. Or was I mistaken? I closed my eyes, tried to imagine the sequence of events. Then a picture of discovering the body came to mind. Vernon had definitely put the paten at the side of the trench as soon as Nathan had finished the first series of photographs. That's when he'd lifted the fragment of slate. So where was that?

Keeping a wary eye out for any of the police, fortunately all engaged in speaking to the others, I slipped under the tape and had a quick look into the trench. Even from this distance I could see enough of it, especially as it wasn't particularly deep. The paten wasn't something easy to mistake: its distinctive shape, almost like an elongated saucer, even if still encrusted with dirt, would make it easy to spot.

There was no sign of it, nor of the slate, anywhere in or near the trench. There was only one explanation. In all the confusion of finding the body someone had deliberately removed both items.

13

'Don't tell me there have been problems already.'
Simon sounded concerned.

Much as I was attempting to talk down the finding of
Benjie's body, it was impossible to do so.

'The police have interviewed us of course, but there
was nothing I could tell them. I didn't meet Benjie.'

'Even so. This project I'm working on will be
finished by the end of the week, so once I've tidied up
all the bits and pieces, I'll be able to come over and join
you. And not a moment too soon by the sounds of it.'

'That would be great,' I said, meaning every word.
Simon has the ability to put everything in perspective,
counterbalance my tendency to overreact.

'Oh,' catching him as he was about to ring off, 'Any
word from Maura.'

'No,' he replied, 'and don't start to worry. I'm sure
if there was any problem she'd have let you know at
once.'

Feeling better after Simon's phone call, putting any
personal difficulties firmly to the back of my mind, I
snapped my mobile shut and sat on the bed, wondering
whether to book us into another hotel or ask for a
bigger room. This one was cramped enough for one
person, never mind two, with the bed taking up most of
the space, and the sensible solution would have been to
move to a different hotel.

The Crannog was increasingly failing to live up to
expectations. My room was only sketchily cleaned, the
cleaner having phoned in sick apparently, the dining
room was tiny with tables cheek by jowl and the quality

of food left a lot to be desired, giving rise to the suspicion there was a problem or two with cash flow.

I'd met Zofia a couple of times in the hotel, but our encounters were thankfully brief, no more than 'Good Morning' or 'Good Afternoon'.

I headed downstairs continuing to mull over this decision about whether to stay here or find a different hotel, but as I reached Reception, Georgie was coming out of the dining room, precariously balancing a tray laden with dirty crockery. Georgie and her husband owned the hotel, but apparently he worked on the mainland, leaving her in sole charge. Unfortunately, these seemed to involve her doing all the jobs, help apparently being hard to find.

'Whoops,' I said moving aside to avoid bumping into her and having her send the crockery flying.

She put the tray down with a thump on the Reception desk as I handed her my key.

'Wouldn't you know it,' she said, running her hands through her hair. 'Neither of the girls has turned up today and Brenda hasn't even bothered to phone.'

'That's very frustrating,' I said, my mind still on whether I should broach the subject of accommodation for Simon and me. 'It's difficult enough at the moment to own a hotel without having to do all the work yourself.'

'That's one way of putting it. I've no idea how I'm going to manage for the rest of the day.'

'Have you been busy with guests then?' There was little evidence of the hotel being full.

Ooops, wrong thing to say. Apparently glad of a sympathetic response and happy to have a willing audience, she leaned against the counter saying, 'It's been a really bad season so far. To be honest, we're relying on this St Blane's theme park taking off. It should bring lots of people over to Bute, from what I hear. And we could certainly do with something to attract more tourists. That's if the discovery of Benjie Anderson's body doesn't put paid to the plans.'

She broke off to answer the desk phone which was ringing incessantly, but before I could make good my escape she slammed down the receiver. 'That was Brenda at last. Claims she's too ill to come in for the next few days. Good grief. What will I do?'

Mumbling more bland words of sympathy I edged towards the door, but she wasn't finished yet.

'You're involved in the theme park, aren't you? They say it has to be finished by August and they're planning to hold a big opening ceremony. Do you think they'll be able to continue now?'

'Yes, I'm sure we'll be allowed to start again soon,' I lied, making another attempt to leave. 'I dare say it'll work out.' There was no point in fuelling the rumour mill.

'Let's hope so. We need something on the island to give us all a boost, to ....'

Luckily at that very moment the phone rang again and, with a loud sigh, she picked up the receiver, giving me the opportunity to make a swift exit, trying hard not to feel depressed after this conversation. It was clear a lot of people on Bute were depending on the income they thought this venture would bring, the large numbers of tourists they imagined would flock to the island. But even if work resumed soon, there was still the problem of the protesters.

In the meantime I had to get over to the Pavilion where Zofia would no doubt be waiting to give us another lecture on teamwork and objectives, trying to pick up the pieces. Pity she didn't practise what she preached. She seemed to lack any such skills, judging by what I'd seen so far and, even worse, she found it difficult to keep her temper under control.

And now with the concerns about the discovery of Benjie's body I'd be counting the days till Simon was able to join me. These past few months had seen us draw closer together after yet another rocky period in our relationship and I was hoping a few days with him on the island would give us space to make a new start.

Today the weather had turned fine with a hint of Spring, buds pushing out on the skeletal trees, and determined to get going on my fitness routine, I walked to the Pavilion, past the Skeogh woods where a solitary dog walker rambled. Along the verges, in odd corners and in the gardens of the houses along the sea front, daffodils had seemingly sprung into bloom overnight and their yellow, nodding heads making me feel more cheerful in spite of what had happened.

Deep in thought, I didn't notice Ryan come up behind me.

Contrary to my expectations, his first words weren't anything to do with Benjie's death. 'So what d'you make of our dear leader, Zofia?' he said.

'She's certainly keen on promoting modern management techniques,' I replied cautiously. 'I expect it's very difficult to cope with a group as disparate as this one.'

'Hey, too right. I should be out there in the field, supervising the diggers, instead of coming in here for yet another meeting. How does she think we'll get everything done on time if we have to keep stopping to examine our navels? Bloody management speak.'

The image made me chuckle. 'Come on now, Ryan. There has to be a certain amount of teamwork. And you can't blame her for the police sealing off the site meantime.'

'Yeah, but wait till she finds out Sven has refused to come along today. That'll make her lose her cool.' He appeared delighted at the thought of Zofia's reaction, making no attempt to conceal his glee.

By now we'd reached the Pavilion, pausing for a moment or two to look out over the bay, relishing the view.

'It's so peaceful here,' I said, holding up my face to the sun.

'Mmm, guess so. If we get the chance to enjoy it. I've another project starting in six weeks in the south of England and I gotta make sure everything is tied up here. Gonna be a tight squeeze.'

Out on the bay a large yacht was creaming along, its pale blue sails billowing in the wind. From this distance a couple of sailors could be seen on deck, their yellow oilskins reflecting the sun as they manoeuvred, tacking into the wind, neatly avoiding the *MV Bute* which was coming into shore in the calm waters of Rothesay Bay. This CalMac ferry was the lifeline for the island, not only for visitors, but for the many people who worked off the island and relied on a regular service.

A couple of bold seagulls strutted up to us, squawking loudly, asking for titbits, then flew off towards a family group ambling along the sea front, hoping for better pickings.

'Might as well go in,' said Ryan. 'The sooner we do, the sooner we get this over with and find out when we can get back to work.'

Inside the building Zofia and Dexter were standing at the front of the meeting room, engaged in a conversation that seemed as tense as it was quiet, but finally patience ran out and, 'Hey, hey, do you think we could make a start,' said Ryan loudly after we'd been sitting waiting for some ten minutes, during which he'd been doodling faces on the letters on the page of instructions Zofia had left on each seat. 'I gotta get back to the site as soon as possible. We're nowhere near finished digging the first section and time's a-wastin'.'

'Absolutely,' agreed Nathan. 'The light's particularly good today and I want to capture as many shots as I can.'

Poor Benjie, to be so easily dismissed because of our individual concerns.

'We're ready now,' said Zofia, implying any delay was our fault.

Dexter moved to the back of the room, pulled round an extra chair to face the front and planted his feet on it, twanging the elastic band on his wrist as he did so and setting my teeth on edge.

Zofia looked round. 'Is *everyone* here?' She stopped. 'Where's Sven?'

'Not coming, for sure,' said Ryan trying, but not succeeding, in keeping the delight out of his voice.

Zofia stamped her foot, then abruptly changed it into a sideways movement almost like a little jig. 'It's essential everyone is here. This is how messages get muddled, when *some* people receive information second-hand.'

She continued, 'I understand we're all upset about Benjie, no one more so than I am...' a snort from Vernon made her pause before she repeated, '...more so than I am. But we must try to carry on, even if some of you prefer to dawdle around and use this as an excuse.'

There was a deathly hush and Zofia appeared flustered, not quite in control, as she started to go through the schedules, breaking off from time to time as though her mind was elsewhere, until Vernon said, interrupting her, 'So, Zofia, has there been any more word about Benjie? What exactly have the police said?'

Zofia looked uncomfortable. 'As far as I know the place where he was found will remain sealed off for a few days, then we can resume work, providing we stay clear of that area. There's plenty we can be doing without going near the escarpment.'

'Suited you, his disappearance,' muttered Ryan, but if she heard him she gave no sign.

Suddenly in the middle of Zofia's spiel about tightening targets and benchmarking something or other (I was only intermittently listening, my mind drifting to more personal matters), Luann said in a loud voice, 'We have to get on, Zofia. There's too much to be done to be hanging round here for meetings that don't make any sense. We all know what we're supposed to be doing and wittering on about targets and fine tuning and team analysis (she'd evidently been paying more attention than I had) isn't going to help us get the job done. I'm off. While we wait to get back on site I can meet with the contractors.'

She sprang to her feet, grabbed her yellow safety jacket and stormed out, leaving the rest of us gazing after her with a mixture of surprise and admiration for the way she'd stood up to Zofia.

At the front of the room, Zofia remained still, as though she'd been dealt a physical blow and, to make matters worse, Nathan stood up and said as he followed Luann out of the room, 'No disrespect, Zofia, but Luann's right. There's so much to be done and we're so far behind we have to make use of every minute. I've the opportunity to take some shots elsewhere on the island and if I don't go now, I'll miss the best of the light.'

As though emboldened by this Ryan said, 'Gotta make tracks. Loads to do,' and joined Vernon heading out of the room.

Zofia glowered at their departing backs, her face contorted with rage. 'None of you understand, none of you. It's all very well talking about what you have to do as individuals but the project will only be finished if we work together as a team.'

Ryan shrugged and left, shutting the door noisily behind him while Harry and I looked at each other for support.

As if encouraged by the firm stance taken by the others, Harry gathered up his papers and from the thickness of the bundle it was evident he hadn't been as cavalier in his attitude as I'd been. 'I think we should make a start on the next section of text for the booklet, Alison. I've been doing more research and I've come up with some interesting facts about Blane and his life here on Bute.' He spoke slowly, carefully avoiding looking at Zofia, as though wary that she might have another outburst.

Taking my cue from this little speech I said, 'Good idea. We can make some progress today.' There was no way I was going to be left with Zofia.

Her bottom lip quivered, a sign she might be about to cry. She wasn't quite as steely as she liked us to think and tears I couldn't deal with, so I added brightly,

'We'll see you soon,' and hurried out to join Harry who was standing in the hallway, gazing at the notice board as though the announcements were of supreme interest.

This defection left Zofia alone with Dexter who'd remained completely impassive during the earlier exchanges, except for the occasional twanging of that wretched elastic band on his wrist.

Things were going from bad to worse and with such dissent among the team, never mind finding out who was responsible for Benjie's death, I was beginning to wonder if this theme park at Kingarth would ever be finished.

14

The next day the rain started in earnest, the temperature dropped and winter was back. It was a day of contrasts: late morning saw the earlier blue sky quickly cloud over as the rain came scudding in across the bay, driven by a strong north easterly wind that whipped up the waves and sent them splashing over the railings along the promenade in a frenzy of water.

By midday the CalMac ferries were on amber alert. Anyone who wanted to get on or off the island was left with the option of taking the short crossing from Rhubodach to Colintraive on the mainland and a long drive over the Rest and Be Thankful – aptly named because of its steep hilly twists and bends. That's if that road was still open, prone as it is to landslips. Late in the afternoon even that short ferry crossing was suspended as the rain and the wind gathered strength, sweeping across the harbour at Rothesay, churning up the waters to a pinkish foam that broke violently against the sea wall, the palm trees bending and swaying as though they might break, the poor daffodils drooping and falling over.

'I wouldn't go out in that if I were you,' warned Georgie as I crossed the hallway at Reception. One of the girls had returned but the elusive Brenda was still too sick to work apparently and Georgie wasn't in the best of moods. I'd the impression this wasn't the first time this had happened and Georgie was decidedly tetchy as she scurried about from task to task, all the while muttering under her breath. Now wasn't the time to remind her yet again about the need to fix the number on the door to my room.

'I'm meeting someone out at the Ettrick Bay tearoom,' I said, piqued at this attempt to interfere in my plans. 'I'll have to go.'

She shook her head. 'Not today, you're not. There's an electricity pylon down at Ettrickdale and the road's closed and will be for some time. They won't be able to get anyone out to repair it till this storm subsides a bit. It's far too dangerous. It was announced a few minutes ago on local radio.'

Thwarted in my bid to leave the stuffiness of the hotel, what could I do but turn tail and head for the lounge. I didn't fancy sitting in my cramped bedroom and instead sought out a corner where I could use my laptop and occasionally look out over the stormy bay. Even at this early hour of the afternoon the lamps on the low tables dotted around the room had been switched on, scarcely dispelling the gloom and eventually I turned my chair away from the window in an attempt to block out the noise of the spates of rain rattling the ill-fitting panes of glass.

After working for an hour or so without stopping, I realised I'd have to phone Harry to check we were agreed on the next stage. His phone rang, then went dead. I shook my mobile, but of course that did no good.

Georgie came through with the coffee I'd ordered. 'The phone signal can be poor at the best of times on parts of the island and it'll be particularly bad today.' She seemed almost to be enjoying being the bearer of bad news.

She set the coffee down on the table in front of me and lingered, clearly keen to chat. With so few guests in the hotel, she appeared to be at a loose end, no matter how much she complained about the workload.

I tried to pretend she wasn't there. It wasn't that I was being unsociable, but if she wasn't busy, I was. There was work to do and I wasn't willing to spend the afternoon in idle chat, but to my shame, I soon discovered I'd misinterpreted her motives.

'The dig over at the theme park will be called off again today, I guess? The police or the weather?' She tapped her foot to make sure she had my attention.

'Mmm.' I didn't lift my eyes from the screen.

'It's not going to be lucky, you know.'

'Lucky?' That was a strange word to use.

'Yes, there have been a number of accidents at that site over the years.'

Now I was intrigued. 'What kind of accidents? So the site's been dug before?'

'Yes, at one time it was a popular place for people to look for treasure till the farmer who owned it put a stop to it. There were accidents, broken limbs, that kind of thing.'

This was news to me, but all I said was, 'That's predictable where you have people digging a difficult site like that one, being so hilly.' I'd no idea if that was correct or not, but it was the first thing that came into my head.

Then I looked up, perplexed as the full meaning of her comments struck me. 'Do you mean the site has been properly excavated before?'

'Of course. There have been all sorts of rumours about the place over the years, rumours that there might be valuable objects hidden there.'

'But it's an empty field. It was only sold by the farmer because the price was so good. It's been used for grazing sheep for a long time, from what I hear.'

'That's as maybe, but I'm only telling you what I've heard. It was used for sheep because the farmer became so fed up with people sneaking on and digging up great swathes of it. So he stopped them. It was all because over a hundred years ago some workmen were digging in a field not far from the ruins of the chapel at St Blane's and came across old coins...and a couple of gold rings I think. Anyway, it was of some value. You can check it out. Of course nothing has been found since, but people started to dig up the fields round about, hoping to find treasure.'

Apparently everyone knew about the Hoard. There might have been treasure discovered near the monastery site but the field being used for the theme park was, from what I'd seen, virtually untouched. There was certainly no sign of it ever having been dug before this project started. Could it possibly be true that there might be treasure buried there? It seemed most unlikely.

'Anyway,' I added, 'if there was anything of worth, it would all have been buried at St Blane's and as far as I know nothing's been found there. There'd be no reason for the monks to bury stuff elsewhere.'

'I'm telling you, it's not good. And there are other rumours, more recent rumours.'

Now I was intrigued in spite of myself. 'What kind of rumours?'

It seemed that she wasn't going to say any more, regretted having said what she did.

'What kind of rumours?' I persisted.

'Well,' with some hesitation, 'I'm only repeating what I've heard.'

'Which is?' There was no way she could leave now, not when she'd whetted my appetite.

'I hear a number of people had been unhappy with that project manager. You know, the one before what's-her-name.'

'Benjie Anderson? But I thought the story was that he'd had enough and wanted out of it all.'

She pursed her lips. 'I'm only telling you what I've heard. I don't actually KNOW anything, but the word was he and that manager of Crombie's, Texon or Dexon or something, had a terrible fight.'

'How do you know that?' In a small place news can certainly travel quickly, but this wasn't the usual kind of gossip.

'You know Elsie who works in that café on the front at Rothesay – the one next to the Co-op? Well Benjie is her cousin. He told her all about it. He was very unhappy with the way things were going at the site. He suspected Mr Crombie wasn't the man he claimed to be.'

'But if it there's more to it than he simply left...?' I left the words hanging in the air.

'No idea exactly why he left, only that he wasn't happy about something. That's as much as I know. I dare say it will amount to nothing. You know how stories get about. And now the poor man's dead.' She turned away, evidently concerned she'd started on this subject, unaware she was making me even more curious by telling me this story. 'Can I get you anything else?'

'Have you told the police about this?'

She shrugged. 'Plenty of people know the story. I'll tell them if they ask me.'

It was perfectly clear she'd no intention of saying another word on the subject, so anxious to get back to work, I said, 'This is fine, thanks. There's plenty left in the pot,' feeling a niggling worry I'd offended her by my too quick dismissal of her tale about the disappearance of Benjie Anderson. It was all nonsense of course. Everyone knew he'd gone because he was fed up with all the petty squabbles on the project and if he'd had a serious disagreement with Dexter this made sense.

None of this explained how he came to be found in that shallow trench. Even so, it might be worthwhile asking round, finding out if anyone else had heard this rumour about Benjie's suspicions.

Georgie had certainly piqued my curiosity about the Hoard discovered at St Blane's. What if the stories were true and there was more treasure buried somewhere, waiting to be found? Anything I knew about the Hoard I'd learned from Harry. I'd have to push him for more details as soon as we next met.

In the meantime I'd plenty of work to do without becoming involved in another investigation. And yet again I'd forgotten to ask Georgie to fix the number on my bedroom door.

15

In spite of all my efforts, it proved impossible to concentrate on the task in hand as my mind kept wandering back to what Georgie had said about Benjie. Tempted to believe her story was no more than rumour, there remained a bit of doubt. Increasingly it seemed important to talk to Elsie as soon as possible, rather than waiting till next time I was in town, a decision justified by a belief Harry and I should have been informed about this change in personnel, not that it would have made any difference to my decision.

Whatever had happened, it must have been serious to make him take off so suddenly with no word of explanation. Unless someone had made sure he wouldn't be available, he hadn't left at all, at least not by his own choice. Surely it was nothing to do with Zofia? She hadn't come over to the island until Benjie had "disappeared". Perhaps it all came down to money and Alexander Crombie had decided it would cost less to use Zofia, but it was nonsense to think he'd murder Benjie in order to get a cheaper replacement.

Stop it, I told myself. There was no reason for me to be caught up in this simply because my imagination was working overtime.

Simon's constant warnings about getting involved in problems that didn't concern me rang in my ears. It was nothing to do with me, had taken place before I arrived on the scene, but even so I couldn't help but be curious. The problem was who to approach first: someone in the theme park team or Elsie. After mentally running through each member of the team I decided Elsie in the café on the front at Rothesay would be the best person to start with and turned my attention back to the task in hand.

To my great satisfaction, free from further interruptions, I made good progress with the visitor guide, managing a first complete draft with only twenty or so gaps where I had to check out facts with Harry.

I sat back, allowing my mind to wander once again. The information Georgie had given me about the St Blane's finds continued to nag away at me. What would happen if the archaeologists did find some treasure on the site of the theme park? All work would have to be halted for some time while it was assessed, properly excavated and recorded. Any time-scale would useless, that was for sure and the chances of opening the theme park on the agreed date in August slim.

A quick glance at my watch showed I'd been working for almost two hours and I saved the latest version of my draft (bitter experience had taught me to do this without fail), closed the laptop and wandered into the Reception area, intending to speak to Georgie again, try to winkle out any more gossip she'd heard about Benjie before heading off to my re-arranged meeting with Harry.

Outside the storm had suddenly abated in that way it can do on this Atlantic coast and although it was still raining, the wind had dropped to a gentle breeze, the waters in the bay no more than a gentle swell.

Georgie wasn't anywhere to be seen and a young girl I didn't recognise was behind the desk, idly examining her nails and occasionally filing one of them before drawing back to admire them again. The tag on her bright blue sweater proclaimed her as being Brenda, Assistant Receptionist. Ah, so this was the elusive Brenda, back at last from sick leave.

She jumped as I approached and said, 'I was looking for Georgie. Is she around?' There were so many part-time staff in this hotel it was difficult to keep track of them.

Brenda clutched her chest in mock fright. 'What a start you gave me. Georgie goes mad if you don't look as if you're occupied when you're on reception, even if there's nothing in particular to do.'

'You're not busy then.' This I could tell from the lack of visitors in the lounge, indeed for a time I was the only one, in spite of the very inclement weather, but it seemed as good a way to start the conversation as any.

'No, Georgie has gone off into town, to the bank, but more likely to take money out rather than put it in. We've had a terrible season so far.' She giggled as though the financial difficulties of the hotel were a source of amusement.

'It's surely early yet,' I protested. 'Perhaps things will pick up as the season goes on.'

She giggled again, before turning it into a cough. 'We're all pinning our hopes on this theme park out at Kingarth. If that doesn't come off I don't know what we'll do. We'll close, I expect.' She didn't appear unduly worried by the prospect.

I've no idea why I said it, it came out of nowhere. 'Have you heard anything about the original manager of the project? Benjie Anderson? The one who took off without a word and was found dead out at Kingarth?'

Her expression changed. 'Why do you want to know about that?' she said warily, avoiding my gaze.

Something in her reaction warned me to consider my next words carefully. 'No particular reason. Someone mentioned it was strange the way he left the project so suddenly, given he'd a contract.'

She sniffed. 'You don't want to be believing all the rumours you hear on the island. Some people can make a big deal out of something simple and straightforward. It was more than likely he got fed up living in such a restricted place, with so little to do. Nothing ever happens in the evenings here. I'll be leaving myself soon. Once I get enough money together for a deposit on a rented flat, I'm heading for Glasgow.'

'Even so. Have you heard anything?' It was extremely unlikely Benjie would have signed up for the St Blane's project on the strength of the night life on Bute.

But she wasn't going to confide in me and the most she was prepared to say was, 'And how do you know what's happening behind the scenes? It might all appear quiet on the surface, but there could be lots going on. And I'd be wary of that Everett who's leading the protest group. ' She began to file her nails again, leaving me with the distinct impression she regretted saying even this much.

'What do you mean?' I could be very persistent when I put my mind to it.

I could see her now wrestling between a wish to close the subject and a desire to show off her superior knowledge. Finally, after a quick look around, though there was no one to be seen, she leaned over the desk and said in a gloomy voice, 'Everett has form, you know.'

'I don't know,' I replied. 'What do you mean?'

'He's been in trouble with the police I've heard. Assault, I think it was. Oh, not here on the island, somewhere else. He's from Birmingham as far as I know and he's only been on the island a short time. One of those newcomers who think because they've a bit of money they can take over.'

Given a "short time" on the island could mean anything from two weeks to several years this was a vague reply, not one to inspire confidence in the value of her judgement.

In spite of further prompting she refused to say more, leading me to suspect the stories about Everett were all gossip. But one thing was certain. Here was another person who believed something odd was going on. I'd a lot of questions, not only about Benjie's disappearance and death, but also about the entire project, doubts I'd pushed to the back of my mind.

Frustrated by these snippets of information, I went through to the lounge and sat again at the table in the corner to ferret in my bag for my notebook where I'd written down the particulars Zofia had passed out on our first meeting. I read them through, this time paying much more attention to the details of the targets and times, annoyed that I'd so easily discarded everything to do with the project except what directly concerned me. I'd have to ask Harry for a copy of his papers, sure I'd be able to come up with some excuse or other.

What I did know was that we were now in late March and if the opening festival was to take place on 12th August it didn't leave much time to complete all the work, given how modest progress had been so far. And today's weather had been an indication of how easily things could be disrupted. A wet summer, not an impossibility on this Atlantic coast, and any timescale would be in complete disarray. How would they manage then?

I thought about the bare site on the hillside at Kingarth, with nothing more than a few trenches dug, a skeleton of one or two of structures that could have been anything, the way in which Zofia was obsessed by targets and teambuilding, the concerns of Ryan about the finds, the death of Benjie and asked myself what exactly was going on at this theme park?

16

On my way back to the hotel after meeting Harry, I decided on the spur of the moment to break my journey and try to find Elsie. Georgie's story had been nagging away at the back of my mind and now Benjie's body had been found in such an unlikely spot, there must be something to this tale.

The little café where she worked was busy, the few tables and chairs occupied, a queue snaking out of the door. For many people a trip to the seaside wouldn't be complete without an ice cream and this café had a reputation for some of the best on the island.

The waitresses were flitting back and forth, balancing trays above the heads of the customers as they squeezed between the close packed tables. At the counter two women were serving while trying to take money and there would be no opportunity to speak to Elsie in this crush. Still, now I was here it was worth a try. As soon as there was a gap in the queue of customers I moved forward briskly. 'I was hoping to speak to Elsie,' I said, 'but I realise you're very busy.'

One of the women smiled as she handed a giant cone topped by raspberry sauce and a milk flake to a wide-eyed youngster, clad for summer in a T-shirt, shorts and sandals. 'You're in luck. She's on her break in the room at the back of the shop. You can go through if you want.'

She lifted the counter partition to let me in and I was relieved I hadn't had to come up with some flimsy excuse or other about the reason for my visit.

I knocked the door loudly before opening it to find Elsie sitting at a table by the window, among piles of boxes displaying the variety of confectionery the shop sold. She had a bowl of soup and a magazine in front of her, but it appeared neither had been touched.

She was younger than I'd expected. Somehow with a name like Elsie, which struck me as rather old-fashioned, I'd anticipated a woman in her fifties at least, but she couldn't have been older than her late thirties in spite of the threads of grey in her very dark hair, tied back in a severe pony tail. Under her apron bearing the logo Brandane Ices she was wearing a pale pink jumper and jeans, comfortable clothing for a busy shop.

She frowned as I came in. 'Can I help you,' she said, 'customers aren't allowed in here.'

Not the best of starts to a conversation.

'Sorry to disturb your break, I'm Alison Cameron, one of the team working on the project to develop a theme park out at Kingarth.' I held out my hand then let it drop to my side as she ignored this greeting.

'What do you want?' She sounded nervous, wary.

Now we were face to face, I realised I should have given more thought to what to say. As usual I'd gone rushing in, somehow assuming she'd be delighted to see me.

'Do you mind if I sit down?' That would pass a minute, allow me to collect my thoughts and without waiting for her reply, I sat down on the chair opposite, grabbing on to the sides as it wobbled a little.

She regarded me in stony silence, making it clear she'd every intention of waiting for me to explain why I was there, then as I said, 'I wanted to ask about your cousin,' she pushed the magazine and the soup to one side.

A blank look was her response.

107

'Your cousin,' I repeated, 'Benjie Anderson.'

'What makes you think he's my cousin?'

This was tricky. I didn't want her to think I'd been listening to gossip (though of course I had) but on the other hand I wanted to find out about Benjie, so I made some vague remark about "someone telling me" and waited.

The silence seemed to go on for ever, but just as I thought I'd have to jump in and make some remark to end the stalemate she said, 'He wasn't my cousin. He was treated like one of the family, but he wasn't.' She looked up at me and I could see her eyes were glistening with tears.

Distressed as she was, I had to ask, 'Do you know why Benjie decided to give up on the project to build the theme park out at Kingarth? Did something happen to make him decide he should leave so suddenly?'

She swallowed hard, evidently trying to regain control. 'Do you mean leave his job?'

This was even trickier. I was getting nowhere fast and the only option was to be honest. Taking a deep breath I said, 'When I was asked to join the project, Benjie was in charge. I'd a fair amount of contact with him via e-mail so you can imagine my surprise when I arrived here to find he was no longer in charge, that he'd been replaced by Zofia Kass.' Surely now there'd be some reaction.

But she continued to be wary. 'So what made you think he'd left on a whim?'

'I didn't exactly say "on a whim",' I replied, trying hard to keep cool in the face of her nippy reply. Wasn't I the one who was supposed to be asking the questions?

She leaned over the table towards me, catching her sleeve in the bowl of soup. She didn't seem to notice as little spots dripped on to the magazine. 'The last time I saw Benjie he told me he was very involved in the project and that he was hopeful that something really big would happen soon.'

This was interesting and I had to know more. 'What sort of thing?'

She sat back again, taking a paper napkin to wipe her sleeve as she realised what she'd done. 'He didn't give me any details. All he said was that there was something very strange going on with the project, that he'd found out things Mr Crombie didn't want known. He wouldn't tell me more, though I did press him.'

'So you've absolutely no idea what it could have been?'

'None at all. But I do know this. Whatever it was he'd found out, he was very excited about it, thought it would be life changing. What's more, I'm convinced it was important enough to have had something to do with his death.'

17

Before I'd time to reflect any further on the strange events at Kingarth, something happened much nearer to home to take my mind off anything to do with finds, or dead bodies.

We'd all been interviewed by the police, "a preliminary interview" they'd said and we'd been warned not to leave the island. As if any of us would, or could, in the circumstances. After my discussions, if they could be called that, with Elsie, I headed back to the hotel, thinking over what she'd said about the discovery Benjie had mentioned. It was clear she knew no more. Whatever had been the cause of his excitement about the project he'd had no intention of sharing any information with Elsie.

In the meantime, while we waited for the police to summon us again we were free to carry on as usual, though much of the site was out of bounds and I was glad to be staying at the Crannog hotel, well away from most of the others. Thankfully, Zofia had made no attempt to befriend me and the few times I'd encountered her had been in Reception where she was usually complaining about something or other.

On arrival at the hotel, I mumbled something noncommittal in reply to Georgie's, 'Back early, Mrs Cameron' and hurried through to the bedroom corridor, concerned she might try to engage me in conversation. At the moment there was nothing to say about the episode out at the theme park site, or nothing I wanted to say.

Not that there wasn't plenty to think about, including what had happened to the paten and the piece of slate. It was perfectly understandable the main concern would be the body, now formally identified as Benjie Anderson, but it was strange that once the preliminaries had been taken care of and we'd gathered once again in the Portakabin, none of the archaeologists had mentioned these important finds.

Why was I imagining problems where there were none? Of course these objects wouldn't have been left lying around, even though the shock of finding Benjie's body had affected everyone. Most likely Ryan or Sven had taken care of them, put them somewhere safe. Yes, there had to be some reasonable explanation and I'd find out soon enough.

So back in my room, I kicked off my shoes, lay on the bed and flicked the remote to switch on the television, not the least bit in the mood for work. Perhaps there would be something about the discovery of the body on the local news. But it was far too early for the story to have transferred from Bute to the mainland, even in this age of twenty-four hour news.

Idly flicking through the channels, seeking something to distract me from the uncomfortable thoughts that kept crowding in, I was startled when my phone rang. It took me a moment or two to locate it in my jacket pocket where I'd hurriedly shoved it earlier that morning.

To my surprise it was Maura. 'Hi, Mum,' she said.

'Hello, Maura, how are you?'

'More to the point where am I?'

'Is this some kind of quiz?' I laughed. 'You know I'm hopeless at that kind of thing.'

'Even if you were, I doubt if you'd guess I'm at Wemyss Bay, about to board the ferry to Bute.'

'What on earth are you doing there?'

'Why coming across to see you, of course. And have a bit of a holiday on the island. You've told him so much about it, Alan is determined to come over to see for himself and it's ages since I've been.' For a fleeting moment I wondered if Simon had sent them to spy on me, make sure I didn't get into trouble, but quickly dismissed this as unkind.

'Dad mentioned something about you coming north, but I didn't expect you so soon.'

Aware of how churlish this sounded I hurriedly added, 'And of course I'll be pleased to see you, both of you.'

Thank goodness Alan was with her. If they were coming over together there could be nothing wrong, in spite of my imaginings.

'Yes...and before you go fretting about where we'll stay, we've booked into one of the hotels in Rothesay for a few days. I know you're working, so we won't interrupt your arrangements too much.'

In spite of her words of reassurance, I couldn't imagine why Maura would make this sudden decision to come to Bute. Now with Deborah, my younger daughter, nothing she does would surprise me. She's had so many jobs, tried her hand at so many diverse careers (often involving some course or other funded by her parents) that I've almost given up on any expectation of her finding a permanent job. And as for Alastair, he's well settled in his career as a lecturer and apart from a brief foray home last year, he's not one for keeping in touch, even using Skype.

We arranged to meet up for dinner, once I'd explained how my day would be taken up working and before ringing off, Maura promised to book a table at the Kingarth restaurant.

Pleased to have solved the problem of where to have dinner I phoned Harry, suddenly revitalised. 'Let's try to make some progress with this work,' I suggested, 'it may be some time before we can get back on site,' and luckily he was happy to agree to meet at the Rothesay library in Moat Street.

I'd another reason for this suggestion. I was intrigued by the story about the St Blane's Hoard, wanted to check it out and perhaps the local paper The Buteman might have some information. I grabbed my laptop, added my notebook to my rather full bag and, well wrapped up in my warmest jacket, headed for the centre of town.

I'd a good hour before my meeting with Harry, giving me plenty of time to find the information I was after, but it wasn't quite as simple as that.

For a start it proved impossible to find a parking space anywhere near the library entrance because there was (as I discovered) a Tai Chi class taking place in the community centre next door. It would have been easy to park in one of the surrounding streets had I not been burdened with my collection of notebooks, my laptop and a large handbag, but eventually, as I'd almost given up hope after cruising round for the third time, a driver suddenly swerved his car out of a parking bay beside the castle and with a feeling of relief I edged my way in to a very tight space. Admittedly it took me one or two unsuccessful attempts.

Once inside the library I hurried to find one of the librarians, but both were busy. One was helping a customer who was searching for a particular book; the other was bent over a computer giving instructions to an elderly man who was finding the experience of being

113

online frightening in spite of her calm, reassuring manner and her patience with his every question.

I sat down in one of the comfortable bright red chairs in the reading area nearest the door and waited, idly flicking through the magazines set out on the coffee table, but after a good twenty minutes there was no sign of either librarian being available any time soon. At this rate I'd have to try to find the information I wanted after my meeting with Harry.

As though he'd read my mind Harry came breezing in and with a, 'Hello, Alison,' sat down heavily on the chair opposite. 'I'm a bit early, but thought I could make a start if you hadn't arrived.'

Before he could become too comfortable, I stood up saying, 'There's a little room at the back between the library and the Moat Community Centre. We can use that.' Sweeping up my belongings and heading off through the side door left him no option but to follow me.

As luck would have it, both librarians immediately became available, but although it would have been useful to have some details about the St Blane's Hoard before my meeting with Harry it could wait till later. That left me with a problem about whether to tell Harry about the missing finds or to keep quiet. By the time we were settled in the room off the Moat centre corridor, with a cup of coffee from the vending machine conveniently located beside the door, I'd decided on the latter course of action. He would only say I'd made a mistake, that one of the archaeology team had taken them for safe keeping and pooh-pooh any concerns.

For the first half hour we were engrossed in going over the draft of the visitor guide. To give him credit, Harry had done a power of work, had taken several of the ideas I'd come up with and turned them into something much more informative.

'And I thought we could use these headers,' he said. 'That will link up the information in the visitor guide with the actual sites and make everything easier to find.'

Personally I didn't think there'd be much difficulty about finding a giant Ferris wheel called the *Devil's Ride* jutting out of the peaceful Bute landscape, but wasn't going to disagree. Harry seemed to have overcome his earlier reservations about the project, about the way the story of St Blane and his monastery was being turned into a travesty of the original and he was embracing this venture with an enthusiasm which surprised me. And so, to avoid any dispute, I approved most of his suggestions.

Harry sat back, drained the remainder of his coffee and crushed the polystyrene cup before lobbing it in the direction of the bin. Unfortunately he missed and saying, 'Damn it,' got to his feet to retrieve it.

'Do you think that's enough for today?' I said, conscious that the library would be closing within the hour and I had yet to investigate the story of the St Blane's Hoard.

'I suppose that would be a good idea,' he agreed, standing up and gathering his papers together. He yawned. 'We've broken the back of it. I don't think we're very far off a conclusion and then I can get back to Manchester.'

'I didn't know you'd moved there?' Somehow I'd imagined Harry had remained in Glasgow where we'd both taught years before.

'I moved there…' a pause… 'afterwards. My sister lives there and at the time it seemed a good idea to be near family.'

Of course by "afterwards" he meant after the death of Greta, but I merely mumbled and nodded, not sure what to say.

'Are you going back to the hotel?'

'Not immediately,' I said, not wanting to lie. The last thing I needed was Harry looking over my shoulder, asking what I was doing.

Harry dithered about, sorting this and that while I tried not to show my impatience, silently trying to usher him along. Eventually he was satisfied all was in order and departed with a, 'See you tomorrow, then Alison.'

With a sigh of relief I returned to the main library and my first idea was to check through back copies of the local paper, *The Buteman*, or the now defunct *The Rothesay Chronicle*.

'That should be easy,' said the librarian when I requested the microfiche. 'Were you looking for anything in particular?' she said, helpfully.

'You know I'm working out at the St Blane's theme park at Kingarth?'

She nodded. 'Everyone on the island knows about that, with very mixed feelings, let me tell you.'

Unwilling to get into a discussion about the merits or otherwise of the project, I hurried on to say, 'I'm doing a bit of research and I understand a Hoard was found at the site in the 1860s. Would you have anything on that?'

'I'm sure there will be something given that it was a very important local find. Give me a minute,' and she sat down at the computer, frowning in concentration as she scrolled through various items.

'Yes, here we are,' she said in triumph a couple of minutes later. 'Got it. There were various articles written at the time then collected together in one volume. *A Short History of Finds at St Blane's* it's called and I'm sure we've a copy here in the library. Give me a couple of minutes.' She hurried off to look and I waited at the counter, idly watching the customers coming and going. Since its recent refurbishment, the library had been given a new lease of life and it was great to see it wasn't suffering the same fate as so many libraries on the mainland.

Absorbed in my thoughts, the sound of a gruff voice beside me gave me a start. 'Are you one of those involved in that work out at St Blane's?'

It was Everett. His face was ruddier than ever and he was dressed in faded brown corduroy trousers and a wax jacket that had seen better days, judging by the cracks and creases in the fabric. As he leaned forward and jabbed his finger at me, I instinctively took a couple of steps back.

'You should know that there are many people on the island most unhappy with this project. You'll find it's not going to be plain sailing, I can tell you. You'd better watch out.'

Before I could recover from this sudden onslaught, he turned on his heel and left, muttering to himself, at the very moment the librarian returned.

She made a face. 'Don't let him upset you. Everett objects to every attempt to move the island into the modern age, though,' she hesitated, 'he does have some very powerful friends.'

She seemed to consider this and I said, 'Does he work on one of the farms on Bute?'

She laughed. 'Good heavens, no. He's a self-styled artist. He's not lived here for more than a year or two. Not that he sells many paintings and if you see them you'll know why.' She gave a mock shudder. 'Very strange they are.'

'I thought by the look of him that he worked outside,' I said innocently.

She raised her eyebrows. 'A fondness for the whisky is what that shows. Still, best to avoid him if you can. Not that he'll be able to do much about the project, in spite of all his blustering. There's too much money invested in it and besides the island needs more visitors. He's one of those people who take on a cause with the sole objective of seeming important.'

Suddenly she appeared to recollect the original reason for my being there and frowned. 'Oh, I've had a good look on all the shelves and there's no sign of the book I thought might be of interest to you. I don't know where it's gone.'

'Does someone have it on loan?' Just my luck that someone else had thought about checking out the story.

She shook her head. 'That's why I was so long. I've been through the record of lending back to last year, but there's nothing there. Someone seems to have removed the book from the shelf. We do lose books from time to time, but this is a strange one to go missing. It's not particularly valuable, although it is of interest.'

Then she added, 'Leave me your contact details and if we come across it, I'll get in touch. It's quite likely it's been put back in the wrong place. That does happen more often than you'd believe. People take something down to read, then can't remember where they found it and instead of asking for help put it back on any old shelf.'

118

I thanked her and leaving my card, headed out to collect my car.

Strange indeed that the book had disappeared. And whatever the librarian thought, it was clear the book was of value to someone.

18

In the meantime, intrigued as I was about what could possibly have happened to the book about the St Blane's Hoard, I had to catch up with Maura and Alan. We'd agreed to meet back at the hotel and I was more than a little curious to find out what had brought them to Bute so unexpectedly. All kinds of scenarios ran through my head as I drove along the seafront, ranging from the innocuous to the downright scary. If they'd decided on a holiday surely they wouldn't have come to Bute with so little notice, particularly when they knew I was working. Both have really busy jobs in London and time off is difficult to arrange.

They were waiting for me in Reception and Maura sprang to her feet to give me a hug. Alan hovered behind her. He's a man of few words, not at all demonstrative, but his heart's in the right place.

Greetings exchanged, I suggested we go into the lounge. 'We can have a cup of tea here. It's a bit early to go for a meal,' I said, guiding them to some comfortable seats in the corner by the window with a view out over the bay where the last of the light was glinting on the waters of the bay, the pink and purple tinged sky reflected in its calm surface.

'I'd forgotten how much I like Bute,' sighed Maura, sinking into one of the armchairs. 'It's so long since I've been here it's like discovering it all anew. We've had a walk along the Tramway out to Ettrick Bay this afternoon and pottered round the graveyard beside the ruined church at Cnoc an Rath. It's amazing what you find.'

'I'm looking forward to doing a bit of bird watching,' said Alan. 'I hear this is a great place for it. I saw the bird hide out by Ettrick Bay and I'll be spending some time there.'

'Bird watching? I didn't think you were a twitcher,' I said. Alan never ceased to surprise me, possibly because he said so little it was difficult to know much about him.

'Yes, I did a lot of bird watching when I was a boy and we lived on the coast in Kent, but I gave it up when I went to live in London.'

'He decided it would a good hobby to help cope with stress,' added Maura, looking fondly at him.

Alan was the last person I'd have thought of as suffering from stress, another sign of how little I knew about him.

'Well, there's plenty of wildlife here,' I said. 'The oyster catchers, the seagulls, the blackbirds...' my voice tailed away as I realised my knowledge of the birds on the island was limited.

Alan ignored my ignorance about bird life on the island. 'I'm hoping to see some gannets while I'm here and some buzzards. Did you know their Latin name is Buteo... another link to Bute. They're pretty elusive, but there's a good chance of catching sight of at least one as we're on the island for a few days.' He sounded positively enthusiastic.

'Anyway,' said Maura as I beckoned over one of the staff to order some tea, 'that's not the reason we're here.'

'Let's order first,' I said, as much to postpone the moment as anything. Whatever they had to tell me, it would require my full attention and while we waited I tried to sneak another look at Maura. She sounded cheerful enough, but her face was pinched and she'd lost her usual good colour. What's more she'd clearly lost weight by the way her jeans hung loosely about her hips. I tried to convince myself she was merely tired out by that manic job in London and hopefully a couple of days of sea air would restore her.

At last I could contain myself no longer and leaning over said to her, 'You look a bit pale. Are you feeling okay?'

'I'm absolutely fine,' she snapped in a way that was so unlike her it made me feel more concerned, but I'd no option but to let the subject drop, especially as Alan came in hastily, 'We're so looking forward to a few days with nothing to do but chill out.'

Fortunately this difficult topic of my daughter's well-being was interrupted by the arrival of tea and we spent a few minutes sorting out who wanted what, though Maura did no more than pick at one of the sandwiches.

I sat back and said tentatively, 'So there is a reason for coming all the way to Bute?'

She looked over at Alan who nodded encouragingly and then said, 'Yes, we wanted to tell you our news in person. Alan's been offered a job in Edinburgh and we've decided now would be a good time to take the opportunity to move out of the South East.' The words came out in a rush as though she was afraid of my reaction, but all I felt was a tremendous sense of relief, given all the possibilities I'd imagined.

'And will this be happening soon?'

'We've already let the house in Kent, which was easier than selling at the moment, the way the market is. We'll rent in Edinburgh of course because it might only be for a year or two. We've been really lucky. One of

Alan's colleagues is moving to take up a short term post in the Boston office and we're going to rent his flat for three months till we find something more permanent.'

I couldn't conceal my delight. 'That's great news, having you so near for a while.'

A ghost of a smile crossed Maura's face as I added, 'And is will be a good opportunity for Alan.'

'Absolutely,' said Alan with enthusiasm. 'It's a step up the ladder and when we go back to London the experience will stand me in good stead.'

'If we go back,' Maura chided him gently.

'But what will you do, Maura? Do you have a job lined up?' Knowing Maura's post with a small advertising agency was more than a little precarious, I was apprehensive about her prospects.

'Oh, I'm sure I'll find something...eventually.' Maura dismissed my concerns with a wave of her hand. Ah, so it was very likely this also solved a problem for Maura. She'd told me how unhappy she'd been these past few months at work. The economic downturn had affected the advertising business very much and on at least two occasions she'd been concerned the agency might close altogether.

We chatted about the move, about the kind of they might be able to afford to rent ('somewhere round about the Marchmont area would be good'), about the prospects for long-term letting their place in Kent ('the rental market is really buoyant at the moment and though it's only a six months' lease, I'm sure the tenants will stay on, though we'd much rather sell'), about timescales and other plans. Genuinely happy for them and more than a little thrilled at the idea of being able to visit them in Edinburgh, see them more often, the time seemed to disappear until suddenly I noticed it was almost seven o' clock.

'We'd better think about dinner,' I said.

Maura put her hand to her mouth. 'Oops,' she said, 'we were so busy I forgot to book. My memory seems to be awful these days. There's so much happening, I'll have to start making lists.'

Reluctant to leave the cosy hotel, especially as it had now started to rain, Maura and Alan decided the hotel would do fine and we had a pleasant enough evening, sharing a bottle of wine with a rather indifferent meal which seemed to owe a lot to the freezer rather than the celebrated local produce.

I waved them off a little after ten o' clock with promises of meeting up again before they left the island. 'Remember we're only here for another two days,' said Maura, frowning. 'I know you're busy, but perhaps we could meet again for dinner? I'll make sure I book this time.'

Was telling me about the move to Edinburgh the only reason they'd come to Bute? I'd have to try to find an opportunity to talk to her on her own.

It had been a long and in some ways difficult day but I felt relaxed, chilled out. I'd phone Simon, have a hot bath, then head for bed. He'd be as delighted as I was at the news of their posting to the capital, even if it was likely to be on a temporary basis.

I slid the key into the lock of my room door, but it opened almost of its own accord. That was odd. There was no way I would have left it open this morning. I stood outside, wondering what to do. Berating myself for being a coward when there was most likely a simple explanation, I took a deep breath and cautiously I peered round, listening intently for any noise. All was quiet.

I crept inside, my heart beginning to pound, making sure to leave the door wide open in case I had to make a sudden exit and walking on tiptoe to make as little sound as possible.

A quick glance round the room convinced me there was no sign of any disturbance: the room looked if anything tidier than when I'd left it that morning. The bed was made up, the towels in the minute ensuite bathroom squared on the rail, the soap and shampoo replenished, a sign the cleaner must be back at work. I stood still for a moment, trying to spot if there was anything out of place, but there was nothing that immediately caught my eye.

It was then I noticed it. Lying on the carpet inside the door was a large brown envelope and I bent down to pick it up cautiously, turning it this way and that, but there was no clue as to who might have left it. And why leave it here rather than at Reception?

I flopped down on the bed and ran my fingers along the outside to make sure it didn't contain anything that might be dangerous, mindful of so many warnings about letter bombs. It seemed perfectly safe, but even so I began to open it carefully and, as I turned it upside down, I caught a single sheet of paper as it fluttered out.

The paper was lined, apparently torn from a standard A4 notepad, but the message was clear. In large block capitals it said

KEEP YOUR NOSE OUT OF ISLAND BUSINESS. GO HOME OR YOU'LL REGRET IT

There was no signature and my first inclination was to laugh at this amateurish threat, then I shuddered. What on earth did the writer mean? Certainly I was involved with the St Blane's theme park, but "island business"?

Resolving to ignore it, regard it as the work of some crank or other, I was about to screw it up and toss it in the bin, then decided for some reason to put it in the drawer in the bedside cabinet. It was hardly worth going to the police about something so trivial and I didn't feel in any danger, though it was unpleasant. I'd have to find a way of checking if anyone else on the team had received a similar note.

I could ask Georgie if she'd seen any strangers lurking about, but as quickly dismissed the idea. No harm had been done and it was most likely the work of one of the protesters intent on frightening us. Even so the question niggled away. Why me?

Best to sleep on it, if sleep would come, but exhausted by the day, worries about Maura and a rather dusty bottle of wine from the minibar, I managed no more than a chapter of my book before drifting off.

19

The next morning, groggy from sleeping through the alarm and unable to decide whether to say anything about the threatening letter, I showered, dressed hurriedly and left the room, but not before double checking everything.

The decision was made for me because as I came out of the corridor, too late now for breakfast, Georgie was on duty at the Reception desk and her cheerful, 'All well, Mrs Cameron,' prompted me to say, 'Did anyone ask to go along to my room yesterday?'

She regarded me with astonishment. 'Not as far as I know. Why? Have you had a problem?'

Her pursed lips showed she was almost daring me to say there had been trouble and all I replied was with, 'I thought someone might have been trying to contact me.'

'Well, if that was the case they would have asked at Reception and been required to leave any message here. What makes you ask? Are you expecting someone?' She sounded prickly, as though I was questioning the hotel security.

'No, no, I thought perhaps....' My voice trailed off as I couldn't think of an excuse for my questions so I coughed loudly to disguise my comment and said, 'Well, I must be off to the next meeting,' leaving before she could quiz me further.

As I went out of the main door I could almost feel her gazing after me, puzzled at this strange behaviour.

I hurried round to the car park at the back of the hotel, cross for not keeping to my original decision to say nothing about the incident and hoping she'd have forgotten about it by the time I returned.

An unexpected stretch of roadworks delayed me for another five minutes, leaving me breathless as I more or less abandoned my car in the road at the side of the Pavilion and ran down to join the others in the Lesser Hall.

All eyes swivelled round as I came in, muttering apologies, though Zofia couldn't have been long started.

Harry patted the seat beside him. 'Sit here. You've not missed anything,' he whispered.

'I have to ask you for some help,' I hissed back before becoming aware of Zofia glaring at me.

'Glad you could *join* us, Alison. If everyone's quite ready,' she said, 'I'll start again for the latecomer.' She was even more wound up today, clicking and unclicking her ballpoint pen as she walked backwards and forwards at the front of the room.

Sadly, it was the same old management speak, targets and outcomes, benchmarking and prepping, reflective exercises and sharing in teams. It was increasingly difficult to see what benefits Alexander Crombie thought she would bring to the project.

In the seat in front of me, Nathan shifted this way and that, looking from time to time at his watch.

Finally, when our general restlessness showed we were running out of patience, she said, 'Is that clear? I'll be starting the individual appraisal sessions in the next few days and I'll put out a schedule.'

'This is a bloody waste of time, Zofia, even if you are the spokesperson for our funder.' Vernon's sudden outburst created a ripple of a sigh round the room as he got to his feet. 'How is it going to be if we can't open on the due date, because we've spent too long faffing about with a whole lot of management gobbledegook instead of getting on with the job? The only thing of any interest to us is if the police have given permission for us to return to the site?' There was a murmur of support, but Zofia stood her ground, her voice rising higher and higher as she continued. 'It's been my experience it's teamwork that gets the project completed. And yes, I've been in touch with the police and they are fine about us going ahead with the work as long as we stay away from that cordoned off area round the trench where the body was found.'

'Exactly, Zofia. Work, the key word is work. That's what we're being paid for. We can go back to the site. That's all we need to know.' Vernon tried to hide a grin as he realised he'd achieved his aim of winding her up.

Zofia stamped her foot, her face suffused with anger. 'I'm only doing what I've been *instructed* to do. Mr Crombie is behind me all the way.'

But by now Vernon was on his way out, muttering, 'I'm off to the dig. That's what I'm good at, what I'm paid for,' leaving the rest of us looking at each other, uncertain about what to do next.

In the end it was Luann who solved the problem. Perhaps she was beginning to feel sorry for Zofia, perhaps she thought it would be a good idea to move the meeting along and let us get out of here sometime soon. 'Can you summarise, Zofia?' she said in a sugar sweet tone that made it obvious she wanted the meeting to end. 'Then we can decide how best to proceed.'

Zofia clutched at this straw, failing to recognise Luann's underlying sarcasm. 'Yes, I know everyone is busy,' she said eagerly, 'and I'll try my best to get through the rest of this quickly. Now if we could look at the last item.'

A collective sigh went round the room as though we were agreed to make as few comments as possible. If we kept silent, let Zofia ramble on for the next few minutes we'd be able to leave before long.

Unfortunately we came to the conclusion this hope was entirely unjustified and that Zofia was determined to make the most of having a captive audience and we wouldn't be finishing any time soon, the door was flung open and the caretaker came running in. My first thought was that the place had gone on fire and in the circumstances that would have been a welcome relief, but if so there'd been no fire bell to warn us.

Zofia was more than a little cross at yet another interruption. 'Yes,' she said frostily, stopping in mid sentence, 'is there a problem?'

'There may be for you,' said the caretaker, trying to keep the note of glee out of her voice at having the opportunity to interrupt Zofia. 'I've this minute had a phone call from one of the diggers. They tried to contact you but I guessed your mobile was switched to silent. The protesters have arrived at the site of the theme park and are threatening a sit-in.'

'What do you mean? What are they up to?' Zofia rounded on her, eyes blazing.

The caretaker shrugged. 'I'm only the messenger,' she said, smugly, 'but if I were you I'd get over there pretty quickly.'

20

We didn't wait to be asked a second time. We crowded out of the Pavilion, scrambling into a couple of cars, a achievement which took longer to organise than necessary.

'Alison, Harry and Luann, you come with me,' Zofia ordered, now back to her bossy self, leaving the others to make a decision about transport as best they could.

I was in no mood to argue though as I soon discovered Zofia wasn't the best of drivers. Even allowing for the circumstances, wanting to reach the site as quickly as possible, she drove like a demon, skittering round corners, accelerating round blind bends, overtaking several cars on the Ascog Road where it narrowed immediately before the Chandlers' Hotel, much to the alarm and consternation of other drivers. Checking and rechecking my seat belt to make sure it was tightly buckled, at any minute I expected to hear the wail of a police car siren behind us.

'Careful, careful,' said Harry, hanging on grimly in the front seat, but she paid no attention and drove on regardless, hunched over the steering wheel, eyes fixed on the road ahead, hammering on the steering wheel with both hands as we came up behind a tractor. Thankfully I was in the back with Luann and could close my eyes at the most difficult bits, though once or twice I sure we were about to crash.

At the farm near the junction where the Kingarth Hotel sits, I thought our last hour had come. We'd sped down the twisting road past Mount Stuart, heading to Kilchattan Bay and suddenly, as we rounded the bend, there was a farmer herding his cows across from the field to the milking barn. Being cows, they'd no concept of someone in a hurry. I doubt the farmer had either. For most people on Bute, residents and visitors alike, the main attraction of the island is the leisurely pace of life and as Zofia jammed on the brakes just in time to avoid hitting the slow moving herd, the cow nearest her windscreen stopped and turned to look at her with an expression that could only be described as disdainful, its mouth moving slowly as though about to speak.

She leaned out of the window and began to shout, 'Get out the way, get out the way,' but understandably the cow only continued to stare at her, standing stock-still in the middle of the road, its eyes regarding her soulfully.

'That won't do any good,' said Harry, pulling her back in to her seat. 'We have to wait till they're in the milking barn. It won't take long. The farmer knows what he's doing.'

She sat back at this, impatiently drumming her fingers on the steering wheel, muttering, 'Hurry up, hurry up,' until at last the farmer and his lively collie came up at the rear of the herd, prodding the last of the cows to move out of the way and into the milking barn.

He raised his hand in greeting as he passed, and sensing Zofia's stony stare in reply, Harry rolled down the window and waved back, shouting, 'Good day.'

He wound the window up again as Zofia revved up the car with a grinding of the gear stick that set my teeth on edge. 'You have to understand these people are working, Zofia,' he said. His tone was mild but his words struck home.

'So? We're also working and may not be today if we don't get to the site in time to stop whatever it is the

132

protesters are up to.' And with that she was off again, her foot flat on the floor to speed us to our destination in the same terrifying manner. It was hard to stop myself stamping on imaginary brakes with every terrifying lurch of the car.

Towards the end of the road leading to St Blane's we could see some brightly coloured banners waving in the breeze and hear the sound of chanting. Luann and I wound down the windows and the sounds came clearly across the still air, 'No theme park here, no theme park here.'

The group of protesters filled the roadway, standing shoulder to shoulder, showing their determination not to let anyone pass through to the site and we had to park the car further along the road at some distance from the entrance. I use the term "park" loosely as Zofia more or less abandoned her car in the middle of the road, yanking on the handbrake as she switched off the engine, then flinging open the door to run towards the nearest protesters at the edge of the group. Harry, Luann and I came along behind her at a slower pace, trying to make a judgement about what was happening, assess the situation before taking action. Not so Zofia: she flung herself towards the group, shouting and yelling in a way that was far from helpful.

As I came up close it was clear to see the group was larger than I'd first thought, straggling on to the site and up the hill towards the Portakabin. I recognised Everett at the front, but the others were unfamiliar to me, though one or two might have been among the crowd we'd encountered at the Pavilion.

The largest banner, held aloft by two women flanking him, bore the legend ST BLANE'S IS NOT A THEME PARK. Fronting Everett were Vernon and

Ryan in what appeared to be something akin to a Mexican stand-off and as we got nearer we could hear some of their angry exchanges.

'This is private property,' Vernon was saying. 'You've no right to be here. You're trespassing.'

'We're trespassing?' Everett sneered. 'You're the ones who're trespassing, destroying our heritage here on Bute, making us a laughing stock.' He turned to address his followers in a style which suggested he was a fan of the film *Braveheart* and the two women waved the flag aggressively as the others cheered. The effect was a little spoiled as one of the women slipped on the wet grass and the flag went down, lopsided, to the sound of a loud crack as the pole splintered.

Everett ignored this mishap and shouted, waving his arms around to emphasise his point, 'We'll continue to protest until you abandon this mad plan. The site of St Blane should be cherished, left in peace for future generations, not despoiled in this way.'

'What are you talking about?' said Zofia coming up beside him, her words coming out in a breathless rush. 'This is an empty field.'

Everett turned to glare at her. 'It doesn't matter. It's near enough the site to be a contamination.' The gleam in his eye said he was a man not to be easily dissuaded from his point of view.

But Zofia was having none of it. 'You *stupid* man,' she yelled, which wasn't the best way to improve relations, 'take your ragtag crowd and your stupid banners off this land at once.' With a well aimed kick, she sent the splintered pole rolling down the hill and only the prompt action of the two women saved it from landing in a heap at the bottom.

There were murmurs in the crowd: some shuffled their feet, others moved back as though anxious to leave before things became ugly. Everett turned round and waved his arms at them. 'That's it, as soon as we encounter a bit of resistance are we going to give in? This is our heritage we're talking about. Do you want people to come from far and wide to see a travesty of our history?'

Zofia went over and stood beside Sven, who'd now arrived with the others, her hands on her hips. 'I won't tell you again. You're trespassing. Clear off this land.'

She moved across to Everett so that their faces were almost touching and he pulled back a little, startled. 'Anyway, I don't know what you're doing here. You're a Johnny-come-lately if I ever saw one. What do you know about the island and its history?'

For a moment it looked as if Everett was about to explode, his face becoming purple with rage, the veins on his neck standing out. Oh great, I thought, that's all we need – for Everett to have a heart attack.

There was a murmuring behind him, a shuffling of feet. It was clear that most of the people in the crowd had come to have a peaceful protest and the notion of things getting out of hand didn't appeal, so one by one, or in little groups of two or three, they trickled away, with a 'Sorry, Everett', or 'What can we do?'

Everett wheeled round on them as they moved slowly off the site. 'Cowards,' he shouted at their disappearing backs. 'Don't you realise how important it is to stand firm against these vandals?' But even the insults didn't stop the exodus and within a few minutes he was left alone at the bottom of the hill with only his two faithful banner carriers for company.

'Well, are you going now?' Zofia folded her arms and glared at him.

Everett leaned close to her and Ryan moved to push him away. Angrily, Everett shook off his arm. 'You may have frightened them today,' he hissed, 'but believe me, we'll be back. You won't get away with,' waving his arms about, 'with this monstrosity.'

He turned on his heel and strode off, the two women trotting meekly behind him, trying hard to keep some semblance of dignity as the banner drooped on its cracked poles.

Although I couldn't say anything for fear of upsetting Zofia or any of the others, he did have a point. From what I'd seen, the theme park was going to be not much more than a glorified funfair with very little educational or historical basis. But it was rather late to be having these doubts and I put such thoughts to the back of my mind, convincing myself that at least Harry and I were trying to preserve some modicum of history in the project.

Nathan was shaking his head. 'You've made an enemy there, Zofia. He's not the kind of man who gives up easily.'

'Nonsense.' Zofia was determined as ever to defend her actions. One thing she would never do was admit a mistake. 'I'm sure he won't be back. And if he and his raggle-taggle mob do come back, I'll *certainly* call the police. Of that you can be sure.'

'It was a peaceful protest,' said Harry, though his voice was timid. 'They are entitled to their point of view.'

Zofia rounded on him. 'Indeed? Since when did you become an expert in all of this? These people are against progress of any kind, they've no concept of the difference something like this will make to the island. Don't worry. Believe me, we've seen the last of Everett and his gang. They won't be troubling us again.'

But she was wrong, very wrong.

21

The mystery of who had sent the anonymous note nagged away at me and now we'd met him again in the latest encounter with the protesters, I came to the conclusion the person responsible must have been Everett. So far, I'd put off telling the others what had happened but now I'd have to find a way to check discreetly, find out if anyone else received similar threats, but if not, I'd no idea why I'd be targeted. I'd no influence, no control over the project. It was a great puzzle.

With no decision made, I headed off to meet Maura and Alan for the last time before they left the island, but it was an uncomfortable evening in many ways and I'd the distinct impression there were underlying issues between them, though whether that was about the move to Edinburgh or something else was difficult to decide. Several times during the meal Maura seemed distracted and only came back into the conversation when prompted. There'd been no chance to have the one-to-one chat I'd hoped for. She shrugged off the suggestion, claiming there'd be plenty of time once I was back on the mainland.

Later that night after dinner, as we said our farewells, I caught her by the arm and whispered, 'I'll come over to Edinburgh to see you as soon as you're settled. I finish here next week with a bit of luck and can do the rest of the visitor guide at home.'

'That would be great,' her brave front disappearing as she answered with a little catch in her voice.

So my guess had been correct. There was something wrong. This I could do without. Of all three children

Maura is the one who's given us least cause for concern over the years.

And as I came back in to the hotel, still fretting about the cause of my unease about her, Georgie said as she handed me my key, 'Someone was here a few moments ago looking for you. You just missed him.'

'Did he leave a message?'

She shrugged. 'No, he wouldn't even leave his name. Said he'd catch up with you later.'

Not much later, I thought as it was past eleven o'clock and I was heading for bed, in spite of being curious. The only person I could think it might be was Harry, but why come to the hotel rather than phone? I was sure I'd told him about meeting Alan and Maura for a meal that evening. It was all very strange.

As I reached my door, I realised I'd yet again forgotten to mention to Georgie the problem about my room number. Ah well, I was too tired to go back down to Reception and complain. I'd make a note to remind myself to do it in the morning.

In spite of everything, I was asleep almost as soon as my head hit the pillow. The excitement of the day, as well as all this fresh air, something I wasn't yet used to, had exhausted me.

When the bedside phone rang a little past midnight it was a few moments before I realised it wasn't part of some dream. Groggily I reached out and felt around in the dark, only to hear the receiver clatter to the floor. I sat up, switched on the lamp at the second attempt and bent down to lift the phone, but as I said 'Hello,' the line went dead.

Late as it was, my first thought was Simon was trying to contact me, but as I became more awake I realised he would contact me on my mobile rather than using the hotel phone. Whoever it was, it couldn't have been my husband and my fast beating heart slowed to a more normal rate as all my imaginings about news from Maura receded. Probably it was a wrong number. It would be someone the worse for wear phoning from some pub or other, making a mistake with a digit or two, an easy thing to do.

Carefully replacing the receiver, I crawled back into bed, snuggled down under the duvet and prepared to sleep. Sadly, having been so rudely awakened, sleep proved impossible and I tossed and turned, a jumble of thoughts crowding into my brain: the problems of the project, Benjie's death, what had happened to the paten and to the slate, worries about Maura and Alan.

Eventually I must have dozed off, only to be wakened again by the shrill sound of the phone ringing. This time, not in such a deep slumber, I managed to grab the receiver by the third ring but the only response to my, 'Hello, who's calling?' was a click, followed by silence.

Someone was playing games, trying to upset me or even frighten me. Was it the same person as had called earlier?

This time, before settling down, I left the receiver off the hook, but even with no possibility of another call, I tossed and turned all night. I awakened a few minutes before seven o' clock as the first light filtered through the gap in the curtains where they didn't quite fit together. I lay for a few minutes thinking about the previous night's phone calls. Much as I tried to convince myself it must have been a wrong number, I wondered if it was anything to do with the note I'd received. Used as I was to cold calls on my landline in Glasgow, I very much doubted if that was the reason

140

behind these. Even the most determined of companies selling double glazing or new kitchens didn't resort to phoning in the middle of the night and no easy explanation came to mind.

Still pondering the mystery caller I went down to the breakfast room, after making sure to check the room door was locked behind me. I was becoming more than a little apprehensive about what was happening: the anonymous letter, the strange phone calls and realised it was about time to confide in someone. The dilemma was who.

'Gosh, you look tired, Mrs Cameron. Did you not sleep well?' Gemma was one of the many part-time waitresses in this hotel and kindly intentioned as her comments were, I'd no desire to discuss my problems with her.

'I've been a bit busy during these last few days,' I replied and then covered my tetchiness by adding, 'I'm sure it's a temporary thing. There's been so much going on.'

She smiled, not the least put out. 'Go into the breakfast room and I'll get someone to bring your coffee over, I'm sure it's what you need,' she said and headed off towards the dining room.

As I passed the Reception desk I stopped, coughing to attract the attention of Brenda who was leafing through a copy of a celebrity magazine, considering how to frame the question that was bothering me.

'Did anyone phone late last night, ask to be put through to my room?'

She looked up. 'No...not as far as I remember, but then I went off at eleven o'clock.'

'So who was on duty?'

141

She shrugged. 'Georgie would be around until about one o'clock and available after that for any emergency. That's why guests have their own front door key.' She waited, then when I made no reply added, 'In case they come back very late.'

'So what happens about phone calls during the night?'

'Emergencies you mean?'

'No, if someone wanted to phone…say for a chat.'

She squinted at me, clearly thinking this a very strange conversation. 'If it was someone you knew well, they'd have your extension number and would phone direct. We've paid a lot of money for this new system. Has there been a difficulty with it?' She sniffed. 'This is a very small hotel; we can't have someone on duty on the off chance someone might want to phone one of the guests in the middle of the night. That's why Georgie had it installed.'

That explained one part of it. Whoever it was who'd been making the calls he or she must have obtained my direct extension. No need then to worry about going through Reception.

I persevered. 'So did anyone call here and ask for my extension number?'

'No one asked me, but of course one of the others might have been on duty at the time.'

'Do you think you could check for me?'

'What, now?' She made no attempt to disguise her surprise.

'No, no, but if you could ask whoever was on duty earlier in the day.'

'Okay,' she said returning to her magazine and leaving me with not the slightest hope she'd do as I asked.

Best to leave it there, not raise any further questions and I headed over to the dining room, my questions to Brenda probably forgotten already.

There was only one couple there, talking in low voices as they demolished the full Scottish breakfast on offer, but I wasn't in the mood for so much food, something unusual for me, especially with the prospect of a day in the open air ahead of me. My stomach was churning over and over, but several cups of coffee and a slice of toast later, I felt able to leave, keeping my phone on silent and planning to check it from time to time in case Simon phoned to update me on his plans to come over to the island. I was beginning to wish most heartily that he'd come soon, even with the unresolved issues between us, veering from thinking our marriage was really in trouble to thinking how much I valued his support, but at the moment I couldn't cope with any more decisions.

22

Along at the Pavilion, Harry was sitting in the Lesser Hall on his own.

'No sign of any of the others?' I said.

Harry shrugged. 'Not so far. I've the impression everyone is pretty fed up with these endless meetings. Perhaps they've all decided to boycott today's.' He chuckled. 'Zofia was going to the site first so she's probably over there, trying to round them up.'

'So what do we do now?'

'No point in getting involved in their squabbles. We can stay here and use the time to review what we've done. Let's get started.'

We spread out our material on the table at the front of the room. With so much subject matter, I had to keep Harry on track, no mean task given his reluctance to leave out any of his research.

'I think we need a bit more about the early Celtic church,' said Harry, flicking through his papers. 'About the disagreements with the Roman church.'

'Mmm,' I said, trying not to sound too negative, sure the kind of people who came to a theme park wouldn't be the least bit interested in the dissensions in any church, far less the early Celtic and Roman.

Sadly, Harry was now in full flow. 'The Romans adopted the tonsure, that bald patch in the middle of their head in memory of the crown of thorns placed on Jesus' head, while the Celtic church shaved the front of their head and let their hair grow long at the back.'

It was becoming clear that Harry was letting the research take over and the problem was how to rein him back. 'Possibly we could have a slim booklet with no more than a few interesting anecdotes about the life of St Blane and you could think about writing a proper book for those with a more academic interest in the life and times of Blane.'

After some thought, he said, sitting back and scratching his head, 'You know, that's not a bad idea, Alison. I've spent a long time on this research and I wouldn't want the material to go to waste. Yes, the more I think about it, the better I like it.'

Heaving a sigh of relief, I continued before he could come up with objections, 'Good. That's the decision made.'

Harry stared at me. 'You seem a bit tired, Alison? Not sleeping well?'

'Probably I need a coffee, that's all.'

It had been my intention to say nothing about the mysterious phone calls, but the sympathetic tone of his voice made me blurt out, 'I had an awful night last night. I kept getting these silent phone calls.'

Harry frowned. 'Don't let it bother you. It happens all the time.'

'Not in the small hours, it doesn't.'

'Ah, that's a bit different,' he said. 'But many of these calls are entirely automated, so if they were coming from, say, India, then the time difference wouldn't mean anything. Don't start imagining things, Alison. I know that's a difficulty you have – an overactive imagination. I'm certain there's nothing to worry about. Forget it.'

We worked on, but there was still no sign of any of the others and I said, snapping my notebook shut, 'It's ten o'clock, Harry. There must be something wrong. We should phone Zofia.'

'Mmm?' Harry looked up. 'I guess so.' Then his mind obviously still on what we'd been doing, he said, 'You realise there were a few attempts to find other treasure, but it was agreed everything had been taken by the Viking looters when they ravaged the site in the 8th century. They burned the place down, as they'd done with Iona, so the guess is they took anything of value.'

So the paten and the fragment of slate were likely to be the only items of worth: anything else had disappeared centuries ago.

'I thought Zofia and the others might be here by now,' I said, looking again at my watch. 'What could be keeping them?'

'Who knows? Think I'll head for the library while I've the chance.'

Together we left the Pavilion, walking out into a day bright with sunshine and a warmth that made it feel like summer.

'It's an afternoon for being outdoors,' I said, turning up my face to catch the sun. 'I think I'll drive over to Kingarth, see what's going on.'

Harry waved to me as he headed for his car, but I was off to the site of the theme park to find out what was detaining the team.

With little traffic on the road I soon reached Kingarth, but before I parked the car I heard the noise: sounds of angry voices, shouting and yelling. It was immediately clear why Zofia and the others hadn't returned to the Pavilion.

Down at the bottom of the field where the archaeologists had finished their survey, some building work had at last begun. The newly started structure of the *Devil's Ride*, modelled on the big dipper common to many fun fairs was no more than a heap of tangled metal and an acrid smell of smoke filled the air. The partly built walls of the monastery restaurant were reduced to a pile of bricks scattered across a wide area, evidence someone had been hard at work with a sledge hammer. Further up the slope, where the outline of the fish farm had been, the earth had been tipped back into the pond, rendering the excavation efforts useless.

The workmen were making half-hearted attempts to clear up while the archaeologists and the others stood round watching them, but it was obvious their hearts weren't in it and the air of dejection was almost tangible.

For a moment I couldn't see Zofia, but suddenly I spied her at the very top of the hill, sitting on one of the recently carved wooden seats made to look like stone and destined to go outside the monks' cells cum holiday homes.

'What on earth has happened?' I said hurrying up to her, slightly out of breath.

She waved her hand round the site, indicating even more destruction. 'You tell me. Someone has been busy destroying everything we've done so far. This will set us back weeks, if not months. There's absolutely *no* chance of being ready for 12th August now.'

'But surely they couldn't have done all this without being spotted?'

There was a note of bitterness in her voice. 'It would appear it was done during the night, when there was no one here of course.'

'The site wasn't guarded?'

She snorted. 'No, not so much as a guard dog. Mr Crombie's way of saving money. Well, he'll regret it now. This will cost a fortune to put right.'

'Have the police been?'

'Yes, they were the ones who spotted what had happened. A patrol car doesn't usually come round this way often, but they have a new constable and he was being shown round the island early this morning. It was only because he'd heard about the building of the theme park, showed an interest in what had been done to date that they got out of the car and came over to look at the site. Too late to catch anyone, of course.'

'They must have some idea who would do all this damage.'

Zofia laughed bitterly. 'Oh, the forensic people have been, they've been all over the site and though they might have an idea who was behind it, proving it will be a different matter.'

She could only mean Everett and his fellow protesters, though surely that was unlikely. Even Everett, opposed as he was to this development, was more bluster than action. Shouting and making protest was one thing, criminal damage quite another.

As we sat there in silence, a bank of clouds came scudding in across the bay, blotting out the sun and leaving the site in shadow as though in sympathy with what had happened here. It was all too much.

Or perhaps St Blane was taking action, incensed by the travesty that was planned in his name, but I didn't dare joke about this to Zofia.

'So what's to be done?'

'There's nothing we can do, except pick ourselves up and try to repair the damage as best we can.' She shrugged. 'The workmen have already started as you can see. We have to hope they can make enough progress over the next couple of days to get us back on track.' Brave words, but she sounded less than hopeful.

She stood up. 'I'll tell you this – we'll have the site guarded night and day from now on. There won't be the chance of anything like this happening again.' She shook her head.

Dexter had come up beside her. It was the first time I'd seen him in several days. For a so-called manager he didn't do much managing. He patted her awkwardly on the shoulder, then drew back, twanging the elastic band on his wrist. 'Don't worry, Zofia. This wasn't your fault. I'm sure it was nothing to do with you. I'll speak to Mr Crombie and we'll get some extra resources in, more hands to help.'

A feeling of anger bubbled up inside me and I felt sorry for Zofia. Of course it wasn't her fault, though she had antagonised Everett, by standing up to him at that last encounter. If it was anyone's fault it was Dexter's. He was supposed to be managing the project.

Almost as if she hadn't heard him, Zofia said, 'Everyone is upset as you can imagine. All that hard work.' For a moment it seemed as if she was about to burst into tears, and I wouldn't have blamed her. However she seemed to collect herself and taking a deep breath said, 'We'll meet at the Pavilion tomorrow morning as planned, try to catch up. We have to go on no matter what.'

As she strode off to where the diggers were huddled deep in conversation with Sven and Ryan, I couldn't help but wonder if I was wrong and this was indeed something to do with the protest group. Unlikely as it seemed, had Everett and his crowd of supporters decided to go beyond mere words?

23

'I'll be on the twelve fifteen ferry. I don't think I'll bring the car. I can as easily get the train from Central Station down to Wemyss Bay.'

This plan of Simon's didn't suit me. 'But I'll need the car for getting round the island. Sometimes we have meetings in the Pavilion, sometimes we have to go out to the site.'

'Not a problem. I can run you to any of the venues. There's no point in having two cars on the island.'

'I don't know what I'll be doing or when. It's difficult to predict.' The idea of Simon ferrying me around, sitting in the car drumming his fingers impatiently as I was kept late somewhere or other, wasn't in the least appealing. Then the solution came to me, a way that would most certainly persuade him. 'You also need some choice about what to do. Won't you want to fit in a few rounds of golf? You know how unpredictable the weather can be on the West coast and you'll want to squeeze in as many games as you can.'

'Mmm,' he said reluctantly. 'I suppose you're right and I had intended to bring my clubs, but it does seem a bit of a waste of money having two cars.'

But having gained the advantage, I wasn't about to backtrack and decision made, we agreed he'd make his own way to the hotel and we'd meet up there.

Now I was running late for the meeting which had been set up with Alexander Crombie and I'd no wish to add to Zofia's troubles. The clearing at the site would continue for a day or two yet, after which a proper assessment could be made. The opening date still hung on a knife edge.

Fortunately one difficulty had been resolved. There had been no more anonymous notes, no further silent calls, though I'd slept only fitfully. Perhaps Harry was right and the phone calls had been a one-off. I certainly hoped so.

It was very likely the damage at the site was proving to be more difficult to sort out than Zofia was leading us to believe. It was in no way her fault, but she might feel a certain responsibility for what had happened and the grand opening on 12th August was looking less and less possible, no matter how hard we all worked. But Alexander Crombie would have the last word.

Many of us were clustered outside the Portakabin, awaiting his arrival, some of the diggers taking the opportunity for a smoke, while others passed the time having a kickabout on the flat part of the site at the bottom of the field. From our vantage point we could see his black car draw up right next to the entrance and Dexter eased himself out, closely followed by Mr Crombie. We watched their progress with interest as they began the climb, stopping halfway for Dexter to point out various parts of the site, waving his hands about to emphasise his words. They were still too far off to make out anything that was being said, but the frown on Crombie's face didn't augur well.

'Oh, oh,' I whispered to Harry who was standing close to Luann, as though to protect her, 'this doesn't look too good.'

'Let's wait and find out what the score is,' said Harry, glancing sideways at Luann to gauge her reaction to this. Certainly she had a lot more to lose than either Harry or I should the project be abandoned.

Zofia was clearly on edge, the shadows under her eyes evidence of how little she had slept. She'd made a great effort with her appearance for this event: her hair was securely tied up in a bun at the back of her head and her normal garb of a navy suit swapped for a stylish coat. She'd even exchanged her usual high heels for a pair of flatter shoes, though they appeared to be more fashionable than robust.

Alexander Crombie wasn't at all what we expected, though Harry whispered as we were introduced to him, 'He's very imposing looking, isn't he?'

He certainly was. He was tall, well over six feet, and broad to match. He sported a thick grey beard which seemed to meld with his thatch of iron grey hair, making his piercing blue eyes look more striking. A deep voice, overlaid with a faint South African accent seemed to suit his appearance, while his baggy grey sweater and combat trousers disguised his incipient paunch.

It was difficult to judge his views on the ravages at the site from the expression on his face. He greeted us affably enough, 'Glad to meet you all at last', gave a spiel about 'terrible losses after all the work everyone had put in', and 'the perpetrators must be punished', but he also stressed how much money had already been spent on the project and now careful consideration would have to be given to the best way to proceed.

'It's a big gamble and I want to be absolutely sure nothing like this happens again.'

Beside him, Zofia fidgeted, twirling a little bit of her hair that had escaped from her tightly wound bun, moving from foot to foot, buttoning and unbuttoning her coat as she appeared to listen intently to every word. The rest of the crew stood in silence, their drooping shoulders hinting at what they thought would be the outcome of this meeting. Although the leaders,

Ryan, Sven and Luann might have work lined up I was sure many of the diggers and the builders would have been depending on this being a lengthy project.

And if it would be bad for any of us if it was now cancelled, how much worse would it be for Zofia. A reputation can be built up over many years and lost in the twinkling of an eye. Still, I had enough to concern myself at the moment and I silently vowed to finish my assignment as soon as possible and send in my invoice, in the increasingly likely event of the project being cancelled.

'I'd like to have a walk up to the far end of the site,' said Crombie, turning to Zofia.

So far Dexter had contented himself with the occasional nod of agreement and twanging the elastic band on his wrist. I gritted my teeth, trying hard to ignore this maddening habit of his.

Zofia went pale and I could understand why. This was the worst part of the site, the one where the proposed fish farm had been completely ruined.

'Man, he'll lose his cool over this,' muttered Ryan. 'It was his pet bit of the project.'

As Crombie slowly began the climb, we all trooped obediently in his wake, not the least bit happy about his reaction to what he would find. The devastation in this part of the site could be the deciding factor.

In the event, it wasn't as bad as we feared and although clearly furious at the vandalism at the fish farm, a little sigh of relief went round as he said, 'Well, it sure is a terrible sight, but I've been told it can be fixed.' Then he added, breaking into a smile, 'I know you've all worked really hard on this and that starting again won't be easy, but I consider this an important contribution to the island economy. It's been my dream for so many years to come back here, repay what the island where I was born has given me. Let's not get downhearted, defeated by people with no sense. It's time to start again. Let's go for it. Dexter and I will be staying on the island for a couple of days, having another look at the site. Keep digging, everyone, make sure you've surveyed the site properly and then the building work can go ahead quickly. The St Blane's theme park will be ready by 12th August.'

A cheer went up from the crowd and he raised his hand in acknowledgement before bidding us farewell and heading slowly back down to the roadway where his car sat waiting.

'Looks as if we can get it all together now,' said Ryan with a grin, signalling to his band of diggers to get back to work. 'No time to lose, friends.'

'Yes, thank goodness,' said Zofia, sighing with relief. 'The police have assured me they'll keep an eye on the place, make sure there are regular patrols round this way. But to make sure,' she added hastily, 'we've hired a firm from the mainland, *Everin Secure Ltd*. That should see off any potential intruders.'

'The police will surely pursue those responsible, won't leave things like this.' Luann sounded anxious for a positive response.

'Absolutely. There's no way they should get away with causing all this damage. We've all a good idea – a very good idea – who was responsible.'

She could only be referring to Everett and his fellow protesters, but I wasn't entirely sure. Certainly they'd been making a lot of noise, protesting about this development every chance they had, putting up posters all round the island, but criminal damage? That was another league altogether.

I stood looking at the archaeologists, closely followed by the team of diggers, as they made their way back to the latest trench, then spied the builders heading for the *Devil's Ride* to make a start on repairing the damage.

Everyone had been so pleased to resume work, delighted the project wasn't to be cancelled; I doubted if any of them had picked up the underlying threat in Crombie's words. He wanted the project to be finished, the site to be opened in time for the feast day of St Blane. Was that achievable? If it wasn't would the site actually be finished? While the others went back to work with a will, a niggle of doubt itched at the back of my mind. In a way I could understand why the opening date was so important and if the project overran Crombie would be disappointed, but surely this theme park was destined for a long life and a week or two would make no difference, especially as the birth date of St Blane was little more than a guess.

Leaving the others to sort out the site as best they could, I said goodbye and headed off, intending to work on the last part of the visitor guide and then phone Harry to update him.

We were well on the way to fulfilling our contract and that was our main concern. And to finish this section of the work all we had to do was meet up with Nathan and agree on which photos to use. There should be nothing difficult about that.

24

The news wasn't good. If the police knew who had
vandalised the site at St Blane's they weren't giving
anything away. Evidence, it would appear, was scarce
and even the most eager gossipers had fallen silent.

'Why should we worry, friends,' said Ryan as we sat
together in the small room in the Pavilion waiting for
Zofia to start what we hoped would be our last meeting.
I wasn't too sure what would happen to the others, but
as far as Harry and I were concerned we'd done our bit,
had produced the draft of a guide we were pleased with,
combining enough of Harry's historical research with
several interesting anecdotes about the life and times of
Blane. Whether they were true was another matter
entirely.

Nathan had been happy to agree he'd send over a
selection of photos for us to make a choice, although he
gave me the impression he was more interested in his
own portfolio than in the visitor guide.

'Don't you want to know who caused all that
damage?' said Luann. For some reason (though at a
guess it might be something to do with Nathan) she'd
changed her glasses for contact lens and had her hair
cut short, really short and every time I glanced over at
her I did a kind of double take. It made her look so
much younger with the cropped, almost boyish look
rather than that mass of hair straggling down her back.
It reminded me a visit to the hairdresser was overdue
and I resolved to phone later, make an appointment for
when I'd be back on the mainland.

Luann made a face, saying, 'As long as they don't
come back, what's the point? If they are caught what

will happen? A reprimand and a few hours of community service. That won't help anyone.'

'Perhaps they'll be required to work at the site, help repair the damage they caused.'

Ryan gave a laugh that was more a snort of derision. 'Do you honestly think they'd be allowed anywhere near the site? No way, my friends.'

Everyone was convinced the damage had been caused by the protesters, but I wasn't so sure. Such action wouldn't help their cause and I didn't see any of Everett's followers being the kind of people to take a sledgehammer to the *Devil's Ride* somehow.

Besides, even those who agreed that the site was a desecration of the story of St Blane wouldn't be happy to support something like this, not judging by the protesters I'd met so far. Most of them appeared to be far too elderly to engage in this kind of vandalism. Everett himself struck me as more bluster than substance, interested in making himself important and the theme park was no more than a way of doing so.

As though reading my thoughts, Harry said, 'It might have been some of the local youths on a spree. I've heard those caves over at Dunagoil are used by youngsters as a drinking den.'

'Who on earth told you that?' Luann looked astonished. 'How would they get out there for a start? Honestly, the stories some people come up with.' She shook her head in disbelief, stopping suddenly as she realised she no longer had that mass of hair to make an impression.

Harry seemed rather piqued by her reaction. 'Well, apparently there's been a lot of activity. Lights seen at night, noise, that kind of thing. What else could it be but youngsters? They're the only ones with the stamina to get across the rugged landscape and out to the caves.'

Fortunately, before things could become more acrimonious, the door was flung open and Zofia came hurrying into the room, clutching a sheaf of papers, her laptop case slung over her shoulder. Today she'd exchanged her usual business suit for a more casual look of trousers and a top.

'Bet those cost a fair bit of money,' muttered Luann.

'Everyone ready?' Zofia said, dumping everything on the table at the front so that most of the papers in the pile slid off on to the floor in a jumbled heap. For someone who was always banging on about management techniques she displayed very little ability.

No one moved to help her and it was a few minutes before she could begin, after sorting out the various papers.

She gazed round, pausing to make sure she had our attention before taking a deep breath and saying, 'There's been some news about Benjie's death.'

No one spoke, the silence stretching out as we waited to hear what she would say next. 'Yes,' she said, as though determined to draw this out for as long as possible. 'Poor Benjie was murdered and thank goodness the police have arrested someone for it.'

There was a rapid intake of breath as the full significance of this sunk in and she smiled, pleased at the impact her announcement had made. At last she had our full attention.

Sven was the first to speak. 'How do you know this, Zofia? There has been nothing about it in the media or on the internet.'

'I only found out a short time ago. I *do* have contacts,' she replied, making no attempt to disguise her pleasure at being the one to deliver the news. 'Some of us were called by Mr Crombie's secretary early this morning.'

'Spill the beans, Zofia. Who's been done for it?' Ryan made no attempt to keep the impatience out of his voice.

'Well...' said Zofia, pausing for dramatic effect, 'they've arrested Everett, the leader of the protesters.'

'Everett? Why on earth would he kill Benjie?'

Zofia shrugged, frowning to show her annoyance at the way her announcement had been received. 'How would I know that? The police have done their work, they've taken Everett in for questioning.'

One thing was for certain. It explained why there had been no sign of Everett or any of the protesters in the past couple of days, though it seemed impossible that he could have been responsible for Benjie's death. Everett was someone who enjoyed being the leader of a protest group, something that gave him status. I couldn't see him as a killer somehow.

'So he's been charged, locked up?' Ryan's question brought me back to the discussion.

Zofia shuffled her feet. 'Not *exactly*. He's been taken in for questioning so they must be sure he's the one responsible.' This latter statement came out in a rush.

'I think not,' said Luann. 'That means what it says. He's being questioned. Let's not spread any more rumours, Zofia. There's been enough of that sort of thing already.'

'And how does this change anything?' Ryan sounded worried, perhaps envisaging yet another hold-up to the dig. 'Please don't josh me about more delays.'

Zofia looked deflated as though this wasn't the reaction she'd been expecting. 'Well, it doesn't *change* anything for us, not really,' she said tetchily. 'We have to continue as normal.'

There was an undercurrent in the room, a feeling something wasn't quite right, but then few of us had met Benjie, so his death, although a dreadful event, didn't affect us greatly. We'd have been pleased to hear Everett was the culprit, close the episode, but with no firm news we could only focus on the task in hand and within a few minutes we were once again engaged in a plethora of management speak. Zofia resumed her chosen role with even more gusto, as though to make up for lost time.

I kept re-running this latest exchange in my head, scarcely paying attention to what she was saying and only came to as she gazed round a few minutes later, as though counting us one by one, and said, 'Where's Nathan?'

25

As happens so often, on my return to the hotel events took an unexpected turn. Georgie was clearly at a loose end, hardly surprising as I'd the impression there were few guests.

She put down the newspaper she was reading and came round to the front of the desk as I tried to slink past. I was already late, having promised Simon I'd join him for lunch at one and it was now nearer two o'clock, delayed as I'd been while Zofia tried to track down Nathan.

'We were supposed to have a presentation of those photos of the site today,' she'd raged. 'They were to be used for pre-publicity articles. He'd even taken some by moonlight to capture the full impact of the history of St Blane's. Calls to his phone are going to voicemail.'

Unfortunately Georgie wasn't to be deterred, no matter how fast I tried to scurry past, reckoning even the briefest word would give her an opening to engage me in conversation.

She stepped out from behind the desk and stood in front of me, barring my way. 'Oh, Mrs Cameron, have you heard the news?'

Now, in spite of my determination to ignore her as politely as I could, her question stopped me in my tracks. How could I resist this?

'No,' I said, not quite stopping, but pausing sufficiently for her to be able to talk to me.

A smile crept across her face. 'You know they had someone in for questioning in connection with Benjie's murder.'

'Yes, yes,' I replied somewhat impatiently, 'I did know that.' I quickened my pace towards the corridor leading to the bedrooms. 'Everett has been charged, or rather questioned, in connection with his murder.'

I was wrong: this wasn't what she wanted to tell me as I soon realised when she grabbed me by the arm. 'Everett was taken in for questioning, that's correct, but he's been released as there's no way he could have been responsible.' She smiled, paused, knowing what she was about to say was a piece of interesting news. 'He can't have been responsible,' she repeated, a note of triumph in her voice, 'because...he has a cast-iron alibi.'

'And what might that be?' Now I was very curious.

'He was on the mainland collecting his new car at the time they think Benjie was killed. It's a brand new Alfa Romeo, from what I hear. For an artist who doesn't sell many paintings he seems to have plenty of money to flash about.'

If it was true, it confirmed my belief that Everett was innocent, but left the question of who'd been responsible for killing Benjie. As this appeared to be the extent of her information, I made my excuses and headed for my room where another surprise awaited me.

Still trying to think through the implications of Georgie's revelation that Everett had been cleared of Benjie Anderson's death (though there had as yet been no other arrest, which still left the whole episode on the level of gossip) I opened the room door to find Simon on the phone.

'Yes, yes, that would be no problem,' I heard him say, motioning me to be quiet. 'I'll look forward to confirmation tomorrow.' He ended the call.

'What would be no problem?'

162

He grinned and punched the air as he swung round to face me. '*Scottish Alignment Limited* have asked me to prepare and deliver three days' training to their new recruits. They've a great reputation and this could be the start of a long run of work if I get it right.'

'They're based in Inverness, aren't they? So you'll have to stay up there for the duration, I expect. Thank goodness we decided to have this break now.'

'Mmm.' He looked sheepish, drumming his fingers on the bedside table, faster and faster till I stopped him by placing my hand over his. 'It's not as simple as that. They want me to start at once. The company they originally awarded the contract to has gone into administration and Calvin, the managing director of the company remembered me from some work I did for a friend of his. Everything has been set up, so it's too good an opportunity to pass up. Sorry about our holiday, Alison, but you do understand, don't you?'

With forced cheerfulness he said, 'There'll be plenty of opportunities for holidays on Bute.' He waited for my reaction, all the while watching me closely.

'So when do you leave?' Much as I appreciated Simon's delight at having another contract so soon, when he thought he'd be hard pressed for work, a little shiver of disappointment went through me, though I tried not to show it.

One reason for our joint decision to start working freelance was to give us more leisure, let us pick and choose our projects, spend more time together. Instead we seemed to be scurrying from job to job, desperately trying to keep afloat in a tough economic climate and now this chance to spend even this short holiday together was vanishing fast. Pleased as I was for him, I knew that if he was successful with this contract, others would follow, giving us fewer opportunities to find time together to sort out the problems in our relationship.

Taking a deep breath, trying hard to sound positive I said, 'There's still time to have a meal out tonight, enjoy the rest of the evening together.'

'Of course, of course,' he said, eager to please. If I'd suggested a picnic on the beach at midnight he'd probably have agreed.

We headed for a restaurant in Rothesay, but it was obvious his mind was on his new job. He kept checking his phone, frowning from time to time until I said, 'For goodness sake, no one is going to be in touch at this time of night,' and he guiltily put it in his pocket, out of sight, if not quite out of mind.

Our chat over the meal was desultory, going from one trivial topic to another, as though a gulf had again opened up between us and I only hoped this was another temporary glitch. Trouble was, we seemed to be having more and more of these lately. We'd have some kind of crisis, then all would be harmonious for a time, then something else would happen to upset the balance. Perhaps it was as well he was heading for the mainland tomorrow morning to make the journey north to Inverness and I wondered if all couples who'd been married for a long time experienced these creaks in their relationship.

Sometimes I looked back on those early days when we first met, when we were newly-weds and wondered if we were the same people.

So there was a kind of false gaiety in our evening, as though we were both trying too hard and problems lay unspoken and unaddressed between us. Best to continue to bury my head in the sand, to hope that everything would work out in the end.

In the meantime, another separation loomed and as we got ready for bed around ten o'clock ('I have to catch the six thirty ferry,' said Simon, hurrying me to finish our not-so-leisurely meal) there was a silence, unresolved issues, between us which didn't bode well.

It was a long time before I eventually fell asleep, lying in the dark thinking back over all the years we'd been together, all we'd been through, while Simon lay gently snoring beside me, unaware of my inner turmoil.

By early morning I'd fallen into a deep sleep, so deep I only vaguely registered Simon pull back the covers and swing his legs out of bed to creep round the room, get ready to depart for the early ferry. And I was only dimly aware of him kissing me gently on the head and murmuring goodbye. Or perhaps I preferred not to acknowledge his departure.

26

To my surprise, Harry was sitting in the reception area as I came down to breakfast later that morning. After much deliberation, I'd come to the conclusion my problems with Simon would have to be put on hold if there was to be any possibility of completing the visitor guide. Our work here was almost complete. In a couple of days we'd be able to leave the island and finish writing and preliminary editing at home. Oh, the value of technology for a co-operative piece of work like this.

'Something wrong?' I said as he jumped to his feet.

'Something very wrong,' he replied, glancing around nervously, though there was no one else in sight. The reception area was deserted as I could see Georgie in the dining room: it appeared she was on her own and having to help serve breakfast, something she was doing with ill will as she banged the plates down on the tables in front of the startled guests, an elderly couple who must have arrived the previous evening.

Harry grabbed me by the elbow and steered me in to the far corner by the door. 'It's Nathan,' he said. 'I've said we'll go along and check his flat.'

'Why on earth should we do that?'

He wrinkled his nose. 'Well, we're the ones working most closely with him and I promised Zofia...' his voice trailed off as he saw the expression on my face.

'Good heavens, Harry. Why can't one of the others go? It wouldn't surprise me if he'd gone over to the mainland for a couple of days to get away from all this.'

'Without telling anyone?'

Harry looked so crestfallen at my display of temper I said grudgingly, 'Oh, let's do it then. Do you have his address?'

Harry pulled a scrap of paper from his pocket. 'He's in a rented flat at Ascog. It won't take us long.'

'And what if he's not there? What do we do?'

'It's a conversion. It's one of a number of flats in an old house on the front. There's bound to be a caretaker and we can leave a message.'

I insisted we travel in my car. Concentrating on the road out to Ascog defused my annoyance at this errand Harry had volunteered us for.

Nathan's flat was one of about ten in a large, very grand house overlooking the little bay at Ascog and we made our way along a curving drive, with regimented lines of trees that would form a canopy of green in summer, but now pointed skeletal fingers skywards.

'It's number three,' said Harry consulting his piece of paper as I parked beside an ornate curving staircase topped on each side by a large stone urn bright with pale yellow narcissi and red tulips.

'Well, let's find it and discover what Nathan's up to,' I said, locking up the car and striding ahead up the steps, forcing Harry had to break into a trot to keep up with me.

Flat Number Three wasn't where I'd expected. It wasn't part of the main house, but round at the back of the building as the arrow at the bottom of the staircase indicated, if only I'd taken the time to look. The arrangement of flats seemed to be haphazard, but we found Number Three with no difficulty and I lifted my hand to rap on the bright red door.

'We're not going to wait,' I said. 'If there's no reply we'll try to find if there's a caretaker's flat or else put a note through the letterbox.'

'That's odd,' said Harry, coming up behind me, pulling me back.

'What now?'

He pushed in front of me, and gave the door a nudge. It swung open easily. 'It isn't locked,' he said.

'Oh, this is Bute, Harry. He's probably gone out and forgotten to lock it.'

'In which case, he can't be far away.'

We stood and looked at each other, at a loss to know what to do next. 'Do we go in?' said Harry at last.

This was a different situation altogether and suddenly I had a feeling of dread, though I didn't want to show it. I'd so easily dismissed Nathan's non-appearance. What if he was ill, had been unable to get in touch with anyone? How callous we'd seem then.

'We'd better find out, now that we're here.' I sounded a lot more positive than I felt.

Harry pushed the door open slowly and together we edged in, calling out, 'Nathan, are you there?' as we made our way at a snail's pace down the long narrow hallway, our footsteps sounding extra loud on the polished wooden floor.

'It's a bit intrusive, going through his place like this,' I whispered, grabbing Harry by the elbow. 'It's clear he's gone out. What if he comes back and finds us? What will we say?'

'If he comes back we've every reason for being here. He should have told Zofia if there was a problem. She's tried often enough to contact him.'

'Yes, but you know what these artistic people are like, he…'

But Harry wasn't listening and I stood back as he opened the first door on the right, leading to what appeared to be the main room in the flat.

'He's not here,' I said, becoming more and more uncomfortable by the minute at trespassing on Nathan's property. 'Let's go. We can leave a note behind the front door and it'll look as if we put it through the letterbox.' Determined not to be persuaded otherwise, I started to scrabble in my bag for a pen and a piece of paper.

Suddenly Harry shouted, 'Oh, no...'

'What's wrong?' I said, spinning round.

He held up his arm. All colour had drained from his face. 'Stay back, Alison. Don't come any nearer.'

'What do you mean?' I tried to nudge him out of the way but he stood his ground, forcing me to draw back.

'I said, don't come any nearer.'

The resolve in his voice took me by surprise and I moved a few steps away, but not before I'd had a glimpse into the room.

We'd been very much mistaken. Nathan was here all right, but he wasn't ill, hadn't fallen out with Zofia. He was lying sprawled across the floor in front of the fireplace and from the amount of blood that had seeped from the large gash in his head into the white fireside rug there was absolutely no doubt he was dead.

27

I sat with Harry in the police station in Rothesay, ready to give a statement, trembling from head to foot.

'What could have happened?' I kept asking over and over. 'Are they sure it wasn't an accident? Couldn't he have fallen and hit his head on the hearth?'

Harry shook his head. 'No one knows for certain but it looks like a break in, a robbery that went wrong.'

'A break in? What could he have of value? Nathan didn't strike me as someone with expensive possessions. It was only a rented flat.'

'I don't know about that. There was all that camera equipment for a start. That might have been what they were after. We'll know soon enough.'

'His camera might have been stolen? You realise what that means?' For a moment the awful nature of his death was overtaken by personal concerns.

'No.' Harry waited for me to continue, a puzzled look on his face.

'If his camera's gone then so have all the photos, including those we needed for the visitor guide.'

'Of course,' said Harry, light dawning. 'What on earth will we do now?'

'What can we do? Hope he had the photos on a memory stick or something.' Suddenly realising this made me sound heartless, I hastened to say, 'Not that any of it matters in view of what's happened to the poor man.'

Harry's phone pinged and he scrabbled in his pocket to pull it out, frowning as he read the text message. He leaned over and whispered, 'That's a message from Zofia. They've done the post-mortem on Benjie and word is it looks very likely he was killed by a blow from a spade.'

'How on earth do they know that? Anyway, there are lots of spades on the island and any one of them could have used to kill Benjie.'

'No idea,' said Harry. 'Perhaps they...'

Constable Goodson came in to the room. 'The C.I.D are on their way over on the eleven o'clock ferry. Anything else you need? More tea?'

I shook my head. More tea was the last thing I wanted.

What could we do but sit and wait as instructed, occasionally exchanging a word or two to break the silence, wondering how soon they'd be able to find out the truth about Nathan's death.

Thank goodness Simon had left the island to take up his new post with the company in Inverness. I dreaded to think what he would say when I told him what I was involved in now.

Just when I thought our wait would never end, there was the sound of voices outside the door and when the police came in they couldn't have been more courteous. Even so, introductions over, Detective Inspector Fulton made it clear from the start that their intention was to clear this new murder up as quickly as possible.

She nodded to the Sergeant, 'You'll have organised an interview room, I'm sure?'

'Of course.' The Sergeant bristled a little at this suggestion he might not be up to speed. 'The room is right across the corridor.'

'Fine, we'll begin at once,' she said briskly and left.

'Did you catch the sergeant's name,' I whispered to Harry but only received a shake of the head in reply.

171

Detective Inspector Fulton grimaced, then spoke quietly to Constable Goodson who said, 'We'll see Alison Cameron first. If you would come with me to the interview room.'

I stood up a little unsteadily and followed her across the corridor. The room wasn't exactly small, but it felt claustrophobic and when I was invited to sit opposite DI Fulton and the sergeant, it reminded me of being called to the head teacher's room for some misdemeanour or other. I'd been interviewed before, on more than one occasion unfortunately, but it didn't make it any easier and I answered nervously, trying to relax and stop myself appearing guilty. Thank goodness Harry had held me back, that I'd had no more than a glimpse of Nathan's body sprawled on the white rug, though the image would stay with me for a long time.

In spite of the fact he was the photographer for our visitor guide I knew next to nothing about Nathan and certainly nothing about his personal life, or who might have wanted to kill him.

We'd been told we could leave once our interviews were over, but outside the police station I sat in my car, waiting for Harry and as he came down the steps I beckoned to him come in to sit beside me. 'Over here,' I said.

For a moment or two neither of us spoke, but sat gazing at the traffic going up and down the High Street. Then I broke the silence, 'What do you think happened? Why would anyone want to kill Nathan? He was only a photographer, for goodness' sake.'

Harry shrugged. 'I've absolutely no idea, Alison.' He turned and stared at me. 'Are you sure you're okay?'

Did I detect a little feeling of guilt that he'd insisted we go along to Nathan's flat? If he hadn't been so determined someone else would have had the task of discovering the body and we wouldn't have been involved.

We sat for a little while longer, watching a pair of seagulls swoop and dive towards the moat at Rothesay Castle and finally Harry said, 'We've very little work left to do here, Alison. I asked if we could leave the island and the answer was yes. They know where to find us if they want to question us again, although there's nothing we can tell them.'

'You're right, though it's strange about poor Nathan. And what will we do about the photos?'

We'll sort something out.' Harry pushed open the passenger door. 'We'll meet this afternoon in the library and try to work out a plan of action, agree a timescale.' He stopped and chuckled, in spite of the gravity of the situation. 'Heavens, I'm beginning to sound like Zofia. What I mean is I've taken lots of photos and perhaps we can make do with those. After that, I suggest we take our leave of Zofia and the others and do as we always intended – finish off the work at home.'

I didn't want to hurt Harry's feelings but I very much doubted if his photos would be of a professional quality and silently hoped Nathan had made back up copies of his photos, though at the moment all I could think of was that image of Nathan's body lying sprawled on the white rug.

In the meantime we each went our separate ways, but with the day being so lovely, I'd no intention of going back to work. I needed something to take my mind off recent events and headed for the beach at St

Ninian's to find a quiet spot to open my E-reader and make a start on the latest book by Norman Deeley. The fictional story of *Murder on the Isle of Bute* might take my mind off what was happening in real life.

28

Later that day, feeling more composed after a walk on the beach and time out with the luxury of reading, the best way to banish the mental image of Nathan lying dead on the rug in his flat was to go back to work. Deliberately concentrating hard on sorting through the latest draft of the visitor guide, with all the sections spread out in piles in front of me on a table in the hotel lounge, it was a few seconds before I realised the phone ringing was mine.

The number that came up wasn't one I immediately recognised and my heart gave a lurch in case it might be the mystery caller of the other night. If it was, I thought it might be the final straw, that I'd be on the next ferry back to the mainland and I hesitated before replying. I needn't have worried. It was Kerry from the Rothesay library.

'Alison? Glad I caught you. I remembered you said something about heading off the island soon and wanted to let you know about that book you were looking for.' So she hadn't yet heard about this latest death.

'Book?' For a moment I'd no idea what she was talking about. 'Oh yes, *A Short History of Finds at St Blane's*?' Has it turned up?'

'We haven't found that one, but there is another which deals with the 7th Century site that you might be interested in.'

My first reaction was one of disappointment then, not wanting to upset her after she'd gone to so much trouble to track down something useful, I said, 'I'll come along and collect it this afternoon. I have to come up to the library anyway.'

'Great,' she said. 'I'm off this afternoon but I'll put it aside and Tina will give it to you. Remember we close from one to two for lunch.'

After thanking her again, I returned to the task in hand, anxious to have everything tied up before my last meeting with Harry, hoping he'd be satisfied with the result. In the circumstances, with so much happening, this final draft would have to do.

Harry had spent so long on the research, had found out everything there was to know about St Blane and his times as far as I could tell, but I had to make sure there was enough information to be helpful, while not overwhelming the visitors with too many dry facts. I'd finally managed to edit some thirty pages of text into a booklet of no more than ten pages, including photos. Every time I looked at those spaces where Nathan's photos should have been I'd a feeling of nausea. I only hoped that somehow or other we could resolve the problem, and quickly.

I slid all the papers into a separate folder, keeping the draft of the guide and placing it at the front of my bag before heading for the library, realising too late I'd forgotten about lunch. No matter, I'd be able to stop by the Electric Bakery in Montague Street and buy a sandwich there, though I doubted if I'd be able to face food at the moment.

By the time I reached the library, Harry was already sitting in the foyer area, leafing through the latest copy of *The Buteman*.

'Look at this,' he said, pointing to the front page. Those protesters have been drumming up even more support.'

But I'd no intention of becoming involved in discussions about Everett and his followers. 'I won't be a minute. I've a book to collect and better do it now while I remember,' I said heading through to the main library.

'Yes, here you are, Mrs Cameron,' said Tina, handing over a padded brown envelope, 'did you make arrangements about having it on long-term loan?'

In the end she seemed perfectly happy with my credentials and I stowed the envelope at the bottom of my bag before returning to Harry.

'Strange to think this is our last meeting on the island,' I said, sitting down beside him. 'After this it's a matter of writing it all up and getting it to the editor.' Pre-empting any comments I added, 'And you'll have plenty to do after we've finished this, writing the book you've decided on.'

Harry looked pleased I'd remembered this plan. 'Would it surprise you to learn I've already made a start on it? There seemed no point in waiting till I was home: better to draft a couple of initial chapters while I was in the mood and on the island to check any facts. Besides I managed to get some cracking photos of the St Blane's site and of the theme park site early on.'

'That's great, Harry, you'll do well with the book and the photos will help sell it,' I said, only half paying attention.

'Yes.' He beamed. 'Tell you what, I'll e-mail you the photos. There are at least sixty and I'm sure we'll be able to use some of them for the visitor guide if Nathan's don't turn up.'

The mention of Nathan's name reduced us both to silence and we sat quietly for a little while before I said, trying to make my voice sound normal, 'Yes, we have to find photos some way or other.'

The last thing I needed at the moment was lots of photos to go through, but we'd no option. We would need them. Without photos the visitor guide would be useless. Trying hard to sound more upbeat I said, 'Anyway, let's get this work finished and then we can head home.'

We set to and by four o'clock we'd completed the task as best we could. I yawned and stretched. 'Do you think we've done enough?'

'Absolutely,' replied Harry, then he frowned. 'Though I wonder if we should put in a bit more detail about the Bronze Age to give visitors more background.'

'I think you want to keep that for your own book,' I said hurriedly. 'Remember this has to be a booklet people can carry in their pocket as they go round the site.'

'I suppose so.' There was a note of reluctance in his voice.

I ignored this and standing up to cram everything in to my bag said, 'We'll keep in touch as agreed. I don't think we'll have to meet up again, though I dare say we'll be back for the opening of the site.'

'And there will be the investigation about Nathan's death,' he said, but I'd been deliberately trying to avoid talking or even thinking about that.

We left the library and shook hands, promising to keep in regular contact. He turned and waved as he reached the corner of the street beside Rothesay Castle, leaving me with the impression he was more than a little sorry that his time on the island was over, in spite of all the difficulties of the past few days.

As for me, I could hardly wait to get back to the hotel and find out what lay between the covers of the book Tina had found for me, but before I could reach the privacy of my room to make a start on the library book, Georgie caught up with me in the foyer.

'I believe you're leaving in a couple of days. Are you planning to come back any time soon?'

'Probably not. What I have to do now can be written at home.'

'Surely you'll have an invite to the opening of the St Blane's theme park in August. You'll come back over for that.'

'Of course. I wouldn't miss it.'

'You could book in now if you wanted to. We'd be happy to give you a discount.'

'I'll wait,' I said, thinking on my feet. 'There may be others who'll want to come over with me.'

'Ah. So you might need several rooms?'

Having satisfied her on this score, I headed for my room and dumped my bag on the floor before ripping open the envelope, releasing a musty smell of old paper and leather.

The book wasn't what I'd expected. It was a slim volume, its age evident from the slightly tatty brown vellum cover, the title on the spine, *Some facts on the Ancient Site of St Blane's*. The date on the frontispiece showed it had been published well before the discovery of the Hoard and as it was hardly the most exciting of titles, I opened it with few expectations of finding anything of interest. Indeed the first few pages, taken up with numerous dedications, revealed nothing new in the way of information and I skipped subsequent pages before stopping at a chapter entitled, *The Missing Treasure of St Blane*.

179

Ah, so there were stories of the monks having valuables at the monastery and I read on with increasing excitement till I reached the final paragraph, rereading it a couple of times to make sure I'd completely understood.

"The monks, having taken cognisance of the many raids and incursions of the Vikings in to the neighbouring islands, are believed to have taken the treasures from the chapel and hidden them well. When the Vikings reached Bute, having laid waste to Iona and the Ayrshire coast, they were aggrieved to find so little booty and took their revenge on the monks, killing all those who had stayed to guard the monastery.

Among the treasures reputed to have been hidden and never again found were the Reliquary of St Blane, the gold chalice encrusted with precious gems, the Holy Rood of gold used for Easter services and a wealth of other items of great value".

Beside the text there were line drawings of what the chalice and the Holy Rood might have looked like, probably as much based on guesswork as anything though the writer was at pains to point out how much research he'd done on similar church items.

I turned back to the beginning of the book. The date of publication was 1816, well before the Hoard had been unearthed and I rummaged around to find my notebook and check exactly what had been discovered. Yes, my memory was right. The workmen had found some twenty seven coins, a couple of gold rings, three gold bars and one silver one, but there was no reference to a reliquary or anything else mentioned in this book.

Was it possible these other more valuable items had also been found by the workmen and they hadn't told anyone? Had offered up these lesser items to throw everyone off the scent. No, that wasn't likely. They would have been found out for sure. You couldn't keep news of such valuables secret for long on the island. Besides, where would workmen of that time know to sell such goods?

Yet if this was correct, if the monks had hidden the treasure as the book described, it must still be out there somewhere, in some location the monks had thought safe. Even with little possibility of success, what harm could it do to make a few enquiries? Somehow there was this niggling feeling that all the events of the past few weeks were linked and although I wished things hadn't happened as they had, I felt this obligation to find out about Nathan. There was more to his death than a mere break-in or robbery, no matter what anyone else thought.

And so, in spite of my determination to do no more than demanded by this commission, not to become involved, I knew there was no way I could rest until I found out the truth. There had been too much happening, too many unexplained events, too much gossip and innuendo. Someone had another agenda, something more than setting up a theme park modelled on the life of St Blane. Of that I was now certain.

29

Now that he'd been released, been cleared of any involvement in Benjie's death, Everett seemed bolder than ever. He was to be seen at almost every event on the island, together with the most loyal of his followers, holding up those wretched banners, making trouble for anyone who was in favour of the theme park.

'He's only produced these notices, asking us to put them up in our window,' said the owner of the Fancy Goods shop on the front at Rothesay. 'I believe he's asking everyone.' And she held up a poorly produced photocopy of a garish hand-written notice NO THEME PARK.

'And will you display it?' I asked.

'Not likely,' she replied, tearing it up and popping the pieces in the recycling bin behind the counter. 'We need all the business we can get.'

I was in town because my plan had been to return the book to the library in the morning after checking out from the hotel and before heading for the ferry, but now I was less sure. I used my phone to take photos of the relevant pages, but soon realised this was going to take forever. Far better to ask for it out on loan with a promise to return it within the month. By then it would be early summer and the island would be at its best, the weather soft and mild. Perhaps I could persuade Simon to come with me, take a couple of days out and have that holiday we'd been promising ourselves.

Whatever came about, there was no way I'd be able to rest until this mystery was solved and with Simon's original words ringing in my ears, 'Make sure you don't get involved in anything except the work you've agreed to do,' words I resolutely ignored, I phoned Harry with the excuse of wanting to include a little more of his research in the booklet. If he was surprised to hear from me so soon after we'd said goodbye, he didn't mention it.

'But you said there was more than enough in the way of dry facts in it, Alison. Why have you changed your mind?'

'I don't want all of it, Harry, I'm only really interested in that bit to do with the Viking invasion.'

'Really?'

'Yes,' then, suddenly inspired, I added, 'lots of schools now study the Vikings as part of their history projects. I'm sure that would be of interest to parents as well as children.'

This reason seemed to satisfy him. 'Okay. I'll e-mail the stuff over and send the photos at the same time.'

I said, 'That would be most helpful, Harry. I look forward to receiving them.'

He rang off and I'd the impression he was pleased I was at last showing the interest his hard work deserved. Quashing any guilty feelings about this subterfuge, I resolved to go back to the library book and make some notes. Perhaps attempting to condense some of the information would make things clearer, help me think through a solution.

I spent the rest of the evening in my room, lying on the bed, reading and re-reading the book, treating myself to another bottle of wine from the minibar, though judging by the amount of dust on all the items it contained, it would seem I was the first person to use this particular facility since it had been originally stocked. For that reason I decided to forgo the packets of peanuts, hungry though I was.

By midnight I'd made copious notes, had scrutinised every last sentence, re-examined all the line drawings of the artefacts likely to have been part of the monastery's treasure, but there were no clues to where anything might have been buried and eventually I had to admit defeat and crawl into bed, exhausted by the efforts of the day. Of course the whole thing might be nonsense. The Vikings might well have made off with all the riches and this story might be one someone had come up with to make the site more interesting. The fact that there had been other excavations, all of them with no success made this seem all the more likely. Why was I getting involved in myth and legend?

Somewhere in the middle of the night, well before dawn, I wakened with a start. For a moment or two I was disorientated, couldn't think where I was and then realised I'd been dreaming. Although it was a dream I'd the feeling there was something very important in my subconscious and I lay there in the dark, trying to recall what it was, trying to force myself back into the dream, but nothing would come and eventually I began to drift off again, hoping if I didn't try to think about it I'd remember whatever it was.

All to no avail and by morning I awoke with that gritty eyed feeling that comes from a bad night's sleep. A stop and start tepid shower (not deliberate, it was the hottest I could get it) restored me to some kind of wakefulness but I envisaged a waste of a day ahead. Thank goodness it was almost time to go home.

It didn't take me long to pack. The only clothes I'd worn of the few I'd brought had been the thick jumpers and warm trousers. There'd been no social occasions for anything lighter and more decorative. Finally I stowed the library book at the bottom of my case though it was highly unlikely that there would be anything of help no matter how many times I read it. But the librarian had gone to a lot of trouble to find it for me and, not wanting to seem ungrateful, I reasoned it was more than likely I'd be back on the island within the month. In spite of the agreement that the rest of the work would be completed in the comfort of my home in Glasgow, I'd this feeling it wouldn't be as simple as that.

A double check of the room to make sure I'd left nothing behind (something I was prone to) and I headed down to Reception to settle my bill. I groaned inwardly when I saw Georgie was on duty again: no doubt she'd try to persuade me to book in advance for the gala opening of the St Blane's theme park, no matter how many times I used the excuse of not knowing how many we'd be. To be truthful though they had done their best, it wasn't the level of comfort I preferred and there were far better hotels on the island.

'Sorry, Georgie, I'm in a rush,' I said forestalling any attempt to engage me in a lengthy conversation as I scrabbled for my credit card, remembering to include the bottles of wine from the minibar.

She laughed. 'Oh, Mrs Cameron, I would have thought some time on the island would have relaxed you. You know no one is ever in a rush here. Why would they be?'

'Yes, but I have to stop by the library on my way to the ferry,' I said, though why I needed to make an excuse I'd no idea.

'If it's a book you have to return, I can do that for you,' she said. 'Leave it with me.'

'No, no, I want to extend the loan.'

'Ah, some interesting thriller then?'

'No.' Before I could stop myself I said, 'It's a book about St Blane's and the treasure the monks are supposed to have hidden.' Then I added, realising I'd said too much. 'It's probably all nonsense, but as I've been writing the visitor guide for the theme park, it's of some interest.'

To my surprise she made a little sound of displeasure. 'Yes, we all know the stories and many people over the years have tried to find the possessions the monks are supposed to have hidden, but no one has ever been successful. A lot of nonsense, if you ask me. These stories are usually no more than that - stories.'

With that she turned her attention to laboriously making up my bill and no more was said.

But if Georgie knew about the stories, that over the years the treasure had been hunted for, who else knew about it?

30

Rothesay Bay was calm, glass-like, as the *MV Bute* left the pier and headed out into the waters of the Firth of Clyde. *The Waverley*, the last seagoing paddle steamer, was tied up on the other side of the pier and as I headed up to the passenger deck the day trippers were streaming down the gangplank, chattering excitedly, calling to friends.

Given the clement weather, I'd a certain reluctance to leave Bute, but kept reminding myself my work here was finished. Unless Simon agreed to a short holiday when I came back with the library book, my next proper trip over would be for the launch of the theme park in August, some months away. Fortunately the library had suggested I could have the book on St Blane's on long-term loan and although I'd still a fair amount of work to do to finalise the guide, I was confident a couple of weeks would see it through and off to the editor. After that it was no more my concern and I could move on to the next commission.

Only the day before I'd received an e-mail from someone I'd worked with a year or two previously, asking if I'd like to be involved in a new project to write health promotion materials for schoolchildren. The most attractive aspect of this opportunity was there would be no need to leave Glasgow and I'd be able to make use of both my skills as a writer and my years of experience as a teacher.

Surely I'd be able to persuade Simon to come over with me in August and, after the formalities of the theme park opening, we'd be able at last to have a proper holiday on the island, unencumbered by work, strange events or other unsavoury happenings?

In the expectation that the house would be quiet when I arrived as Simon had returned to Inverness, I was startled to hear loud music as I opened the door. Even stranger, Motley, our cat, came purring down the hall to greet me, wrapping himself round my legs as though genuinely pleased I'd returned, though it was probably no more than a sign he hadn't been fed for a while.

'Hello,' I called. My words were drowned out by the noise of thumping music and I pushed open the door to the living room, knowing there was only one person who had that kind of taste.

'Hi, Mum, you're home then.' Deborah uncurled herself from the sofa and deftly turned down the volume before coming over to give me a hug. Each time I saw her she had changed her appearance: lately she'd let her curly dark hair grow long, but had a feathery fringe almost covering her eyes and was conservatively dressed (for her) in a pair of smart navy trousers and a bright yellow jumper.

'I didn't expect to see you here?' I was genuinely surprised and only hoped it wasn't a sign there was a problem with yet another job.

'I've a few days' holiday and thought I'd come home for a bit.'

I ignored the various empty coffee cups on the table and the plates she'd used for lunch. Now wasn't the time to scold her about her untidiness, given I'm no paragon myself.

Motley jumped up on my lap as soon as I sat down and settled himself, purring loudly.

Before I could ask she said, 'Oh, I collected him from Ella next door, but he seemed reluctant to leave.'

'He would be. Ella spoils him, but we're lucky she's happy to look after him whenever we go away. Let's hope she doesn't decide to get a cat of her own.'

We exchanged news, caught up on Deborah's latest venture, though from her vague answers I'd this feeling she was about to want to try something new yet again.

'Have you had a chance to see Maura? Did you think she looked well?'

Deborah's eyes widened. 'I did meet her briefly for coffee. She looked fine to me. Why, is there something wrong?'

Perhaps it was all down to my imagination after all: either Deborah was less observant than I gave her credit for, or Maura was feeling better.

I said, 'No, no, she looked a bit tired last time I saw her,' before quickly changing the subject and updating her on the progress of the visitor guide.

After a good ten minutes of this, during which she attempted none-too-successfully to disguise her boredom, she said, 'Oh, by the way, in case I forget. There was a phone call for you – Ryan something or other? He asked if you'd get in touch.'

What Ryan could possible want with me? 'Did he give you any idea of what it was about?'

She shrugged. 'Nope. All he said was to ask you to get in touch as soon as possible.'

'I'd better call him then.' It was the last thing I wanted to do: there was nothing I could help with surely. At the moment all I wanted to do was get back to some kind of normality, finish off the contract and address the other problems in my life.

Deborah stood up and stretched, yawning. 'I'll go and make us some tea, give you peace to talk to him. Do you want anything to eat?'

I shook my head. 'I had a sandwich on the ferry, but tea would be good.'

She swept up most of the cups and the plates and headed for the kitchen and about to call Ryan on my mobile, I hesitated. If he'd wanted to he could have called me directly instead of phoning me at home on the landline. Best to return his call the same way and I went out into the hall to fetch the receiver, hoping he'd be available.

He was, though from the background sounds of chattering, thudding and the swoosh of the wind he was out on site at Kingarth.

'Whoa, can you speak up, Alison, I can hardly hear you,' he shouted in response to my, 'You asked me to call you.'

'Yep, give me a minute. Are you at home? Then I'll call you back out of the way of all this noise.'

True to his word he phoned a minute or two later. 'That's better,' I said. 'What's this all about, Ryan?'

'Well…this is difficult, Alison, but I don't know who else can help. Truth is, I tried to catch you before you left.'

All sorts of possible scenarios went through my mind, none of them my field of expertise.

'Hope I can. What is it?'

He waited for a moment and I heard footsteps stopping beside him, then, 'No, you gotta go on with it for a bit longer,' and the footsteps receding.

'Hey, sorry about that,' he said, 'one of the diggers wanting instructions.'

'Ah, so you're out on site.'

'Yep, right this minute I'm in the Portakabin.'

That explained the slight echo on the line. 'So what is it you want me to do?' I deliberately avoided asking how the work was progressing.

'It's this business of what someone from the monastery at St Blane might have hidden in that trench. Those finds in the same trench as Benjie's body?'

'Yes, yes,' I said, curious to know what Ryan would say, if he was also suspicious about their disappearance.

'The piece of slate hasn't been found, though Vernon removed the paten to a place of safety, he's swearing he didn't touch the slate. In fact, everyone is denying all knowledge of it so much so I was beginning to doubt I'd ever seen it.'

'Oh, you saw it all right. We all saw it.'

'I didn't have much time to examine it before it disappeared but I'm damn sure there was something on it. Yep, it was exactly like... like one of the slates the monks used to scratch stuff about their life in the monastery, including their possessions.'

Suddenly a thought occurred to me. 'You're not accusing me of stealing it, are you?'

'Whoa, no way,' he hastened to reassure me. 'Nothing like that, sure. But there are pieces of slate tablets in the National Museum of Scotland in Edinburgh and I'm sure the fragment from St Blane's will help us with the one that's gone missing. Hey, trouble is I didn't have time to examine it closely in all that to-do of finding Benjie's body, but I'm sure as sure it's the other part of that slate in the National Museum. Nathan took some photos but nothing of his has turned up.'

'I think I may be able to help you,' I said, trying to contain my rising excitement.

191

'How come?'

'Harry took lots of photos of the site and,' frowning as I tried to recall this one among the many photos he'd sent over to me, 'I'm certain there was one of the slate. I'll check at once and e-mail it to you.'

'Great stuff, Alison, but I'd still need you to go to the National Museum.'

'How on earth could I help with that? I wouldn't be able to read any inscription.' This was a call too far on my abilities.

'No, no,' he said impatiently. 'All you have to do is photograph the fragment of slate from St Blane's in the museum and get it over to me, like, quickly. There's no way I can leave the site. We seem to be getting further and further behind with work and Zofia is driving me mad, loitering everywhere, and constantly asking questions about our progress, though she can see for herself how it's going. I think Dexter's putting pressure on her.'

'Even so, wouldn't it be better if you did it? I've no idea what I'm looking for. Couldn't you be spared for an afternoon?'

'Hey, no way. I can't get off the island and a trip to Edinburgh from here would take the best part of a day. It won't be too difficult for you. I don't want to get any suspicions going here and for sure someone has taken the slate found with Benjie's body. You're the only person I can trust.'

Then something else struck me. 'But surely the museum slates have been recorded somewhere, deciphered? Can't you use those?'

'Yep, sure there've been attempts but the photos in the books available are all old stuff, of poor quality and today's digital images are just the thing, much sharper and together with Harry's photos…' He broke off again and I heard a muttered conversation before he came back on again. 'Listen up. You have to do this, Alison.'

Reluctantly I said, 'I should be able to manage that, but I'm not too sure about my skills as a photographer. I'll keep in touch.' Surely Ryan was making a lot of fuss about a piece of slate?

And with that I was about to end the call but he said, 'Whoa, whoa, not so fast.'

He broke off again and I heard him say, 'Yeah, yeah, take that up to the finds tent and tell them to give it priority.' Then he came back on line. 'Oh,oh, sorry, Alison, thought we might have something of interest there but we won't know till it's been cleaned up.'

'So have the excavations revealed anything of significance?'

'Nope. That's the point and why this slate is so important. Very important. Come on, you have to help me with this. There's something mighty strange going on at this site and I have to find out what before anything else happens.'

Swayed finally by the urgency in his voice, I reluctantly I agreed to his request, not the least convinced it would be any way as important as he was trying to suggest, but it was easier to agree rather than argue with him. I intended to visit Maura and Alan soon anyway and I could combine that with the visit to the Museum, but I wasn't going to rush over to Edinburgh on Ryan's say-so.

'I'll do it,' I said, 'but only if I can e-mail any photos from the museum to you. I can't get involved, Ryan. Any suspicions you have, you should alert the authorities.'

Someone else came to speak to him because abruptly he said goodbye. 'Gotta go, Alison. Remember this is important else I wouldn't ask you to help.'

It was only as I put the phone down that it occurred to me that there was one vital question I'd forgotten to ask him. He said I was the only person he could trust but was that really why he'd chosen me to do this?

31

The train from Glasgow pulled into Waverley Station in Edinburgh exactly on the dot of nine fifty. It was some time since I'd been in the capital and the station upgrade had been at last completed with a wealth of glass and chrome, making the building airy and light, though there was little that could be done about the platforms, retaining the dusty grey appearance of an earlier age. I joined my fellow travellers in the crush to pass through the automatic ticket barriers: since the building of the Scottish Parliament at Holyrood, it would seem the trains are always busy, even outwith the rush hour, although there was one every fifteen minutes.

The escalator up to Princes Street was a welcome alternative to the steep Waverley steps, though I dare say the exercise would have been of benefit. Next time, I promised myself.

The drizzly rain in Glasgow had given way to clear blue skies and a cold wind here in the East of the country, but I stopped to look along Princes Street at the new tramway system which had caused so much disruption and grief to the good people of Edinburgh for so long. At last it was finished, though not quite operational and the sleek carriages would be a hit with tourists, though the scope of the ride was limited, curtailed by spiralling costs.

The request from Ryan had certainly intrigued me, but I had the perfect excuse for a visit to Edinburgh: Alan and Maura had moved here within the last couple of days. My plan was to pay them a quick visit before heading for the National Museum of Scotland in

Chambers Street. It saved explanations to Simon, temporarily back from Inverness, about why I would suddenly decide on a trip to Edinburgh when I kept complaining there was work still to do on the tourist guide.

Contrary to my expectations, Harry had been in touch several times with questions. My suspicion was that he was reluctant to let so much of his research go, wanted more included, something I fiercely resisted. I soon found out the reason for his persistence. In our last phone call he'd said, 'I've been thinking about the book you suggested I write and I've made some enquiries, but the publishers I've spoken with have been reluctant even to discuss it. They keep talking about "times being hard" and "not much call for academic books of this kind". One of them did look at my proposal but it came winging back almost by return.'

Sympathetic as I was towards Harry's situation, I was determined the visitor guide should be as we agreed: a slim volume with lots of photos and light on hard information. This was designed for visitors to a theme park, for goodness sake.

Fortunately as Alan and Maura's flat was in Marchmont, a short bus ride took me to their front door. Less pleasant was that fact the flat was on the third floor of the building, but that made up for my laziness at the Waverley steps.

Alan was at work at this time of day, but Maura said she was delighted to see me and we were soon ensconced in her airy front room with its large bay windows giving a view of the bustle of the street below.

After some general chit-chat I said, 'So how are things going with you? Are you pleased to be back in Scotland, even on a temporary basis?'

196

'Of course. And it's a great opportunity for Alan. What's not to like about it?'

This prickly response caught me off guard and I racked my brains for something to say that wouldn't sound critical. Unfortunately what I came out with didn't help matters. 'And what will you do while you're here? I guess you've given up your job at the advertising agency, or will they keep it open till you return?'

She laughed with a bitter undertone. 'Well, it looks as if the agency might not be there much longer. Tom's had an offer for the business, to incorporate it into *Cravic Media Services*, one of the biggest advertising agencies in the country. So the question is pretty academic. I'm sure he'll accept. He has a hankering to go travelling for a while.' She sighed. 'Alan says not to hurry to look for another job. He's frantically busy and we have to find somewhere more permanent than this.'

It was difficult to guess how she felt about being at home, even on a temporary basis, and I was about to move on to other topics, when she said suddenly, 'I've been desperate to tell you, but was so afraid something would go wrong as has happened a couple of times.'

I said nothing, merely sat and waited for her to speak again, swallowing hard to dispel the dryness in my mouth.

She grinned and said, 'Thing is, I'm pregnant.'

I jumped up out of my seat and went over to hug her, delight flooding me, plying her with questions in my excitement until she said, 'The baby's due in early November, but we've been on edge for the past month in case anything would go wrong.'

I'm sure the relief there was such a happy explanation for my concerns showed in my face and we spent a pleasant hour in general talk about her pregnancy, what they would do about somewhere to live and babies in general before I said reluctantly, 'I'll have to leave soon. I've still to go along to the National Museum. You should come through to Glasgow for the day and we can have a shopping trip, catch up properly.'

In spite of the task awaiting me at the museum, I was easily persuaded to a last cup of tea, and we chatted about the rest of the family, caught up on general gossip, every now and then reverting to her good news. Eventually we said goodbye, promising to arrange a day out soon and I hugged her again before going back downstairs with a much lighter heart.

In the meantime I had to put all thoughts of Maura and the baby to the back of my mind and head for the National Museum of Scotland to track down the slate from St Blane's as Ryan had asked, but my confidence in my ability to carry out this task was becoming less by the minute.

What's more, in the light of Maura's news, it no longer seemed important.

32

The museum was quiet: at this time of day there were few visitors, though I spied the usual contingent of tourists making their way round in a tight group led by a guide with a strident voice. I edged past them and within a few minutes, thanks to the excellent map and details provided on the leaflet available at the front desk, I found the room with the Monymusk Reliquary and the slate from St Blane's with no difficulty. Perhaps I could learn a trick or two from the way the information beside each exhibit was laid out. At the moment I was struggling to make the text as user-friendly as possible and with no sign as yet of Nathan's camera, or any kind of memory stick, it looked as if we might have to use Harry's photos after all.

Viewed through protective glass, the Reliquary was impressive, even without the alleged link to St Columba. Small as it was, there was something appealing about its structure like a tiny house, its highly decorative surface testament to the skills of these people from the early Bronze Age. I spent a few minutes viewing it from all angles, taking photos as best I could, but glad that on the way in I'd glimpsed a good array of postcards and books in the museum shop. That might be helpful if my photographic skills weren't up to the task Ryan had set me.

Still musing on the magnificence of this little box for holding precious relics, I moved through to the next room where the slate tablets recovered from St Blane's and other sites in Scotland were displayed to best effect in a large glass case. In a way these were very moving, the scribblings of monks so long ago, yet at one time they had been living breathing people like us and somehow, having been involved in the plans for the theme park, they were all the more affecting.

The accompanying notes gave examples of the common alphabets of the time: Latin, Ogham and Runes. The text on the slate from St Blane's was in Latin or a form of Church Latin and I photographed it from every angle, trying to make sure I captured the details of the inscription.

Taking care to avoid the reflection of the lights, I tried to decipher what was on them, but to no avail. The cards beside each one provided a translation, though warned the visitor that various parts of the text were either missing or difficult to decipher because of their condition and I peered more closely at the St Blane's slate, rereading the suggested translation several times. That was strange. Perhaps because I was so attuned to what was happening at the moment over at Kingarth, the words seemed to show there had been some event of great consequence at the monastery. There was a reference to *r_a pretio...* followed by *diri mag...* and the rest was lost apart from a few strange scratchings.

Beside the translation there was an information card alerting visitors to the fact, by no means certain, some scholars believed this was a reference to the Hoard that had been found in the last century, or even other treasures as yet undiscovered, though that was unlikely given the power of the Viking raids.

In the quiet of that room, alone with the writings of the monks of so long ago, my mind turned over all the possibilities. I was no expert, but for the past few months I'd been immersed in the story of St Blane and the monks who'd lived at Kingarth. Was it at all possible that there was indeed a treasure to be found but that everyone had been looking in the wrong place? If so, I'd a strong suspicion that someone had come to the same conclusion as I had. It was the only explanation for the events at the theme park site and for the deaths of Benjie and Nathan.

Not even sure I could trust Ryan, I pulled out my mobile phone again and scrolled to the camera. There must be some way to decipher this slate. Clearly Ryan had some idea that it was of value, or led to something of value. Precisely what I didn't have an idea and I concentrated on taking a last few photos of the St Blane's slate just to make sure I hadn't missed anything.

Job done, I stood and stared at these relics of another age, thinking of those monks so long ago scratching on to the hard surface, wondering if this belief of Ryan that there was something of significance was all so much imagination. Plenty of people had examined these and in much more detail than I was able to do and there had been no clue to anything of worth buried at the site. Yet why would someone steal the slate found at the theme park? It was true there was a huge market in such antiquities, especially with clients from overseas but surely none of the archaeologists would do such a thing?

Suddenly I'd a flash of insight, remembering what had been there at the back of my mind, what I couldn't recall. There was a small engraving on this slate, almost too tiny to be seen, but it bore a strong resemblance to the drawing of the chalice in the book from the library. I was certain the slate found at Kingarth had a similar etching, although I'd seen it only briefly.

Ryan had put me in an impossible situation. There was only one option. I had to go back to Bute, speak to.... who could I talk to about this? Certainly not Zofia and I didn't know Dexter well enough. I ran through the various archaeologists and finally decided on Sven. Though he kept his counsel, he struck me as the most practical of all of them. I'd have to pass the information and the photos to Ryan but I'd tell Sven what was going on, ask for his advice. Now all I'd have to do was come up with a good reason for going back to the island.

As luck would have it, I didn't have to think of an excuse to go back to Bute. No sooner had I arrived back in Glasgow than there was a call from Harry. 'Have you been in touch with Zofia?'

'I've not been in touch with anyone on the project,' I said, evading a direct answer. 'Why? What's happened?'

'Alexander Crombie wants another meeting with everyone who's been working on the site.'

'Surely that doesn't include us? All we have to do is finish off the text for the visitor guide.'

'So I thought. But apparently he wants to make sure that "all the pieces of the jigsaw fit together". Zofia's been trying to phone you.'

I thought guiltily of the missed calls on my phone I'd resolutely ignored. 'So when are you heading over?'

'The meeting is scheduled for next Wednesday and I want to spend as little time away as possible so I'll come up on Monday and head to the island on Tuesday, stay over and then catch the evening ferry back once the meeting is over. It means I won't get back to Manchester till Wednesday, but I can stay with my elderly aunt in Glasgow. She's always complaining I don't visit enough. The CalMac summer timetable is operational so you would be fine if you wanted to make a day trip of it.'

Simon was perplexed when I tried to explain to him as we chatted on the phone later that night. 'Seems very odd,' before adding, 'I hope they're paying you for this extra trip.'

'Of course,' I replied though in truth I'd no idea. Even if they weren't, I couldn't have missed the meeting. I was too consumed by curiosity.

And I wouldn't let the others down, no matter what. And that's how I came to head back to the Isle of Bute once more.

33

Now, in mid April, the island was beginning to spring back to life after its long winter sleep. The daffodils were in full bloom along the verges, the Rothesay Marina was crowded with boats, there was a smell of early summer in the air, a mixture of sea brine and warmth. As I came off the ferry, I indicated right to head along the sea front through Ardbeg and Port Bannatyne towards Ettrick Bay, deciding to take advantage of this good weather before meeting up with the others at the Pavilion. In the centre of town the traffic was unexpectedly snarled up as a policeman solemnly performed the annual task of shepherding a mother swan and her young across the road from their safe haven in the moat at Rothesay Castle to swim at last in the sea.

The Ettrick Bay tearoom was busy and I bought some coffee and cake to take out and sat on the bench overlooking the bay. There was still a little chill in the air. It was fine if you were walking, but fortunately I was well wrapped up and sat for a while after I'd finished, throwing the last crumbs to the ever hungry seagulls. A big mistake, as they came crowding round strutting and squawking loudly, unaware there was nothing left.

Time to leave, but before I did so there was time for a stroll along as far as the little arched bridge spanning the Drumachloy burn, now reduced to a trickle. The stone bridge was still there, built wide enough for a cart and horse to pass over, now overgrown and encircled by trees, beneath which there was a tiny area of sand, scarcely big enough to accommodate four or five picnickers. The yellow gorse at the top of the bank was beginning to show pinpricks of yellow blossom, a sign winter was finally over.

I stood leaning over the mesh railing on the modern bridge, gazing into the water below, suddenly startled to hear a voice at my side. 'Two minds with one thought, Alison?' and turned to face Harry.

'Yes, thought I'd take the chance for some fresh air. I'm heading back to Glasgow tonight as soon as the meeting is over.'

A wistful look came over Harry's face. 'I thought I'd come out here for a little while. It's the anniversary of Greta....' he hesitated '...of our wedding.'

'Oh, Harry, I am so sorry.'

He seemed to draw himself up and shook his head. 'No matter. Time to head off.'

We walked together to the car park, each of us with our own thoughts. This was the first time Harry had mentioned the incident of Greta's death in that house fire in my friend Susie's house high up in the hills above Ettrick Bay. One or twice I started to say-something, but stopped as I saw the grim set of his face.

Harry arrived at the Pavilion before me and was seated beside Luann, chatting to her like a long lost friend so I chose a seat at the back of the room beside Ryan. 'How are the excavations going?' I said, by way of covering up my real question. Then, 'Did you get the photos from the Museum of Scotland that I sent over?' I whispered, after looking round to make sure no one was listening.

'Yes, they came through fine.'

'And... were they of any help?'

He frowned. 'It's too early to say. I've not had the opportunity to study them closely. It'll take some time.'

'Ah, so things are difficult?'

'They're not going very well, if that's what you mean. We've had even more delays.'

'Because of the deaths?'

He shook his head. 'Not only that. There have been problems with the site itself and Dexter keeps interfering, delaying the next part of the excavations and we're very far behind with everything.' He shook his head again. 'Added to which Sven has been complaining about almost everything. It won't be long before the diggers are in revolt. It's all dragging out much longer than any of us anticipated. What's more one or two of them have had to go off to other contracts.'

Was Ryan trying to distract me from questions about the slates? I stole a furtive glance at him at him, but he was now resolutely facing the front. How much did I really know about him? I felt a little sick. I'd taken his story at face value, had supplied him with the photos from the museum in Edinburgh all on the strength of a very shaky belief that he was one of the good guys, interested only in getting to the truth.

Any further questions I might have had were cut short by the sudden arrival of Zofia. I was shocked at the change in her. Her usual suave appearance had been replaced by someone who was gaunt, pinched and had a defeated look. Even her voice had been modulated by a couple of degrees and we had to lean forward to catch what she was saying.

It was a few minutes before she had control of the group: Sven was scrolling through his phone and Harry and Luann were deep in conversation as she tried to gain our attention and it was only when Ryan turned to us all and said, 'Hush everyone, the sooner we hear what Zofia has to say, the sooner we can get out of here and on with the work.'

'Sorry you've all had to come together like this,' she said. 'I'd intended this should be a meeting to clear up a few issues to let us get on with the final stage of the excavations before the rest of the building work could continue, but there have been some unexpected events.'

'You can say that again,' muttered Ryan.

She had our full attention now.

Luann was the first to speak. 'What events, Zofia? We know that there have been problems, though most of them have been caused by all these changes to the schedule.'

A hint of the old Zofia as she flared up. 'Nothing to do with *me*. Dexter keeps saying he's only following instructions from Mr Crombie.' She stopped and looked round. 'Where is Dexter? He said he'd be here to explain everything.' She looked close to tears. 'None of this is my fault.'

'Perhaps we should wait for Dexter and get the full story from him. We've already lost some of the diggers to other contracts and if others go off there's not the slightest chance of finishing the archaeological survey in time for the rest of the building work to start on schedule.'

We seemed to have reached an impasse. Without Dexter it was evident Zofia had no intention of going ahead with the meeting, afraid perhaps of our reaction.

Sven stood up. 'Do you not think it would be a good idea to phone Dexter, find out when he will appear?'

'Yes,' muttered Luann, 'it's bad enough Crombie's decided not to make an appearance.'

There was an undercurrent, a tension which made us feel very uncomfortable and I still had no idea why

Harry and I had been asked to come over to the island, to make a special trip. Our work could easily be completed at home and it was clear, in spite of what we'd been told earlier, that Crombie had no intention of appearing. Apparently he preferred to send Dexter to deal with any resentment.

Zofia said angrily as Sven sat down again, 'I was about to do that. I do *appreciate* you have some questions that only he can answer.'

She pulled her phone from her capacious bag after rummaging round for a bit and went out of the room to make the phone call. As she passed, Vernon muttered, 'Bloody waste of time. If we'd been able to get on with digging instead of spending hours in meetings we'd have been finished long ago.'

If Zofia heard this she completely ignored it and while she was out making the phone call, the rest of us sat in silence, Vernon tapping out a tune with his fingers on the chair in front until Harry leaned forward and said, 'Do you think you could stop that, it's getting on my nerves.'

Vernon glared at him, but did as he was asked.

Truth to tell we were all on edge and there was a little ripple of noise round the room as Zofia returned.

'He says he's on his way, he'll be here in a few minutes.'

Which left us with nothing to do in the meantime except sit around, engaging in desultory conversation, waiting for Dexter to appear. At one point I thought Zofia might start expounding on her management techniques theories again, but for some reason she didn't appear to have the heart for that and sat at the front of the room, fiddling with her phone, frowning in concentration.

Just as it appeared that Zofia had been misinformed, that Dexter had no intention of joining us, the door was flung open and he marched into the room, straight down to where Zofia was sitting. She jumped to her feet, saying, 'At last. We're waiting to hear what you have to say.'

He ignored her and faced the rest of us, saying with no preamble, 'We've had a difficult time as you know. The project has been held up on several occasions.' Twang, twang, twang went the elastic band on his wrist.

'Not our call, man,' muttered Ryan, but if Dexter heard he pretended not to, continuing, 'There's a question over the site. Problems with the nature of it.' The elastic band twanged again.

'What do you mean? The St Blane's site? We know it's a heritage site and can't be touched, but the site we're working on is surely not of any value.'

There was a long silence and Dexter gazed from one to another, waiting for comments.

When there was no response, he said, as though searching for the right words, 'I don't think you... understand... the work we're engaged in here.'

Vernon stood up. 'Of course we understand,' he shouted. 'Do you think we're simpletons? We're archaeologists for heaven's sake.'

A look of pleasure crossed Dexter's face and he paused, clearly for effect. 'The field Mr Crombie bought near St Blane's was not supposed to be of any value, that's why it was thought a good place to build a theme park. Close to the site itself with all the ruins and other artefacts associated with the saint.'

'Yeah, yeah, we know all this.' Ryan was finding it difficult to contain his impatience.

'What's the latest, man? Problems?'

'I suppose you could say that,' said Dexter, speaking very slowly, stringing out his words for effect and starting to twang again at the elastic band on his wrist.

Vernon looked round at us, one by one, before saying, 'Of course something has been found at the site: that silver paten and the fragment of slate.' He waited for a reaction, but no one spoke so he went on, 'There's no problem about them: they've been properly recorded and I assume safely stowed somewhere, not that I've been informed where. I only found them, after all.'

As he was speaking I tried to read the faces of those listening but not one of them betrayed by so much as a flicker that they had any more information than Vernon had.

'Hey, what's this all about? We can go on now surely.' Ryan glared at Dexter.

Dexter paused before replying. 'There have been further difficulties at the site and in the meantime Mr Crombie has decided the whole place has to be closed down. There's to be no argument. I'm afraid you'll all have to be content with his decision.'

The reaction was a stunned silence, not least because Dexter, far from seeming upset by this announcement, looked mightily pleased, whereas we were all too astonished to say anything. If the site was closed, the project would come to nothing; our hard work would be in vain. Surely this wasn't right: Alexander Crombie couldn't have decided this on a whim. There must be a reason Dexter wasn't willing to share with us.

Sven was the first to find his voice. 'What exactly is the problem, Dexter? And how can it be so important that you have to shut down the site?'

Dexter grinned and looked round at everyone, licking his lips and pausing for effect before replying.

'You'll find out soon enough,' he said and, twanging the elastic band, he stood up as though ready to leave.

34

There was a sudden clamour of voices as the significance of Dexter's words struck home.

Questions came from all directions. 'What do you mean?' 'What's this all about?' 'Are you trying to alarm us?'

But it was Harry who asked what was uppermost in everyone's mind, no doubt seeing all his hard research coming to nothing. 'So how will this, whatever it is, affect us and the work we're supposed to be doing for the theme park?'

'That's still under discussion,' said Dexter, a tad pompously. Twang went the elastic band.

'Whoa, whoa, no way,' said Ryan, raising his voice. 'We've other work on offer and no way is my team to be laid off like this, man.'

'It's far from being a whim,' retorted Dexter. 'The death of Benjie and then of Nathan has thrown the time scale out completely and Mr Crombie is concerned that the project will not be completed in time for the great fair he'd planned for 12th August.'

'B... Mr Crombie,' said Vernon. 'There's no real evidence that St Blane's birthday was actually on that date. What would a few weeks matter? Do you think we're going to let ourselves be dismissed like this?'

But Dexter wouldn't be drawn further and refusing to answer any more questions, he marched out, looking neither to left nor to right.

'What do you think that was all about?' I heard Harry say to Luann but didn't catch her reply.

Zofia meanwhile, had sunk down into the chair at the front, her head down as though she was intent on reading, though I knew she was doing nothing of the sort.

No matter what the problems, I couldn't understand how they could affect Harry or me. We'd no involvement with the site and I asked Zofia why we'd been asked to come back over to the island.

'I only did as requested. Alexander Crombie was apparently insistent that every one of you attend this meeting.'

'Did you know what Dexter was going to say?'

This from Sven who was standing up at the back of the room the better to be heard.

'Of course I didn't,' she replied angrily, then, 'I knew there was something wrong, but not exactly what.'

Trouble was none of us believed her and as the others continued to bombard her with questions, questions she tried hard to fend off, I had a sudden flash of insight. Was the halting of the work at St Blane's nothing to do with finds, nothing to do with the deaths of Benjie and Nathan?

The truth of the matter might very well be simple. Alexander Crombie had run out of money and didn't want to lose face by admitting it. That was why he'd sent Dexter, had decided not to come himself. And if that was the case, it was quite likely none of us would be paid. As we filed out of the hall, speaking in low voices, I grabbed Harry by the elbow.

'Nonsense,' was his sharp rebuff. 'Alexander Crombie is a man of means, else he wouldn't have taken on this project. As usual you're worrying about nothing, Alison.'

Unconvinced by this reply – if I'd lots of imagination, Harry had none. I resolved to investigate

213

further. Having put in a power of work I didn't want to find I wasn't going to be paid. In spite of my bravado, I could see my dream of that once-in-a-lifetime trip to Canada disappearing rapidly.

Harry walked off with Luann, trying to cheer her up after the news from Dexter, while I lingered, aiming to have a word with Zofia. As he passed, I whispered to Ryan, 'I'll catch up with you later about those slates and the inscriptions.'

'Yeah, yeah,' he said gruffly, 'give me a call.' If I hadn't been so anxious to speak to Zofia I'd have delayed him, but she was packing up ready to leave and I had to make a quick decision about what to do.

'Have you any hard information about what's happening,' I said bluntly. 'It's important to know if the problem Dexter spoke of is true or no more than a ruse to get us off the site, to stop the work.'

From the expression flitting briefly across her face, I could almost see her wondering how much she should say, eventually settling on, 'There is a problem and yes, Dexter was covering up a bit, but it isn't what you think.'

'So how do you know what I'm thinking, Zofia? We're owed a bit more of an explanation than the one Dexter didn't give us.' I was angry as well as confused.

'So you believe I've been privy to more information than the rest of you? All I've been told is that there is some genuine problem.' She glared at me. 'It's not closing completely for goodness sake. It's only a temporary blip. Don't go spreading rumours. That doesn't help anyone.'

She gathered up her belongings and hurried out leaving me staring after her.

All she said only made the situation more confusing than ever, but one thing was for sure. If I had to make a guess at what was wrong, at the reason for closing down the site, it could only be that money troubles were at the root of this decision by Alexander Crombie to halt the project and I had this awful sinking feeling it wouldn't restart again any time soon.

35

I had few hours left on the island. My preferred option was to head back to Glasgow that evening, but after the news we'd received at this latest meeting, I was tempted to stay the night to try to get to the bottom of this decision by Crombie. I'd invested so much in hoping the opportunity for Simon and I to have time away from the concerns of our daily lives, do something we had long wanted to, would give us time to rescue our relationship.

I'd believed Ryan when he'd said he was suspicious about why the slate had disappeared, had even made that special trip to Edinburgh to help him, yet every time I tried to speak to him about it he dismissed my questions out of hand. Now it would appear he was taking every opportunity to avoid me and I was no wiser than I'd been at the beginning of this mission.

And Zofia obviously knew more than she was willing to reveal about what was behind mothballing the site. Besides, the more I thought about it, the more certain I became my suspicions about Alexander Crombie's reasons for halting the project were correct. It was all very well playing the philanthropist, but you'd need to have very deep pockets given what had happened with this particular scheme.

With so many questions and so few answers, I called Simon to tell him I'd be staying on Bute that night, trying as I punched in his number to come up with a plausible excuse for doing so. Luckily, the call went to his voicemail, providing the opportunity to leave the briefest of messages, before stopping off in town to buy a toothbrush and a few essential bits and pieces and heading for the Crannog Hotel, convinced I'd have no trouble securing a room for the night.

I was correct, although Georgie as usual made a great show of looking through the bookings before agreeing I could have exactly the same room as I'd had previously.

'I didn't expect to see you back so soon, Mrs Cameron,' she said as she handed me the key.

'I didn't expect to be back so soon,' I said, 'but it's only for one night.' Then to forestall any questions about my reasons for this impromptu stay I asked, 'So what's the news, Georgie? Any good gossip?'

'Sadly, no,' she said. 'There've been no developments in the hunt for whoever murdered your colleague, Benjie Anderson. And there's been nothing more about that photographer either. The only recent news is there's been some trouble with youngsters, I believe, out at Kingarth.'

'Not at the theme park site?' Perhaps this was the reason for Dexter's announcement.

She shook her head. 'No, over at Dunagoil. Lights have been spotted at night and it's rumoured a crowd of local youths is using the caves there as a drinking den. There have even been stories they might have set up an illicit still, but to date nothing's been found.'

'A strange place to do that.' Someone else had mentioned this recently, but I couldn't recollect who. 'Anyway, I dare say the police will sort it out.'

She grinned. 'Lucky they've got that new young constable. He should be fit enough to scramble across the rocks. They've investigated once, but found nothing.'

'Is that not odd?'

217

'No. There are lots of caves over there, a warren of caves. They were used at one time by smugglers so they must be well hidden. It might take them some time to find out what's been going on.' She sighed. 'So apart from the story about Neeta Gambie who's left her husband and five children to run off with one of the contractors who came over to the island to rewire the shop they were supposed to be opening at the far end of Montague Street, no, there's no gossip.'

As I'd no idea who these people were, this story was of little interest and, ignoring the fact that this lack of scandal seemed to annoy her, I took my key and headed for my room to make some kind of plan of action, noticing that at least the number on the door had been fixed. With so little time at my disposal I'd have to make best use of every minute and sat on the edge of the bed to take out my notebook. Perhaps I should call Harry, tell him what I was about to do? Then I thought better of it. He'd only fuss and say I was wasting my time. He appeared to have complete faith in Crombie and his promises.

Ryan would certainly have to be tackled. Apart from anything else he owed me an explanation. I'd gone to so much trouble to find the information he needed and now I wanted to know how he was going to use it. Zofia was hopeless: she'd made it clear whatever she knew she wasn't going to tell me. I'd originally decided to try Sven, being almost the only one left, but there was something about the man, something that I didn't like. Perhaps it was no more than a kind of Scandinavian reserve, but I couldn't recall an occasion when I'd seen him smile, never mind laugh.

And if he rebuffed me, would he tell the others? Dexter didn't enter into the equation and I wasn't brave enough to tackle Alexander Crombie in person.

I ran my pen down the list of names, wondering if this was a complete waste of time, but my mind kept drifting back to those photos I'd taken in the National Museum of Scotland for Ryan.

Photographs! Of course, that was it. I could have a look through the photos Harry had e-mailed over and I set up my laptop to look at what he'd sent to me, feeling a little annoyed I hadn't thought of doing so earlier.

As I'd suspected, there were so many I couldn't think where on earth to start, but I made a brave attempt and as they downloaded I scribbled down a list of the things I had to do if I was to make any sense of what was going on.

Trouble was, I needed some help with this, scarcely knowing what I was looking for. I'd done as Ryan requested, but instead of taking me into his confidence, he'd hedged any answers to my questions, avoided being alone with me and all I felt was a total sense of frustration.

Then I thought about Vernon. He'd found the original; he would surely have a good idea of the importance of the slate. Harry's photos could wait.

I saved the photos, closed down the computer and scrabbled in my bag for the contact list Zofia had given us at the first meeting of the team.

As I was about to give up hope of finding it among the contents of my handbag, now emptied out in a heap on the bed, I located it stuck inside one of the small pockets in the back and dialled his number before I'd the chance to change my mind. To my surprise he answered on the first ring and in response to my request to meet up, didn't even ask what it might be about, instead saying, 'How about we meet in the Black Bull in Rothesay this evening.'

That suited me well, but as I rang off I sat on the bed for a moment gazing at the silent phone and hoping I'd made the right decision about taking Vernon into my confidence.

36

Before I reached the Black Bull, I'd an encounter I'd rather have done without. Having parked in Guildford Square I hurried round to meet Vernon, hoping not to be late. I'd been detained by a return phone call from Simon, perfectly friendly, but there was little doubt he was puzzled by my decision to stay on the island and I explained as best I could without giving too much away.

As I passed the Post Office a figure turned round from posting a letter and bumped in to me.

'Sorry,' he said, then 'Oh, it's you.'

It was Everett and I recoiled as he pushed his face up close to mine so that I could smell the whisky on his breath. He moved in front of me as I tried to sidestep him. 'So all your plans have come to nothing.' He laughed as I said, 'I haven't time for this.'

His face grew redder than ever as he said, 'I would have thought that's something you'd have plenty of now. There's no way that wretched theme park will ever be completed. What a mad idea it was anyway.'

Exceedingly annoyed by his manner I replied, 'Of course it will be fine. It's only a temporary glitch.'

He laughed again and pointed his finger at me. 'If you think that, you're very wrong. We're determined there's no way it will be built.'

I drew back and started to head for the Black Bull, leaving him staring after me, shouting, 'You mark my words. There are too many people who want to see the legacy of St Blane kept for future generations, not ruined.'

This was too much and I turned back, his rude manner giving me courage and I faced up to him. 'I should report you to the police for threatening behaviour.'

'What?' He drew back a little. 'What do you mean?'

'I MEAN,' I shouted, seeing I'd gained the advantage, 'I mean the note you put under my door at the hotel, the silent phone calls.'

He looked genuinely puzzled. 'I never threatened you.' A hollow laugh. 'You've no clout, no way of influencing anything.'

'Even so, there was a note pushed under my door at the Crannog hotel, silent phone calls in the middle of the night...'

He visibly blanched, staggering back. 'What do you mean? They weren't meant for you. It was Zo...' Realising he had said too much, he turned on his heel and stomped off.

So that was the explanation. He'd made a mistake about the room number and all those threats had been intended for someone else, for Zofia. I wanted to laugh out loud. Well, for sure his efforts had paid off in the meantime, but the idea that if work didn't resume it was down to him was no more than wishful thinking on Everett's part.

The newly repainted black and white frontage of the Black Bull looked inviting and I pushed open the door into the lounge, all dark wood and plush red seats on a tartan carpet. The bar, adorned with shields from a variety of ships that once sailed in these waters, was busy, the barman diving back and forth, working at speed to serve the crowd of customers. The adverts for *Real Ale*, the low beamed ceiling, the stout wooden pillars, the barley sugar twist bar rail all spoke of a long established business, but the notice offering *Free Wi-Fi* showed the modern world had intruded even here.

Vernon was seated on one of the corner benches in front of the mullioned window, well away from the tempting aroma of food wafting through from the restaurant situated down a dark panelled passageway. He was nursing a half consumed pint of beer. 'Wasn't sure how long you'd be,' he grinned before going over to get my order of a glass of white wine.

We perused the menu in silence for a few minutes then he took a long swallow of beer, wiping the foam from his upper lip with the back of his hand as he said, 'Well, Alison, what's this all about? You made it sound very mysterious on the phone.'

Now that I was here, face to face, I wasn't sure where to begin. 'I've some concerns about this theme park project,' I began only to be interrupted as he said with a note of bitterness in his voice, 'Haven't we all some concerns, like whether we'll be paid or not. I haven't seen a penny piece so far. Have you?'

'Well, I haven't sent in an invoice yet. The agreement was that Harry and I would do that once the guide for the visitors' site was finished.'

'I wouldn't delay too long. The finances are looking pretty ropey if you ask me.'

This was not what I wanted to hear and my heart sank. If Vernon was right (and it was what I'd suspected) I'd been working for nothing for the past few weeks, a realisation that made me feel angry.

'So what do you plan to do about it? Not being paid, I mean.'

He shrugged. 'I suppose I could try to pursue Crombie for what I'm owed, but I'm only part of the team of archaeologists, even though we work on a freelance basis.'

As soon as the words were out of my mouth I regretted them, but it was too late to take them back. 'Perhaps we can salvage something from this. Harry was talking about writing a more detailed book about the island history. He's interested in the early history, especially the links with the saints. What you've done so far could go into that. My booklet was designed to be much simpler. It was something for the tourists who would visit the site and it could easily be turned round to make it a picture book for children.'

Vernon drained the last of his beer and went over to the bar for another pint. When he came back carrying his drink and a glass of wine for me, he said, 'Is there a market for that kind of thing? I'd be surprised if there was.'

'Possibly not, but we could self-publish. There would be interest of some kind, I'm sure.'

He seemed to consider this idea for a moment. 'There's nothing to be lost. Better than wasting the work we've done.'

'Yes, yes,' I said, enthusiasm for this idea which I hadn't considered till a few minutes before, now exciting me.

'Well, how do you want to organise it?'

'If you could send me a rough outline then I could see how that would fit in to the text.'

I couldn't claim Vernon was overcome with joy at this suggestion, but the practical side of his nature no doubt thought it was worth taking a chance on this new venture.

We chatted a little more about how we might follow up this idea, including ways to sell it. 'I'm sure there would be outlets on the island and the Print Point would take copies,' I said.

We eventually ordered a meal - after two large glasses of white wine I thought it prudent - and chatted about this and that. Vernon had no further news for me. Island gossip wasn't his field, but he was an interesting person and some of his stories about his adventures as a field archaeologist had me laughing heartily.

In this relaxed atmosphere I decided it was the right time to ask him the question about the slate found at the theme park site. 'Did you get a chance to look at the slate?' I said, as though this was a casual enquiry and I was only passing interested in his answer.

He frowned. 'Yes, strangely I did have a good look at it, but I'd like to check it again. If they ever find it.'

'So it's been lost?'

'Mmm. Either that or someone had deliberately removed it. I took it back with me to the Portakabin and made a copy.' He shrugged. 'I've no idea what happened to it after that. There was so much confusion when all the others came in and when I looked for it, it had gone.'

'I wouldn't mind seeing what you have,' I said, adding hastily, 'not that it would be of much use to me, but it would be something else for the book, if you decide to come in on it.'

Vernon grinned and stood up to reach into the back pocket of his jeans. 'It so happens, Alison...' With a flourish he pulled out a somewhat tatty piece of folded paper and laid it on the table, smoothing it as he opened it out.

I leaned over, trying to decipher what was on it, but with little success. 'Would you mind if I took a copy?' I pulled out my phone and snapped the piece of paper before he could reply.

'It won't mean much to you,' he said, laughing. 'It's only a fragment. You'd have to have the other part of it.' He traced his finger over the drawings on it. 'It appears to be a direction of some kind, but who knows? It could be anything, no more than a monk doing some practice writing.'

He folded the paper up once more and slipped it into his jacket pocket.

I tried to look as if this was of little interest, but my heart was beating fast. Was it possible the slate in the Museum in Scotland in Edinburgh was the missing piece of the puzzle, the other part of this one and if it was, would I be able to decipher it?

Ryan must surely know already what it was, have put the information together, but for some reason hadn't done anything about it.

I tried to make conversation, finish my meal, but the food stuck in my throat. All I could think about was going back to hotel and trying to find some link between these two pieces of slate.

So, all in all, as the evening ended, I thought rather smugly that I'd made a wise choice in deciding to meet up with Vernon. He might not have been able to provide any information about what was really going on at the theme park site, but he was able to co-operate on a venture that would hopefully make sure I didn't lose out on writing the guide. Who knows, I thought, I might even make enough money for that trip to Canada.

37

The information from Vernon created yet another problem. I'd a vague recollection of a few Latin phrases from my schooldays, but the museum card beside the slate had said it was written in 7th Century Church Latin, as much a mystery to me as Swahili and I didn't have time to start learning now.

In the quiet of the hotel room, I looked at the photo of Vernon's drawing, then scrolled down to the photo of the slate that I'd taken at the museum. This wasn't as easy as I'd hoped. The drawing from Vernon was faint, smudged and unlikely to be of help.

How I came up with the idea I don't know, but in a sudden flash of inspiration I remembered the great number of photos Harry had sent over. Surely there would be some of the missing piece of slate among those? There was only one way to find out and I started my laptop, opened the photo file and began the task of finding those Harry had taken early on in the project.

As luck would have it, they were easy to find being in a separate sub file, all carefully labelled up - thank goodness for Harry's organisational skills - and after clearing a space on the bed I checked all three: the photo of Vernon's drawing; the photo from the museum and the last one from Harry. Putting both pieces of the slate together seemed to reveal some kind of what looked like a compass marking, but it was difficult to tell in this strange arrangement, no matter how much I squinted and moved one or other this way and that. Finally I decided this was a useless way to proceed. I'd have to get hard copies of the photos, but the problem was deciding where this could be done without arousing too many suspicions. The Discovery Centre, the tourist information centre in Rothesay, had a computer and a printer you could use, its advantage being it was well-screened from prying eyes.

Decision made, I e-mailed the photos to myself and grabbed my bag to head into town, carefully avoiding being detained in the Reception by the simple method of almost running across the floor, waving as I went to a very bemused Brenda.

At this time of day the Discovery Centre was quiet with only an elderly German couple at the desk enquiring about hotel accommodation and it was easy to sidle past and settle at the computer. A quick look round to make sure there was no one else in sight and I downloaded and printed off the photos in double quick time, unusually easy for someone like me who isn't exactly a technology buff.

Feeling self-satisfied at having accomplished this task so easily, I headed for a quiet spot along by Ascog. For some reason I was reluctant to return to the hotel and, using the passenger seat as a desk, I spread the photos out in front of me. There was no doubt about it, this was a direction of some kind and I could feel my heart begin to beat faster and faster as I realised the implications. It was a direction to something, but exactly what I'd no idea. For a moment I considered telling Vernon about this, then as quickly dropped that idea. Harry? Or Ryan? Or even Luann? But what if this was a lot of nonsense, no more than practice scratchings of some monk or other, trying to pass the time one day and idly drawing something he could see from St Blane's? Some of the marks were faint, difficult to make out, but there was no mistaking the sketchy outline of the vast looming shape that was Dunagoil and the little compass mark directing the reader to something inside the vitrified fort.

There was nothing else for it. With no desire to become a laughing stock if my guess was wrong, I determined to go over to Dunagoil and have a look. Then I could decide what to do.

38

For a few minutes I was completely disorientated. The light from my torch made little impression in the absolute darkness at the edge of this headland at Dunagoil. Yet I was sure I'd seen some lights only a few moments before, winking and swaying as though being held by someone who was walking along down by the caves.

It wasn't too late to turn back or look for help, but the opportunity might not come again. Whatever was happening here, tonight might be the last chance to find out the truth.

I pointed the beam of the torch downwards, illuminating the rugged path across to the headland, concerned that one slip would land me in serious trouble. Out here it was unlikely there would be a mobile signal, my phone would be of little use, so I picked my way with care over the rough terrain.

As I rounded the rocky outcrop leading to the complex of caves, I stumbled in a patch of boggy ground and had to grab on to the nearest rock to regain my balance. I stood there for a moment, breathing deeply, waiting for my heart to return to a more normal rate. This was completely mad, better to turn back now before everything got out of hand. Yet I knew I'd go on, wouldn't rest until I found out what was going on in these caves, if it had anything to do with the theme park.

That light again. It came on and went off as though giving a signal, but this site was almost inaccessible from the sea side, the sheer cliffs rising straight up to the headland. It was unlikely, though not impossible, anyone would be attempting to come in by boat.

I crept a little further on, slowly and cautiously, seeking cover whenever possible. The light disappeared and apart from the glimmer from my torch there was complete darkness once more. Had the lights gone out because whoever it was had realised I was there? And if I did come upon them, what was I going to do? I could hardly confront them. Pity I hadn't thought about this before rushing off in my usual disorganized way.

No, all I'd do was have a good look and see what they were up to, then I'd be able to make a judgement about what to do next, whether it was all part of my imagination, or whether I should alert the police. If it really was no more than youngsters using this area as a drinking den, it was no concern of mine.

By now, by dint of crawling forward bent almost double, I'd reached the first cave. The light, if it was a light, hadn't come on again. Perhaps it had been no more than the glint of the reflection of the moon on the water or glow worms. Was that likely? I knew nothing about glow worms, but it was the first thing that came to mind as an explanation.

It was then I heard them: low, muted voices from within this cave. So it hadn't been my imagination after all, there were people here and I stopped at the entrance, wondering what to do next. The island gossip might well have been right. It was no more than some of the youths indulging in a spot of illicit drinking, well away from the prying eyes of the inhabitants of Bute. What would I do if that was all it was? Say, 'Good evening, I was passing and thought I'd drop in.'

I put my hand over my mouth to stifle a giggle, recognising my laughter was no more than a nervous reaction to the situation I'd landed myself in. Well, too late now. Best to have a quick look before heading back to the main road, curiosity satisfied.

Feeling more positive, I switched off my torch and crept in to the mouth of the cave, treading as lightly as I could. My foot slipped on a bed of scree and I stopped, my heart pounding wildly in case I'd been heard. But there was nothing, no one came tearing up from inside the cave to challenge me and after waiting a moment or two to make sure, I breathed a little more easily. A few steps more and I hesitated again, wondering if I could risk using my torch. The floor of the cave was so uneven, slippery with algae and water left behind by tide.

The tide! Was it coming in or going out? I'd absolutely no idea. I tried to recall what I'd learned about tides round the coast, but sadly my knowledge was very limited. Surely if the tide was coming in whoever was in the cave would be leaving soon. I was, as usual, worrying about nothing and I inched forward again. By now I was about a hundred yards into the cave and the voices were getting louder so either I was getting nearer or they were coming out.

Unsure what to do, which way to go, I stood stock-still in the darkness, scarcely daring to breathe. The noise became louder, so they must be coming nearer, making for the entrance to the cave. Something ran over my feet and it was with difficulty I stopped myself from screaming. I couldn't bear this darkness another minute and dared to switch on my torch, directing the beam all round, looking for a place to hide. The only possibility was a rocky ledge right above my head, though the handholds up to it looked difficult, uneven and slippery.

232

There was no option: it was the only place that looked safe and, stowing my torch in my jacket pocket, I began to pull myself up. When I say I'm not the fittest person, I'm not exaggerating and time on the island, sitting writing most of the day hadn't helped. Several times I slipped back, had to stop and cling on tightly till I regained my balance and was able to grab on to the next piece of rock. My hands were cut in several places, raw, but I scarcely noticed as I tried to maintain my rate of climbing, aware the voices were getting ever nearer.

Eventually, my trousers torn, the blood from several cuts on my hands making it difficult to get a grip, I heaved myself by a last great effort on to the ledge, in time to hear what sounded like two men come round the bend in the cave and pass beneath me. I scarcely breathed, my throat parched and dry, terrified I'd cough and alert them to my presence, but they were so deep in conversation they passed me by without noticing.

I craned down, trying to see if I recognised either of them, but it was too dark and the light they carried only made giant ghostly shadows on the walls of the cave, too indistinct to be of any help.

One thing was for sure: whoever they were, they were most certainly not some young lads out on a drinking spree in the caves at Dunagoil.

I waited for some time, listening to their voices receding into the distance and counted slowly to a thousand before I began my descent, which was a lot more difficult than the climb up. With every movement I felt myself slipping and had to grip hard on to the nearest bit of rock, making progress down painstakingly slow. My heart was beating fit to burst and I had to keep wiping my hands on my trousers to get a decent grip on the wet rocks. My heartbeat thumped in my ears. Surely it could be heard?

At long last I was back on solid ground, bent over trying to regain my breath, feel my heart subside to a more normal rate. Well, having come this far, I was determined to see what they had been up to in the far reaches of the cave.

Pausing only to listen for any sound of either man returning, I moved quickly on in to the far part of the cave, tempering my natural inclination to hurry with a reminder that if I slipped and fell here I'd be in serious trouble.

Emboldened by being so near my goal, I switched the torch on to full beam and suddenly found myself in a clearing in the cave, almost like a circular room, vaulted as though it were a proper ceiling. I directed the torch round, scanning the surface, suddenly spying a large chest, much covered with algae and sand, sitting askew in the far corner.

I'd no expectation of being able to have a look inside, thinking it most surely it would be locked, but to my surprise the lid yielded after a few determined tugs and I was able to have a look at the contents, illuminating them with the torch. At first it was difficult to make out what was there amid a jumble of pottery and items wrapped in old cloth, damp and rotten with age. Carefully I moved the items one by one, ignoring the gritty feel of the decaying material they were wrapped in. Most importantly I had to try to remember their exact order and location in the chest, in case the men would realise someone had been tampering with them.

The last object lying at the bottom of the pile was heavy, securely wrapped in a number of layers and I lifted this one out slowly, before unwrapping it and placing it on the ground the better to see. I shone the torch on it, the light catching the glitter of gold as I did so. There was no doubt about what it was: in spite of the dullness of the metal after so long lying hidden, the faint bloom on the gems, this could only be one of the items I'd seen illustrated in that book from the library and etched on the slate. It was the chalice of St Blane in all its glory. Or was it?

39

I sat back, trying to make sense of everything. I'd only seen those sketchy drawings of the chalice in the book from the library, but as I moved it round, examined it from every angle it looked very much as if it was the precious cup the monks were reputed to have hidden from the Viking hordes. It must have been the chalice that I'd noticed faintly scratched in the corner of the slate found with the paten. A little scrabbling noise nearby and I stopped, clutching the chalice tightly, standing still as a statue. Had the two men come back? But it slowly passed and I realised it was no more than a creature of some kind who was probably as much disturbed as I was.

The question I couldn't resolve was what to do now: take this with me or leave it and come back with the police. After wrapping it up, I began to unwrap some of the other items I'd put to the side.

Was it possible this was the treasure of rumour, precious items hidden by the monks to keep them out of the clutches of the Vikings? Trouble was I needed confirmation my guess was correct. In this poor light I began to have doubts. This might be later copies, nothing to do with the monastery of St Blane. How would I feel if I brought the police out here only to discover they were of no worth at all? I had to come up with a plan and the best I could think of was heading back to Rothesay and finding one of the archaeologists who'd be able to tell if they were of value.

It wasn't a good idea to linger here longer: the men might come back at any moment, so carefully replacing the items as near as I could recall to the way I'd found them, I began to feel my way out of the cave, hoping to remember the route I'd taken into the cave. Luckily the sounds of the water swishing round the headland guided me, but nevertheless I made my way slowly, stopping every now and again to listen warily as the noise grew louder. At the entrance, the water was now lapping round: the tide was coming in and I sighed with relief to have made my escape in time.

Once outside, I ran over the bumpy ground for a few yards and then stopped to regain my composure, realising I was shaking uncontrollably. The night was overcast, but suddenly the moon sailed out from behind the clouds, illuminating the landscape, bathing the fields across to St Blane's in a ghostly silver light, providing the opportunity to move quickly but carefully over the rocks, knowing that the slightest slip could land me in trouble.

At last I reached the wooden gate and with what little strength I had left stumbled towards the roadway to collect my car from the turning area where I'd parked it, all the while looking round fearfully. But there was no sign of anyone in this deserted spot.

Back in the car, I waited for a few minutes, trying to collect my thoughts, my hands grasping the steering wheel tightly in order to steady them, until I was sufficiently recovered to begin the drive back.

Was it possible one puzzle had been solved and an ancient one at that? If these items were indeed genuine, there had indeed been another hoard, just not in the place where people had been looking. Or else someone had found the treasure and hidden it in the caves until they came up with a way of taking it off.

Either way, it left me with the problem of what to do next. I had to confide in one of the others. I couldn't do this on my own. Mentally I ran through the list of options, finally deciding on the person I'd originally considered. It had to be Sven. He was the most experienced of the archaeologists, the most sensible and the least likely person in the team to be thrown by this great discovery, if indeed it was what I suspected. Besides, given his taciturn nature, he wasn't likely to tell everyone if I'd made a error and these items were worthless. It was one thing to make a mistake, quite another to become a laughing stock.

Having started up the car, I drove slowly away from the site and headed down the long, twisting road towards Rothesay. It was too late to contact anyone to night, but I'd get in touch with Sven first thing in the morning.

40

Another sleepless night, unable to dismiss thoughts about the possibility of a hoard lying in the cave at Dunagoil. Should I have taken the most important items with me? Why had I left them there? Eventually, sick through lack of sleep, I rose early to stand at the window and watch the sky grow light over the waters of Rothesay Bay. The plan to involve Sven which had seemed so clear-cut the night before now looked full of problems. What if he didn't believe me? Thought this was no more than the ramblings of a silly woman? Underneath that quiet exterior I'd the distinct impression Sven was rather contemptuous of the rest of the team and given his apparent age, probably the only reason he'd engaged with the project was because he needed the money.

I ran through the list of options again, if only to reassure myself Sven was the right choice. Harry wouldn't be fit enough to make the journey over the rocks to the cave: I could scarcely manage it myself. Zofia was too hysterical, Luann didn't know enough and there was something about Ryan that I didn't trust, given what had happened over that business with the photos of the slate at the National Museum. I was still annoyed at the way he'd dismissed my questions, had deliberately avoided me after the trouble I'd taken to do as he asked. It had to be Sven. Decision made, I dressed and left for the site, too uptight to consider coffee never mind breakfast.

Georgie was at the Reception desk as I passed. 'You're out early this morning, Mrs Cameron,' she said as I hurried out, making only a mumbled reply to her greeting.

If I didn't carry through my plan as quickly as possible, my courage would fail me.

The Portakabin was still at the site, standing out against the green of the open field. The remnants of the proposed theme park had been tidied at the bottom of the field, though there had been no attempt to dismantle the skeletons of the structures of the refectory and the *Devil's Ride*. That would come later.

The archaeologists had another few days to complete the survey of the site and then it would be mothballed until a decision could be made, another buyer found to take the project forward. That seemed most unlikely in the circumstances, especially if the feasibility study of running such a venture here was ever published.

There was a certain sadness about the place, I thought, as I climbed towards the Portakabin, though Everett and the rest of the protesters would be delighted, claiming the decision to abandon it was all down to them. *The Buteman* had carried a front page story this week, Everett's face grinning out, his pleasure at his "victory" evident and in all fairness it was likely there had been many silent protesters who supported him, didn't want to see the island spoiled by something they considered a monstrosity.

I was in luck. As I pushed open the door to the Portakabin, Sven was sitting on his own at the table in the far corner, smoking and gazing into space. My entrance startled him and he whirled round saying, 'It was only the remains of a cigarette.'

I tried to hide my laughter: he thought he was about to be scolded for smoking indoors.

'Not a problem for me,' I said and pulled out a chair to sit down opposite him. He regarded me through narrowed eyes and began stroking his beard.

'I wanted to have a word with you,' I said.

'With me? What about?' He almost barked out the words.

This took me aback. This prickly response wasn't what I expected and I began to think I might have chosen the wrong person. Too late now and I ploughed on, 'It's about that chalice and the other treasures the monks are supposed to have hidden to save them from the Vikings.'

A spark of interest, then he said, 'Yes, I have heard those stories.' Then almost bitterly, 'But they are no more than that. They are only stories, tales for round a winter fire to pass the long nights, like the Sagas of old. There is no treasure, or if there was it has been found a long time ago.'

'No, no, that's where you're wrong,' I said, leaning forward eagerly. 'That's why I wanted to talk to you.'

At that very moment the door was flung open and one of the young volunteer diggers came rushing in. 'Sorry,' she said, 'I need to collect my jacket. Looks as if rain is on the way.'

We sat in silence, deliberately ignoring each other as she grabbed her jacket from the peg near the door and hurried out.

Those few moments evidently had given Sven time to think. 'So you have heard something about this treasure?'

'Better than that. I think I know where it is.'

He leaned back, opening his mouth and guffawing loudly, the first time I'd seen him laugh so heartily. He stopped abruptly, but not before I'd caught sight of his teeth with what looked like deliberate patterns filed into them. Tobacco stains highlighted the grooves, making him look fiercer than ever and sent shivers through me. I took a deep breath and tried to ignore what I'd seen, but this explained why he always looked so solemn. He wouldn't want anyone to notice this peculiarity.

'Tell me this story. It will be a good one to pass on to my friends.' He leaned forward. 'But that is all it will be, a story. We have dug over almost this hillside and apart from the paten and the piece of slate we have found nothing, not so much as a coin.'

'That's just it. The monks didn't bury the stuff anywhere near the monastery. That's why only a few items have been found.' I tried hard to keep the excitement out of my voice.

'And you know where it is?' His scepticism showed in the way he raised his bushy eyebrows as he stared at me, unblinking. I dropped my gaze, unsettled by this.

'It's hidden in one of the caves over at Dunagoil.' This came out in a rush and he said, 'What do you mean? How do you know this?'

So I told him.

41

The decision was made. We'd wait till nightfall and then head back over to Dunagoil. I was becoming more and more uncertain about this whole idea, but the alternative of going to the police and finding I'd made a huge mistake, that it was all fake stuff left over from some theatricals and that the youths alleged to be using the place as a drinking den were responsible didn't appeal. I'd made enough mistakes in the past. Sven had the right kind of experience, would be able to tell at once if the contents of the chest were of genuine or not.

Sven took some convincing that I'd found something, that it wasn't some mad idea, though whether he believed there might be something of real worth was hard to determine. He said little and if he was excited about the prospect of finding the valuables hidden by the monks, he didn't show it, but then he wasn't a man given to displays of emotion.

Sven insisted we use his four by four, in spite of my protests that it would be better each to take our own transport. 'That is foolish, Alison and if the terrain proves to be difficult, mine will be better.'

About to object that we weren't likely to be driving as far as the caves at Dunagoil, I thought it more prudent to say as little as possible and he picked me up outside the Bute Sailing Club as we'd agreed a little after ten o'clock.

'Did you tell anyone where you were going?' were his first words.

'No, I should have, shouldn't I? Or at least given some indication about where we'd be.'

'No matter,' he said, shrugging. 'If no one knows that is better. This may be a wild fowl chase.'

I was too much on edge to correct his misuse of language.

Even so, now he'd mentioned it, I was annoyed I hadn't thought to leave some kind of message about our trip to Dunagoil and pulled out my phone, but as I did so he took one hand off the steering wheel and put it over mine. 'Leave it, Alison. If this turns out to be a waste of time, you do not want to look foolish, do you?'

He was right and I put my phone back in my bag, but the idea nagged away at me. If Sven hadn't been out to Dunagoil, he would have little idea of how dangerous the ground could be, especially in the dark, no matter how good your torch.

We parked not far from the entrance to the field leading to the headland and as he opened the boot to get out his walking shoes, I snuck my phone out of my bag while his back was to me and sent a quick text to Harry. I wasn't sure this would do any good – he might not even pick it up – but it gave me some kind of reassurance that if there was an accident, he might eventually realise we were missing and summon help.

'Ready, Alison?' Sven came up beside me so quietly I didn't hear him. He was wearing a pair of stout walking boots and a weatherproof jacket, carrying a torch which was much larger and more powerful than mine. We set off across the field, with me leading the way, urging him to be careful on the slippery stones and almost falling myself in the process.

Eventually we reached the first of the caves located under the overhang of the cliff on the landward side. 'This is it,' I whispered. 'I hope there's no one here.'

244

'We have seen no lights, no sign of anyone else. And you cannot reach this without a car to take you to the edge of the field. Now, let us move on, Alison.'

He pushed me in front of him into the cave and we progressed slowly through the entry, where the ceilings were dripping with damp. I put my hand out to steady myself and pulled back with a shudder as it came into contact with the spongy lichen covering the walls. 'There seems to be more water in the cave than last time I was here,' I whispered, jumping a little as my words echoed mockingly in the empty space.

Sven ignored this comment. 'We must get on, Alison.'

After only one wrong choice, we turned a corner and came out into the clearing where I'd found the old chest last time. As we got nearer I'd a sudden thought. What if the men who had been here last time had taken the treasure away? Damn, why hadn't I considered that possibility? If there was nothing here, it would be even worse than discovering the "treasure" was no more than a pile of old rubbish.

But we were in luck. The chest I remembered was still there in the corner. 'There it is,' I said pointing.

'I shall get it.' Sven pushed me roughly aside and dragged the box forward into the centre of the cave. Without a moment's hesitation he tugged the lid off and lifted out what was on top, then faster and faster, bringing out the pieces one by one much less carefully than I had on my previous trip.

'What do you think?' I said. 'Is it real or is it fake?'

He didn't answer me immediately, but continued to examine each piece, finally alighting on the chalice and holding it up to examine it by the light of his torch. Dirty and dull as it was, there was a glimmer from it that took my breath away. Why had I so lacked confidence in my own judgement that I'd felt the need to involve Sven in this? A niggle of fear began to gnaw at me as I watched Sven again take each item and scrutinise it carefully, as though I wasn't there. He held the chalice again turning it this way and that, muttering softly as he did so.

'Is it real?'

He ignored me and I repeated the question. 'Is this the real treasure?'

At last he faced me and I shrank back. The gleam in his eye was not encouraging. 'Of course it is. This is what I have so long looked for.'

'So,' more hesitantly, 'we should get back, take it to the authorities.' I moved towards him. 'We should be able to manage most of this between us, surely.'

As I got nearer he pushed me hard. 'This is not for any authorities. It is mine.'

I laughed. This was a joke, surely. Then another look at his face and I knew otherwise. All my worries and fears came rushing back. This was a different Sven. He was like a man possessed. My heart began to beat loudly and I edged towards the entrance to this part of the cave, trying to think of a way to get out of here, away from him.

'There's no point in trying to leave, Alison. You are not going anywhere, I am afraid.'

Not nearly as afraid as I was, but didn't want to show it. Some vague memory of "facing down your enemy" came to mind, but as Sven was a good foot taller than I am and twice as broad, this was hardly a viable proposition. Besides, I suddenly remembered those sharp incisors. I was well and truly stuck and it was entirely my own fault.

Once again Simon's words of caution "don't get involved, Alison", came to mind, but the fact I should have listened was of no help now.

42

There was a long silence, broken by Sven saying, 'Now what am I going to do with you, Alison?'

'Have the treasure if you want, Sven. I'm not interested.' At least that's what I think I said, but it came out as a squeak.

He appeared to consider this suggestion, then shook his head. 'I don't think that would work, do you?'

The notion came to me that I could make a run for it. If Sven was burdened by the treasure he'd either have to abandon it or leave me. But as though he'd read my mind, he said, 'Don't even think about trying to run. You are not going anywhere.' He stepped closer. 'I am sorry about this, you must believe me. You have led me to the treasure and for that I am truly grateful, but if you were to tell others about this it would never be restored to its rightful place.'

'Its rightful place is the monastery at St Blane's or the National Museum,' I replied, sounding braver than I actually felt.

'Nonsense,' he growled. 'These are the treasures my ancestor Vikings came for, travelled across the seas, braved tempests and storms, overwintered on the shore at Little Dunagoil, built their noosts. Now we will have what is rightfully ours.'

In spite of the danger I was in, a picture of flocks of chickens on their perches sprang to mind and I blurted out, 'Roosts?'

'Noosts,' he growled. 'Shelters for their boats while they lived nearby during the long winter. They deserved any treasure they found.'

I paid little attention. Once again my mind had gone completely blank, no bright idea of how to escape came to me and there was no point in appealing to his better nature. He was completely mad. So much of what he had said, of what Ryan had said now made sense.

'So it was you who killed Benjie? Did he find out what you were doing? Why you were on the dig?'

He stared at me blankly. 'What do you mean? I did not kill Benjie. I had no reason to. He did not know where the treasure was hidden. He was a very stupid man, but I had no reason to get rid of him.'

Whether that was true or not didn't matter now. Of more concern was what Sven had planned for me. Somehow I didn't think it would be something I'd enjoy.

He turned away and began to put the items back in the box, slowly and reverently. This was my one opportunity. If I could go now while he was distracted I might manage to escape. It was a slim chance, but it was a chance and better than anything else I could come up with. Staying here would determine my fate for sure.

On tiptoe I moved backwards out of the cave, watching him all the time as I inched away and then turned and gathered speed once outside his line of vision. By the time he realised I'd gone, I was a good distance off, but I could hear him roaring as he came after me, the sound echoing and re-echoing in the caves. I had to use my torch: in the inky darkness I risked falling and breaking an ankle or worse, but it was a give-away to my position and once I'd made it to the bend in the cave at the entrance I switched it off.

The sound of Sven's footsteps grew louder and louder. Was it possible to phone from here? I pulled out my phone and pressed the number for Harry but there

249

was no reception. I tried a text, with no confidence it would reach him, but the very action made me feel better. There was some light from my mobile, a glimmer that was less than my torch but better than no light at all. I swept it round this part of the cave, willing there to be a ledge, an inshot, anywhere I could hide, but the walls were smooth with not even a sign of a handhold. Regaining my strength, I had to go on, stumbling in my haste. Suddenly the battery in my phone died and, left in total darkness, I caught my foot on a jagged piece of rock, twisting my ankle as I went down.

The pain was excruciating and I bit my lip to stop myself from crying out, with no option but to try to stand up and hobble on, conscious there was almost no hope of escaping before Sven caught up with me.

And if I did manage to get out of the cave what good would that do? There was still the long trek across the field to the main road. At this time of night there would be no one around on the site at Kingarth and I didn't have my car to make my escape. Too late I understood why Sven had been so insistent on bringing only his car. And with the battery on my phone dead, there was no possibility of calling for help. It was all over. Better to sit down, nurse my bruised ankle and hope that when Sven caught up with me he would take pity on me or dispatch me quickly.

Breathing deeply, trying to maintain a modicum of calm I sat on one of the larger rocks and waited.

A few minutes later Sven came into view, his torch picking me out in the darkness, shining in my eyes and I put my hand up to shield them against the sudden glare.

'So you decided it would be better not to run? Very wise. There is nowhere to go, nowhere for you to hide. You are a very silly woman, Alison.'

While I didn't want him to know how I felt, I had to agree. I was very stupid indeed, to have chosen Sven to trust for one thing.

'So what are you planning to do with me?'

He laughed. 'You have put yourself in an ideal position. I will tie you up here and the tide will do the rest. By the time they find you, it will be too late. I will be long gone.'

That seemed unlikely. How was he going to get off the island? The last ferry had gone – not unless he had a boat of some kind. Of course. That was the answer. He had a boat round the headland and all he had to do was transport the treasure there, while I sat by helplessly and watched and waited for the tide to come in and drown me.

There was a noise outside the cave. I looked at Sven, wondering if he had heard it, but apparently not. He was too busy ferreting in his jacket pockets, no doubt to find the rope to tie me up. He'd certainly come prepared.

My heart gave a leap. The noise could only be Harry. Thank goodness he'd picked up my message after all. What's more he'd had the sense to bring someone with him. I was saved. I coughed loudly, partly to cover the noise, partly to attract attention to my position. The noise stopped, but I knew they were there.

'You'll never get away with this,' I shouted and he looked over, puzzled, as my words echoed round.

By listening carefully, I could detect the noise coming nearer. Only a few more minutes and I'd be safe. I called out again, as loudly as I could. 'You won't succeed, Sven. You have to let me go.'

Sven heard the noise, but it was too late. 'You see,' I said in triumph, 'you thought I was a silly woman, but I had the sense to let a friend know what I was doing. You're the one in trouble now.'

But Sven wasn't listening. He was staring straight ahead. 'What are you doing here?' he said.

I swivelled round, smiling with relief as I prepared to greet Harry. But it wasn't Harry.

Standing in the gloom at the entrance to the cave was Dexter. The man with him was Alexander Crombie and he was holding a gun.

43

Sven sprang forward, only to draw back as Alexander Crombie waved the gun saying, 'Be careful. This isn't a toy and I'll use it if need be.'

I backed off into a dark corner of the cave, trying to come up with a plan of escape, but all I could think of was my stupidity in getting myself into this mess. It wasn't as though this was my first time and you'd think by now I'd have learned a lesson about minding my own business, but as usual I wanted to be the one who'd solved the problem, found out what was going on. It wasn't that I imagined myself on the front page of *The Buteman*, grinning as I showed off the treasures I'd found, it was more to do with a never-ending curiosity. If only I could go back a day or two, come up with some other decision about who to trust. Far too late now.

Sven growled, 'It is rightfully mine, this treasure. My ancestors should have had it many, many years ago. They were the bravest of warriors, real men.'

Dexter laughed, the sound echoing round the cave as Alexander Crombie said, 'Yours? It's mine. Why do you think I invested all that money in the so-called theme park at Kingarth?'

Before I could help myself I blurted out, 'You never meant to build it?'

'Of course not,' said Crombie, swinging round to look at me. 'Who would want to come to a theme park out here in this isolated spot?'

Well, that was very clever giving away my position. There was little chance of escaping now.

But Sven wasn't going to give in easily. 'And how are you planning to take it out of here? Carry it across the boggy land to the road?'

A shadow crossed Alexander Crombie's face and I realised in his haste to get the treasure this was something he hadn't thought about.

'Of course not,' he blustered, 'we have a plan.' In spite of this assertion it was clear he hadn't thought that far. He turned to Dexter, 'We need to get rid of these two,' he said, 'and quickly.'

That was a big mistake. In that momentary lapse of concentration, Sven sprang forward, knocking the gun from his hand and leapt upon him with a loud roar. Crombie was a big man, but he wasn't at all fit, and a single blow felled him. As he staggered backwards, he bumped into Dexter who, taken by surprise, was unable to resist and all three men went down in a heap, to the sound of Dexter's skull cracking on a rock.

There was a struggle as the three men fought to gain control, the noise of thumping, of breaking bones but all I wanted to do was escape.

I didn't wait to see the outcome, but as Sven and Crombie wrestled on the floor of the cave while Dexter lay prone, unconscious beside them, I scrambled from the corner and hopped as quickly as possible along the tunnel leading to the entrance, the pain from my ankle almost forgotten in my desperation to get away.

The sounds of their fight followed me as I clambered with difficulty over the last rocky outcrop before the field leading to the main road, stopping every now and then to regain some of my strength, hoping they'd continue this struggle long enough to let me escape. I needn't have worried. In spite of falling a couple of times, getting covered in mud, any time I looked back

254

there was no sign of any of them and I eventually reached the main road, my heart pounding fit to burst.

Behind me I was aware of the menacing shape of Dunagoil and I flopped down on the verge to recover a little, think what on earth to do next, marvelling I'd managed to come this far. There was no time to be complacent. Sven or Crombie might appear at any minute and with no means of transport my only hope was to gather enough strength to walk to the nearest farm and summon help.

I stood up, coaxing my wobbly legs to move and set off down the road, trying to remember how far it was. Twice I had to stop, sit down and breathe deeply before starting off again, all the while watching in case Sven or Crombie would appear, but there was no sign of either man. After what seemed like hours, but could only in reality have been fifteen minutes or so, the outline of the farmhouse came into view and never had the light spilling out from a window been so welcome.

A red sports car sat in the driveway, an indication someone must be at home and I skirted round it, relief flooding through me. With my last remaining bit of strength I knocked loudly on the door, hoping my story would be believed, that they wouldn't think I was some crazy woman landing on their doorstep at this time of night.

The door jerked open and I managed a half smile. At last I was safe. 'Sorry to trouble you…' I began, then stopped as I realised the man I was looking at was Everett.

44

The reception wasn't what I had expected. 'Good gracious, what are you doing here? And what's happened to you?

I shook my head, unable to speak and almost fell into the hallway as Everett caught me. 'It's a long story,' I gasped, but he hushed me and helped me in to the nearest room where a fire blazed in the hearth and settled me down in a large easy chair. 'What's going on?' he said.

'You have to call the police,' I said, struggling to get up. 'The St Blane's treasure is over at Dunagoil and I only just managed to escape from Alexander Crombie and from Sven. You have to call the police, it's urgent and…'

'Calm down, calm down,' he said, lifting his hand to silence me and easing me back. 'You're in need of something to help you.'

He disappeared out of the room and returned a few minutes later with a large brandy. 'Get that down you,' he said. 'You look as if you need it.'

I wasn't sure this was the best of ideas, but I wasn't in any mood to argue and gulped it down gratefully as he sat in the chair opposite in silence, watching me carefully, a perplexed expression on his face. It was an incredible story and I wouldn't blame him if he didn't believe me. Unused as I was to brandy I tried to ignore the taste on my tongue, wincing as the fiery liquid hit the back of my throat and a feeling of warmth suffused my whole body.

A few moments later he leaned forward and said, 'What on earth have you done?' and I sprang up, flinching as the pain in my ankle caught me, shouting, 'You have to phone the police at once.' This time I managed a very garbled version of the events leading up to the confrontation at Dunagoil ending with, 'Time is important. You have to contact them.'

'Sit down,' he said soothingly, gently pushing me back into the seat and I sank down gratefully as he added, 'Make yourself comfortable. I'll go and phone them right away, but not until you've had another brandy.' He lifted my empty glass and as soon as he'd returned with a refill, he went into the hallway, closing the door behind him with a soft click and I could hear him speaking softly.

In the comfort of the cosy room I at last began to relax, sipping this brandy more slowly. I still didn't like the taste but it was certainly helping me unwind. The soft light from lamps dotted round illuminated a couple of battered sofas and several small tables piled high with books, but I'd little idea about the colour of the walls, covered as they were by numerous paintings which could only be by Everett himself, every bit as garish as Georgie had said. He was evidently a great fan of gouache judging by the thickness of the paint on most of them.

Everything in the room was beginning to take on a fuzzy appearance and I was finding it almost impossible to stay awake. I glanced at one or two of the books at random, the usual collection of books found in any home: a mixture of thrillers, guides to Bute, a couple of books on renovating an old property. Then a chill went through me as I idly fingered one at the bottom of the pile. I recognised that title from somewhere *A Short History of Finds at St Blane's*.

With trembling fingers I picked it up and opened the front cover to see the familiar slip showing it was on loan from Rothesay library. It had to be the book the librarian had been trying to trace for me. Had Everett stolen it from the library? And if so, why? I replaced it carefully in the pile, trying to make sense of this latest discovery.

For the moment I was too exhausted to come up with any answers and putting my head back I closed my eyes, trying desperately to resist the desire to sleep.

Soon the police would be here and it would all be over. One thing was for sure, I'd be on the first ferry out on the morning. What did the treasure of St Blane matter to me? I was glad it had been found, had been saved for the nation, but in a way I wished I'd never heard about it.

The door opened quietly and Everett came back into the room. 'Don't worry, Alison. It will all be over soon. Would you like another brandy?'

I shook my head. I felt dozy enough as it was and I'd need all my wits about me to explain to the police what had happened and to come up with an excuse for my involvement in the affair. Whatever I said, I didn't think they'd be too happy with my reasons and I wasn't looking forward to the interview.

The minutes passed, marked by the ticking of the pendulum clock on the only space on the wall not taken up by one of Everett's paintings and its rhythm must have lulled me to sleep in spite of all my efforts to stay awake.

I came to with a start and squinted at the clock to see that almost an hour had passed. I was alone in the room. Where was Everett and more importantly, where were the police? Surely they should have been here by now?

I was about to get up and investigate, though I felt so woozy it was hard to make my legs obey my command to do so, when I heard the sound of the front door being opened and the murmur of voices and I sank back, flooded with relief. No matter how much of a telling off I'd have to endure from the police, no matter how many lectures about how foolhardy I'd been, I would at last be safe.

The voices came nearer and as the door opened I stood up shakily, holding on to the arms of the chair for support, ready to greet them. But the words died on my lips as Everett came into the room, closely followed by a bruised and battered, but very much alive, Alexander Crombie.

Alexander Crombie sat down in heavily the chair opposite, running his hand over his head, wincing as his fingers encountered a large gash above his left ear. It was clear that if Sven had lost the fight in the cave, it had been a hard one.

Everett raised his eyebrows. 'Dexter?'

Crombie shrugged. 'Hit his head on a rock. A goner, I'm afraid.' This demise of his manager didn't appear to trouble him much, but I now had this terrible feeling Dexter's death was only one among many. He laughed. 'And that fool, Sven.'

'So Dexter was in on it?'

Crombie stared at me, rubbing his bruised cheek. He gave a snort. 'Dexter was useless, supposed to be trying to get back on to the straight and narrow, give up the drugs, but that proved impossible for him, no matter how many elastic bands he twanged. He was easily persuaded to help. He couldn't do anything right, not even getting rid of Benjie.'

'What happens now?' Everett jerked his head towards me.

Crombie appeared to be considering the situation. 'She can't stay, that's for sure.'

For one brief moment my heart leapt. Surely this meant he was going to let me go free. A false hope of course as he continued, 'We'll have to do away with her.'

Everett held up his hand to stop him. 'Fine, but not here. I don't want any association with this place if the police come snooping around.'

'What about that barn of yours? We could put her there meantime.'

'My studio, you mean. Look I spent a lot of money converting that, there's no way it's going to be used to store a body.'

With a horrible realisation I understood the "body" they were talking about was mine and at last I found my voice. 'You won't get away with this, you know. I've left messages; people will come looking for me if I don't return soon.'

Crombie seemed to find this highly amusing as he let out a long guffaw, saying, 'Rubbish. No one is going to miss you. Or if they do, they won't be able to find you. There are plenty of places on the island to dispose of you.'

This wasn't what I wanted to hear and I shrank back in the chair, hoping against hope that some miracle would happen and I'd be saved.

'So,' said Everett, 'you found the hoard, did you?'

'What?' Crombie seemed distracted for a moment before rousing himself to say, 'Yes, we did. Strange to think it was in that cave at Dunagoil all this time.'

In spite of my awful predicament, I couldn't help but ask, 'How on earth did you find out about it? The photos Harry took weren't common property. I was the only one who had a copy.'

'Harry?' Crombie said as though trying to remember who he was. 'Oh, the researcher? It was nothing to do with him. Once Dexter had the piece of slate we had to get Nathan's photos to enhance what was on it. We knew the answer would be there. A great pity wouldn't play along. Didn't seem interested in money.'

'That's beside the point,' said Everett briskly. 'Let's get on with what we have to do and then we can retrieve the hoard at Dunagoil.'

'I don't understand the connection between you two,' I came in with, hoping to postpone what looked inevitable for a little longer.

They looked at each other and a slow smile crossed Everett's face. 'Don't tell me you haven't worked it out. There never was to be any theme park. That was a ruse to let Crombie explore the site. The original Hoard was found near there, so there was a good chance the rest of it would be somewhere nearby. It was my job to cause as much disruption as possible, make sure the plans were delayed and in the end Crombie could walk away from the project, hopefully having found any other treasure.'

'Could have saved myself a lot of effort and money,' added Crombie gloomily, 'but how was I to know the stuff would be hidden at Dunagoil?'

'Come on, come on,' said Everett, dragging me to my feet. 'Let's get this done with. Keep an eye on her. She's a slippery customer. She's escaped once already.'

He headed off to the kitchen, coming back with a length of rope which he then proceeded to use to tie my hands tightly behind my back. I recalled reading somewhere about flexing your wrist so that the bands weren't quite as tight as the other person thought, but either I hadn't remembered the instructions correctly or it was another urban myth because the rope bit into my wrists in a most painful way.

He dragged me over to the hallway, assisted by Crombie. 'There's no point in trying anything,' he said.

Crombie stopped as they reached the hallway. 'What was that?' he said. Everett clamped his hand over my mouth and listened. 'Can't hear anything.'

'Shh, there it is again.'

'You're imagining things.' Everett pushed him forward. 'Open the door and we'll get her out of here.'

Crombie opened the door and began to march me towards his car at the side of the farmhouse but as he did so we were suddenly engulfed in a blaze of lights.

'Stop where you are, police,' shouted a disembodied voice.

Blinded by the sudden brightness, Everett and Crombie hesitated, Everett still holding tightly on to me as the voice came again. 'It's all over. Give yourselves up.'

Everett flung me down unceremoniously and both men began to run back towards the farmhouse as I struggled to my feet, suddenly aided by a welcome arm. 'You're all right, now,' said Constable Goodson.

Then everything seemed to happen at once and several police gave chase. Everett and Crombie stood no chance of escape, even if they had been fit, against this well-planned operation and there was shouting and yelling as they were overcome by several burly policemen. The last I saw of them they were being bundled, struggling and still resisting, into one of the waiting police cars.

'How did you know where to find me?' I said, rubbing my wrists as the rope was untied.

'Ah,' said Constable Goodson, 'we've been following you for some time. We've had a good idea what was going on, it was proving it that was the problem. Fortunately we had that senior archaeologist, Ryan McNab, to help us. He alerted us to what was going on as soon as the trouble at the theme park began to get out of hand. And then when the photographer was killed and the paten and the slate seemed to go missing…' He shrugged. 'There were too many coincidences.' He grinned. 'You were never in any real danger.'

This wasn't my impression, but I wasn't going to say anything. I was glad it was finished, though it was hard to believe how Crombie had set the whole thing up, had colluded with Everett. It was just his luck Sven also had an interest in the hoard hidden from the Vikings by the monks at St Blane's. No matter. It was all over now, thank goodness.

As I sat in the police car, being driven back to the safety of Rothesay a most inappropriate question popped in to my head. Who was going to pay me now for all my hard work?

EPILOGUE

In the half light of the Kingdom of the Scots room in the National Museum of Scotland the illuminated glass case shone out brightly.

'This is a momentous occasion for Scotland,' the Minister for Culture was saying. 'At last this treasure has been restored, is here in its rightful place for everyone to see and enjoy.'

She stood back and the treasures could be seen in all their glory: the chalice encrusted with jewels, the gold monstrance, the reliquary of St Blane, even the silver paten all lovingly restored, winking and glittering beneath the strategically placed lights.

Pride of place was a little piece of slate, mounted in a silver case, the very piece of slate that had led to the treasures being found.

'This is such a great ending to those terrible events,' I whispered to Simon as Ryan McNab came forward to speak.

Simon put a finger to his lips. 'Let's hear what he has to say.'

Ryan had certainly spruced himself up and it was strange to see him in a smart suit and tie, though the dreadlocks were still in place, albeit tied back very firmly.

As he began to speak I remembered all that had happened on the way to discovering the treasure and how close I'd come to not being here at all.

I glanced over at Simon who was gazing with rapt attention at Ryan, as were the rest of the audience. A burst of applause greeted the end of his speech and he made a little bow as he grinned. Then he spotted me standing at the back of the group and winked as he gave me a thumbs up. It was kind he'd acknowledged my help in securing the treasure, but it wasn't really necessary.

I had other matters on my mind. Of course there had been no payment for the visitor guide, because there was to be no theme park, but I had received a nice reward for being part of the team that had brought the treasure to light.

For the first time in ages I felt worry free, looking forward to the future. A lot had to do with Maura. She was safely through the early stages of pregnancy and was looking better than ever, "blooming" as Alan kept saying with pride in his voice.

Simon had signed a new contract and appeared happier than he had been in a long time. I'd agreed to write the school health promotional materials and was enjoying doing the research from home. As long as this lasted life was good.

Simon turned to me and whispered, 'What are you thinking, Alison? You must be pleased it's all ended like this?'

'I'm satisfied it's all over,' I replied.

What I didn't add was that I'd used the reward money to book that special holiday to Canada. That surprise was for tomorrow.

Acknowledgements

Sincere thanks

To Joan Fleming[+] and to Bill Daly[*] for reading an early draft of the manuscript and making many helpful comments, to Paul Duffy for technical advice, to Joan Weeple for proof-reading and comments, to Judith Duffy for suggestions and to Peter Duffy for checking all the details about weather and geography and for the support and the help he always provides.

[+]What the Future Holds by Joan Fleming
(http://www.tirgearrpublishing.com/authors/Fleming_Joan)

[*]Black Mail by Bill Daly
(Old Street Publishing 1 April 2014)

COMING SOON

The New Alison Cameron Isle of Bute Mystery

Death at the Kyles of Bute

Read an extract on the following pages

PROLOGUE

'I tell you, I heard a noise.' Anna sat bolt upright in bed, scarcely breathing in the darkness, straining to hear.

'Oh, for goodness sake, go back to sleep. You're imagining things.' Her husband, Freddie, stirred and then turned over, muttering and pulling the duvet over his head.

Anna swung her legs out of bed and felt for her slippers in the dark before pulling on her fleecy dressing gown. The heating in the hotel was turned down low overnight and at her age she felt the change in temperature keenly.

'Where are you going?' Freddie asked, half raising himself on one elbow, but it was clear he had no interest in what she was doing.

Anna didn't reply, but stood still in the middle of the room, listening. 'Shh - there it is again, a faint crying sound. Can't you hear it?'

Freddie grunted in reply. 'It's the heating system in this hotel, that's all. It sounds loud in the silence of the night.'

Ignoring this explanation, Anna moved forward and cautiously opened the door to peer out into the corridor.

'There's no one there,' she said.

'Of course not.' Freddie manoeuvred himself into a sitting position, pulling the pillow up to support his head. 'Will you stop this nonsense? This is the third night we've been here, supposedly for a pre-Christmas break and you've come up with the same nonsense every night. Now come back to bed and let's get some sleep.'

Anna closed the door quietly and padded across the room, shrugging off her dressing gown before slipping back into bed. Thank goodness Freddie hadn't brought up the subject of why they were having a *Tinsel and Turkey* week at the Kyles of Bute Hotel, instead of the holiday in the south of Italy that had been his first choice. She couldn't help being terrified of flying.

She tossed and turned and no matter how many sheep she tried to count, sleep wouldn't come. It wasn't her imagination, no matter how much Freddie pooh-poohed the idea.

Each night, in the middle of the night, she'd heard the same sound. A low weeping, as though someone was distressed, was in deep trouble. She was sure there was something going on in this hotel, something strange.

Eventually she drifted off to sleep, her last vague thought being that she must speak to some of the other guests, find out if anyone else had heard it.

If someone was unhappy, Anna knew she would have to find a way to help.

CHAPTER ONE

If this speaker went on for a moment longer, I'd soon be fast asleep. In this over-heated room, I felt so drowsy I could scarcely keep my eyes open. The topic wasn't the only problem. There was also the monotonous tone of voice he'd adopted.

A brief glance round the ornate carvings, dusty crystal chandeliers and scuffed and pitted wooden floor of the room, the original ballroom of this ancient hotel, made me wonder if rebuilding the Kyles of Bute Hydro hotel and Spa had been such a good idea.

'If you look closely at this next picture,' the speaker was saying, 'you can see the consequences of not using the right knot when securing your boat to the jetty. It causes a fluctuation in the stability which can be a serious problem when it's high tide. It could even be fatal.'

He chuckled at what he thought was a joke, but there were too many people in this room with a close proximity to death to find his comments funny.

He fiddled with the old-fashioned projector, eventually succeeding after several tries. A grainy picture of an upturned day boat, scarcely visible in the surging waves, flashed up on to the screen. 'The important thing is to make sure you keep hold of the boat, use its buoyancy to keep you alive until help arrives.'

A quick glance round the audience confirmed my belief none of these hotel guests would have the need for this information any time soon. Several were asleep and others were chatting in soft tones to their neighbours.

When I'd told my husband, Simon, of my plans to take up a contract to give a series of talks on the history of the Hydro during their *Turkey and Tinsel* weeks, he'd said, 'But it's only the middle of November. Christmas is ages away.' He put down his newspaper and stared at me, a perplexed look on his face. 'Why would people want to celebrate Christmas this early?'

'It's a way of bringing in customers to the hotel at a quiet time of year,' I replied, trying to keep the defensive note out of my voice. 'It would appear it's very popular, according to the information they sent.'

'Even so, even if they need all the custom they can muster, it seems an odd thing to do so early in the season. Who wants to be thinking about Christmas already?'

As Simon belongs to that group of men who think any shopping for Christmas before Christmas Eve amounts to deviant behaviour, I didn't pay much attention to his comment.

'Well, I've agreed to go now. It won't involve much work for me over the two weeks I'll be there. All I have to do is spend time chatting to guests, answering their questions about the history of the building. You can come down and join me for the middle weekend.' I'm now a freelance writer, after leaving teaching some years ago, and a contract like this was welcome.

With a jolt I came back to the present. The speaker had at last finished his talk and Clive Timms, the hotel manager who doubled as the compere, stood up a little

273

too quickly it seemed to me. 'Thank you, Mr Gibbon, for a most interesting and helpful talk. Are there any questions?'

The compere gazed around in desperation and rather than have this embarrassing silence continue, I raised my hand, not quite certain what my question might be. Finally I managed, 'What's the most dangerous experience you've had with your own boat.'

This was a mistake, a big mistake. Mr Gibbons leapt to his feet and started on a long, rambling story about a time when he'd been foolish enough to go out in bad weather, the difficulties he'd faced trying to keep the boat upright, the problems with the rigging in the wind.

From a little further along the row came the sound of gentle snoring and I caught a glimpse of an elderly lady digging the man beside her in the ribs. He came to with a start, shouting, 'What, what's happened? Is there a fire?'

The speaker was too absorbed in his story to notice this interruption, but the rest of the audience did and as a subdued titter went round the room the compere interrupted him saying, 'Well, thank you so much for a most interesting and enlightening talk.'

Hardly pausing for breath, he went on, 'And now the bar is open for the pre-dinner drink included in your holiday package.'

If I hadn't seen it with my own eyes, I'd have found it hard to believe so many elderly people could move so quickly, bumping into one another, jostling for position as they hurried out of the door and down the stairs leading to the bar on the ground floor.

Perhaps that was their reward for sitting through another boring talk, because this one about boats hadn't been the first one of limited interest, misrepresented on the programme as "entertainment".

Not everyone was willing to suffer. As I came into the bar one of the guests was already firmly ensconced in the best position, downing a large whisky. And by the look of him, it wasn't his first.

'Oh, there you are? I wondered where you'd got to.'

A tall, thin woman, dressed from head to toe in pale lilac, with her hair coloured to match, strode over to him. It was obvious her calm demeanour was only for the benefit of the rest of the guests, because she grabbed him by the lapels and whispered something in his ear. She was clearly scolding him and he jumped up with a start, splashing little drops of whisky on his trousers.

She tutted and fussed as he turned red with embarrassment, hissing, 'Leave it alone, Calla, it's not a problem.'

She shook her head and turned away. 'Well, I'm going in to dinner, even if you prefer to stay here in the bar all night.'

As she moved off, his look at her retreating back was murderous, but before I'd the chance to reflect on this, a voice beside me said, 'Are you going to have the dinner on offer here, Alison, or shall we escape and try one of the restaurants in town?'

Hamish McClure, the person responsible for organising the week's "entertainment" had crept up beside me.

'I don't think that's allowed,' I laughed, thinking he was making a joke. 'It wouldn't look good if the organiser opted out of the meals on offer.'

Rather than returning my smile, he frowned. 'I think I've had about enough of what they serve up here,' he said. 'This isn't what I'd anticipated when I signed up for this job.'

Now it was my turn to frown. 'What do you mean?' I said.

He shrugged. 'It's not exactly the kind of group I'm used to dealing with. Nor,' he waved his hand expansively to take in the sweep of the antiquated bar, 'is this my usual kind of venue. I'm used to somewhere more modern, much sharper.'

A nippy reply sprang to my lips, but all I said was, 'I've promised to sit beside the Herringtons at dinner. They seem VERY interested in the talk I'm giving tomorrow night about what happened to the hotel during the Second World War.'

If he thought most of the events he'd organised were rubbish, I wasn't letting him put my talks in that same category.

He wasn't in the least put out by my refusal. 'Suit yourself. But I warn you, don't have the Shepherd's Pie. It's suspiciously like the mince and potatoes served up yesterday at lunchtime and the Scottish hotpot of the night before.'

He turned on his heel, leaving me staring after him, as the Herringtons sisters, twins identically dressed in flowing garments of many hues and adorned with a wealth of sparkling jewellery, came bustling over to claim me as their table companion.

It wasn't an evening I was particularly looking forward to if I was honest, but their company was much preferable to that of Hamish and I smiled encouragingly as we made our way to the dining room, each of them twittering like a little bird as we went.

As we left the bar I glanced back to see Hamish failing to persuade yet another of the guests to join him in his plan to escape from the hotel and he trailed behind the group heading for the dining room.

It was only later, much later, it became clear Hamish should have taken his own advice about the Shepherd's Pie.